Praise for Haughton Murphy
and
A VERY VENETIAN MURDER

"Haughton Murphy's sophisticated style evokes fond memories of a kinder, gentler type of mystery; and his septuagenarian sleuth is cut from the same cloth as Nero Wolfe and Ellery Queen."

The San Diego Union-Tribune

"Haughton Murphy's latest Reuben Frost mystery moves the septuagenarian lawyer hero from his customary Wall Street haunts to the more exotic but equally lethal (at least when Frost is around) streets and canals of Venice. . . . Flashes of nasty wit."

Chicago Tribune

"Even if you aren't a lawyer (or a murderer) Haughton Murphy's new novel is the ideal mystery to take to Venice."

Sarah Caudwell

"Murphy writes a measured, agreeably old-fashioned prose that properly complements Frost's gentlemanly deportment and calm lucidity of mind."

The New Yorker

Also by Haughton Murphy
Published by Fawcett Books:

Murder for Lunch
Murder Takes a Partner
Murders & Acquisitions
Murder Keeps a Secret
Murder Times Two
Murder Saves Face

A VERY VENETIAN MURDER

A Reuben Frost Mystery

Haughton Murphy

FAWCETT CREST • NEW YORK

A Fawcett Crest Book
Published by Ballantine Books
Copyright © 1992 by James H. Duffy

Library of Congress Catalog Card Number: 92–767

ISBN 0–449–22066–4

This edition published by arrangement with Simon & Schuster Inc.

Manufactured in the United States of America

First Ballantine Books Edition: May 1993

For
Teresa and John D'Arms
Anne and Charles Fried
Angelica and Neil Rudenstine

Lovers of Venice—and Friends

I could not write a book set in Venice without thanking members of the staff of the Hotel Cipriani who have made stays there so pleasant, especially Sergio Agugiaro, Walter Bolzanella, Mauro Casagrande, Gianni Cavallarin, Virgilio Mancin, Gastone Moretti, Massimo Nason, Michele Ossena, Gianni Passaglia, Claudio Pittoti, Gigi Raccanelli and Silvano Tagliapetra.

—H.M.

The author gratefully acknowledges the kind assistance of the following Venetians and would-be Venetians: Louis and Anka Begley, Barbara Bergreen, Alfredo Cavallaro, Massimo Cristante, John H. D'Arms, Robert Fizdale, John Hohnsbeen, Robert Morgan, Dott. Cesare Porta, Patrizio Rigobon, Natale Rusconi and Avv. Augusto Salvadori. None, of course, bears responsibility for what follows.

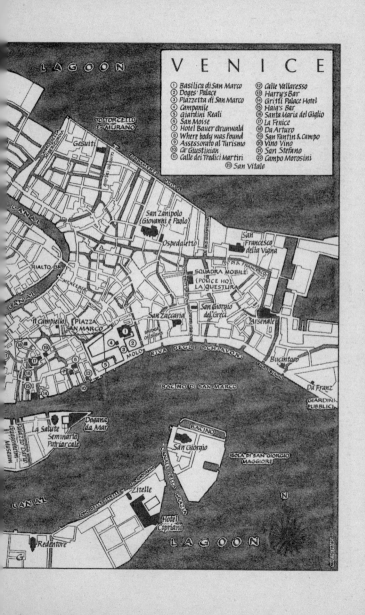

VENICE

1. Basilica di San Marco
2. Doges' Palace
3. Piazzetta di San Marco
4. Campanile
5. Giardini Reali
6. San Moise
7. Hotel Bauer Grunwald
8. Where body was found
9. Assessorato al Turismo
10. Ca' Giustinian
11. Calle dei Tredici Martiri
12. Calle Vallaresso
13. Harry's Bar
14. Gritti Palace Hotel
15. Haig's Bar
16. Santa Maria del Giglio
17. La Fenice
18. Da Arturo
19. San Fantin & Campo
20. Vino Vino
21. San Stefano
22. Campo Morosini
23. San Vitale

If every museum in the New World were emptied, if every famous building in the Old World were destroyed and only Venice saved, there would be enough there to fill a full lifetime with delight. . . . Venice with all its complexity and variety is itself the greatest surviving work of art in the world.

—EVELYN WAUGH

GETTING THERE

1

"IT'S LIKE OLD HOME WEEK."

"What did you say, Reuben?" Cynthia Frost asked her husband as they stood in line at Charles de Gaulle Airport, waiting to board the Monday morning Air France flight from Paris to Venice. "You're muttering and I can't understand you."

"I say it's old home week. All these familiar faces."

"*What* familiar faces?"

"Well, that tall brunette up there, for one," Reuben said, pointing to a woman some eight places ahead in the queue. "Isn't that Gregg Baxter's Girl Friday—if I can use such a politically incorrect term?"

"Where? Oh, I see. The one with the florid complexion. Yes, that's Doris Medford."

"On her way to the party, I'm sure," Reuben said, referring to the well-publicized dinner that Gregg Baxter, the designer of the moment in American fashion, was throwing in Venice on Wednesday. "She's a great admirer of yours, as I recall."

Reuben knew this from past encounters with Medford in New York, when she always claimed to be a fan of Cynthia's, going back to the days when his wife had been a leading ballerina with the National Ballet.

1

"It's not just me, she's a fan of NatBallet," Cynthia said. "She's the one who persuaded Baxter Fashions to underwrite the Company's tour last year. A million dollars plus." The former artistic director of NatBallet, a post she had held for several years after giving up dancing, Cynthia remembered the details of contributions to the Company.

"The tall, fat guy she's talking to is a lawyer named Cavanaugh," Reuben said. "I was on the other side of a deal with him way back when. He looks like an Irish sumo wrestler, but he's really quite genial."

Cavanaugh and Medford were conversing in the friendly but slightly stiff way acquaintances do when they meet by chance. They both towered over a second man, who appeared to be traveling with Cavanaugh.

"Who's the dried-up old fellow, do you suppose?" Reuben asked.

" 'Dried-up old fellow,' indeed," Cynthia said, after taking a closer look. "That's Eric Werth."

"All right, *rich* dried-up old fellow," Reuben said, realizing that he was staring at the most successful marketer in the perfume business since Charles of the Ritz. "He looks like he's on his last legs." Reuben, a healthy seventy-seven and a happily retired Wall Street lawyer, had no hesitation in commenting on the aging process in others. "I assume he's going to the Baxter thing, too. Though it does seem a bit odd to bring your lawyer along."

Cavanaugh's presence was explained after takeoff. The Frosts found themselves in the same row with him and Werth in the small business-class section of their Airbus A-320, the best seating available on the 100-minute flight. Doris Medford was in the aisle seat a row ahead, diagonally across from Reuben.

She had greeted the Frosts as they passed by. Now Jim Cavanaugh, formidable as he stood in the aisle, reintroduced himself to Reuben, then reached over to shake hands with Cynthia. Eric Werth, already settled, looked up and smiled at the Frosts.

"Vacation?" Cavanaugh asked, as he eased his bulky frame into his narrow seat.

"That's right," Reuben said.

"Ever been to Venice?"

Frost smiled. "Every September for the last twenty-two years. It's our annual escape from Manhattan."

"This is my first time. Never had any interest in the place. Those canals smell pretty bad, I understand."

Ah yes, Frost thought. The uninformed Cavanaugh had fixed on one of the two most common misconceptions about Venice, the other of course being the unshakable conviction that the city is irretrievably sinking.

"Maybe in the hottest part of the summer, but not in September," Reuben assured him.

Doris Medford, who had been listening to the conversation, turned and agreed with Reuben. "I've been there for two weeks now," she said, "and I haven't had any trouble with the smell."

"You're not coming from New York?" Reuben asked her.

"Lord, no. I've been holed up at the Hotel Cipriani getting ready for this insane dinner Gregg's having. Right now I'm returning from a crash trip to Paris to buy—don't laugh—*dried flowers*. Gregg decided last Friday that he couldn't deal with the florists in Venice—any of them—so it had to be *dried* flowers from Lhuillier in Paris. Good ol' Doris was packed off to make sure the Frogs worked all weekend to turn out the centerpieces he wanted."

"Are you going to Venice for Ms. Medford's 'insane' dinner?" Reuben asked Jim Cavanaugh.

"We've been invited," the lawyer replied. "But we're really hoping to do some business with Baxter and Dan Abbott, his partner." Then he added, irritably, "It's a matter we could have wrapped up right on Seventh Avenue, but Abbott insisted we traipse over here."

"Dan thinks that Gregg will be more relaxed in Venice and more receptive to making a deal," Medford said. "I hope he's right."

"So do we," Werth interjected.

"Nothing wrong with seeing Venice," Frost added.

"Maybe," Cavanaugh said skeptically. "You've been there so much, you got any bright ideas about restaurants?"

Given Cavanaugh's girth, his interest in eating places was not surprising. Reuben reeled off thumbnail descriptions of two favorites and Cynthia added a third, the names of which Cavanaugh carefully wrote down. Medford, still listening, had been to all three and commended the selection.

"Where are you staying?" Eric Werth asked, leaning forward to see across Cavanaugh's ample stomach.

"The Cipriani," Frost said.

"Like it?"

"Absolutely! For my money, it's one of the best hotels you can find anywhere."

"I disagree with you," Werth said. He had a deep and authoritative voice, out of proportion to his tiny size. "The Cipriani's too far away. I feel marooned over there on the Giudecca, away from the action. You're totally dependent on that boat of theirs to get anywhere. It's the Gritti Palace for me—a first-class hotel right in the middle of everything."

Reuben recalled a hundred debates over which hotel was better. "I can't knock the Gritti, but the Cipriani's unique," he said. "It's a well-run resort, but when you get bored with the resort life—as I do—you just hop on that boat you don't like and five minutes later you're in the Piazza San Marco, the greatest urban space in the world."

"To each his own, Mr. Frost. I'd rather walk to St. Mark's." Werth smiled and sat back, all but disappearing behind his lawyer.

Cynthia and Reuben refused the food being doled out. They had decided to wait for lunch at the hotel; two airline meals in a row, dinner and breakfast aboard the overnight flight from New York to Paris, were quite enough.

"I'm surprised there aren't more passengers heading for the party," Cynthia said to her husband, once their companions turned to their lunch trays. "This crowd doesn't look swank enough for Gregg Baxter."

"He probably chartered a plane. Or the beautiful people came early to spend the weekend."

"I still can't figure out how we got invited," Cynthia said.

"My bet is that Baxter's people asked the Cipriani who would be staying there Wednesday night. Your friend Ms. Medford probably saw our names and put us on the list. You know, even though we're not beautiful people—for which we can be thankful—we do wear shoes and don't smell bad."

"Unlike the canals," Cynthia whispered, provoking a laugh from her husband.

"Why do those who've never been to Venice always bring up the stinking canals? The garbage at night outside our supermarket in New York smells worse than anything I've ever come across over there." While he was talking, Reuben noticed that Doris Medford had attracted the attention of a stewardess and commandeered a second of the splits of Beaujolais being served with lunch.

"We've never met this Dan Abbott they were talking about," Cynthia said. "I've read about him, though—the smart businessman who keeps Baxter Fashions going."

"Actually I have met him," Reuben said. "Before he became so famous in the fashion industry, he was a banker. He worked at First Fiduciary until he hooked up with Baxter and got rich. I'm sure I worked with him on a couple of loan transactions where we represented the bank."

"The long arm of Chase & Ward," Cynthia commented, taking an affectionate dig at the Wall Street law firm where her husband had been a partner for over forty years, including eight when he was the Executive Partner presiding over its affairs.

"Whoops, we have to buckle up," Reuben said, as the seat-belt announcement was piped into the cabin in impeccable recorded French, Italian and English.

Cynthia fastened herself in and squeezed Reuben's hand.

"We're almost there, darling, and I can't wait. Except for Gregg Baxter's extravaganza, I'm looking forward to a quiet, restful vacation. It will do us both good."

"D'accordo, signora."

The confused hotbox terminal at Marco Polo Airport had been improved since the Frosts had first begun coming to Venice. When a full planeload of tourists arrived, the lines at passport control could still be slow, but at least now there were more than two luggage carts to be fought over.

The Frosts always checked their bags through from New York, which meant there were sometimes anxious moments at Marco Polo when they feared the transfer had not been made in Paris. This time their suitcases were among the first to appear on the baggage carousel. Reuben pulled them off under the alert gaze of Sacco, the drug-detecting German shepherd of the *guardia di finanza.* On every arrival he half expected the placid canine to turn into a fearsome monster, savagely—and mistakenly—attacking the Frost luggage, but so far it had never happened.

Reuben wheeled his cart toward the exit without incident, stopping only to invite Doris Medford to share a water-taxi. She declined, saying she had to wait for her boxes of dried flowers to come off the plane. He and Cynthia also paused to wish Eric Werth and the less than excited Jim Cavanaugh a good trip.

"We'll see you Wednesday night for sure," Reuben told them. "And since Venice is really such a small town, we'll probably run into you ten times before that."

Outside the customs area, Gianni, the smiling greeter from the Cipriani, waved to the Frosts, rushed to shake their hands and maneuvered them outside to the *motoscafo* he had reserved. He told Reuben that the cost of the water-taxi would be charged to his bill at the hotel. Reuben knew from experience that this was more costly than shelling out lire directly, but it meant that he did not have to worry about whether he had enough Italian money left over from the last visit to pay the $75 fare. It also lessened the initial shock of having a dollar price multiplied by 1,200 or so to get a lire equivalent. The absurd result—a 90,000-lire fare for the twenty-minute water-taxi ride, for example—required getting used to all over again.

Reuben and Cynthia sat in the open back of their *motoscafo*, drinking in the September sunshine as it sped along. They were exhilarated, realizing that again they had confounded the actuarial tables and the health statistics. Venice cheered them up; and, as Reuben had remarked when he turned seventy, "Forget Thomas Mann and *Death in Venice*. Titian lived and worked here until he was a hundred and three. That's the place for me."

Now he observed to Cynthia that "it looks like the *gabbiani* had a good season," as he pointed to the plump seagulls comfortably perched atop the wooden channel markers they swept past.

The belching industrial plants of Marghera on the mainland came into view far on the right, followed by the garbage-strewn landfill at the end of the island of Murano on the left. Then the scenery improved vastly as the spires and steeples of the clustered, interconnected islands of Venice proper, the *centro storico*, appeared in the midday haze: the campanile of the Madonna dell'Orto, then the tallest ones of all in the Piazza San Marco and at the church of the Frari, then the steepled bell tower of San Francesco della Vigna to the east, then six, eight, ten more.

Their *motoscafista* slowed down as he maneuvered into the Rio di Santa Giustina and across to the Riva degli Schiavoni and postcard Venice: the Doges' Palace and the Piazzetta di San Marco on the right, Santa Maria della Salute and the Dogana da Mar, the triangle-shaped customs house, on the other side of the Grand Canal, and the island and church of San Giorgio straight ahead.

Reuben observed his own personal Venetian talisman, the statue of Fortune atop the Dogana, turning in the breeze, as they again picked up speed in open water and crossed to the front landing stage of the Cipriani on the Giudecca.

Virgilio, the crew-cut, bass-voiced doorman (if that is what one calls the attendant at an open entrance on the water), showered the Frosts with words of welcome as he helped them from the water-taxi.

Alfredo Cavallaro, the black-suited reception manager, added his greetings once the Frosts were inside the lobby. He apologized for the absence of Dr. Rusconi, the managing director, away at a sister hotel in Portofino.

"I'm sorry we can't give you the room you had last year, 301," Cavallaro explained. "But we have 201 saved for you."

"My letter said we wanted 201 or 301," Reuben said. "Either is fine with us." Many years earlier, a friend, Neal Protest, had given Frost a tip that the end rooms on the second and third floors—201 and 301—were slightly longer than the hotel's standard double.

A young woman assistant manager showed the Frosts upstairs. Reuben inquired whether the hotel was full.

"Completely," she replied.

"People here for Gregg Baxter's party?" Cynthia asked.

"Yes. We're fully booked to Thursday with the party guests, and il signor Baxter and his colleagues as well. Then we have for three days some American bankers. Plus very many of our old and good friends, such as you, signora, and you, signore."

Room 201 was exactly as the Frosts remembered it: light and comfortable, with twin beds and two windows looking out on the Venetian lagoon. They changed their clothes as soon as their bags were brought up and went downstairs for lunch.

"I don't know about you," Reuben said as they finished, "but it's now thirteen hours since we left New York—twenty-four hours since I've been to bed. It's *pisolino* time."

Despite his intention of taking only a little nap, Reuben slept until six o'clock, when he groggily agreed with Cynthia that they should dine at the hotel. They had an early and quiet dinner, and then retired immediately.

"As my Pakistani dentist says, 'very excellent,' " Frost remarked as he readied for bed. "It's wonderful to be back."

"No argument about that," Cynthia replied.

PEACE AND QUIET: TUESDAY

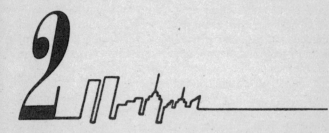

TUESDAY MORNING, REUBEN ATE A LIGHT BREAKFAST ON the terrace outside the Cipriani dining room, delighted to take in the view of San Giorgio and the Lido.

He and the other September regulars had often joked about spending so much money at the hotel that they really had bought a part of it. If they did not have an actual financial stake in its operation, they had an emotional one. After breakfast Reuben took a stroll about the grounds to make sure unwelcome changes had not been made. He was pleased as always to see the garden in the front, with its absurdly but somehow attractively clashing masses of color: explosions of pink begonias next to flaming red salvia, pink and white petunias at war with orange impatiens.

Reuben had decided to take a swim, so he went through the lobby to the pool at the opposite end of the building. Here again he was satisfied with what he surveyed: a lawn studded with flowering trees and evergreens, surrounding the enormous pool itself; the fading red brick walls of the church of San Giorgio in the distance; the terrace where he and Cynthia had lunch most days; the landing stage on the Canale della Grazia used as the main entrance at night; the balconies and skylights of the luxury suites tucked away behind trees at one end of the pool. Bearing out what he had said to Eric Werth, the place had the look of an elegant, immaculately kept resort. It was a quiet, private enclave.

He tipped the pool boy (actually a longtime retainer whose boyishness was giving way to baldness) for bringing him a towel and setting up a chaise longue in his favorite spot, near a cluster of purple-flowering acacias. It was secluded, yet afforded a clear view for seeing anything of interest that might be going on; Reuben gladly ceded more visible perches to those more concerned with being seen.

After a half-dozen laps in the warm water, he put on the white terry-cloth robe furnished by the hotel and settled down to work on the vacation project he had thought up for himself. He believed firmly that each year he should have a definite agenda of places to visit; otherwise there was the risk that he would spend far too much time lazing where he was right now.

He and Cynthia had agreed years before that they would do their Venetian sightseeing separately. Each had a different pace and much preferred to view art objects in silence. Which was not to say they didn't exchange reports on—and discuss and argue about—what they had seen. But sightseeing was, by their preference, a private, independent affair.

On Reuben's part, he loved to walk in the city's automobile-free byways. Years before he had done the walks described in Giulio Lorenzetti's exhaustive *Venice and Its Lagoon*. It had taken three vacations to finish the author's twelve itineraries, but at completion Reuben felt that he knew Venice well. Then he had done the four walks outlined by J. G. Links. (He was a great admirer of Links, a London furrier who became an amateur expert on Venice and wrote the splendid *Venice for Pleasure*.) Next he had used two vacations to view (as best he could in the unsatisfactory light) the mosaics in the Basilica di San Marco, spending a large part of the year between the two holidays reading the remarkable commentary by Professor Otto Demus, who had studied them for the better part of his adult life.

During his reading and sightseeing, Frost had become

fascinated by the Doges, the ducal rulers of the Venetian Republic from the eighth century until its collapse in 1797. The Doges, 118 of them, had been a quirky lot, with endless foibles and eccentricities.

Frost had started his education with John Julius Norwich's *A History of Venice* and then, with ambition exceeding ability, had tackled Andrea Da Mosto's *I Dogi di Venezia,* a massive Italian text. This was slow going, given Reuben's embryonic knowledge of the language, and he finally concluded that he could only make limited use of the Da Mosto.

Part of Reuben's fascination with the Doges came from his amusing discovery that there were similarities between the Dogeship and the position he had once held as the Executive Partner of Chase & Ward, his old law firm. Each Doge had possessed the trappings of power, starting with the extraordinary Doges' Palace, just as Chase & Ward's Executive Partner occupied a breathtaking corner suite overlooking New York harbor. And deference was paid by the colleagues of each. Yet, when all was said and done, both were essentially figureheads. The Doge had been checked and contained by the so-called Council of Ten and the Grand Council of 1,500-plus; Reuben and his successors at the law firm had been kept within bounds by an informal executive committee and ever shifting alliances and coalitions among the partners.

A newly elected Doge had been required to sign a *promissione,* carefully spelling out what he could and could not do. There was no such formality at Chase & Ward, but there did not have to be. A new Executive Partner and those around him implicitly knew what the boundaries of his power were: to make decisions that had to be made but that no one else really cared about; to build a broad consensus on those issues considered important; to preside at meetings of the partners; and to represent the firm to the outside world when a front man was needed. If the Doge had been a "gilded icon," as one historian had described him, the Executive Partner was somewhat the same, though without a great deal of gilt and with a following that paid him something less than full respect; he was more anodized than gilded.

Thus predisposed to the Doges, Reuben had decided, as Da Mosto had, to study them through their tombs and monuments. This would goad him to revisit favorites among the city's churches. It also would provide an excuse for dipping again into John Ruskin's *The Stones of Venice*, which contained comments, often enraged ones, on many of the Doges' monuments. He found the Victorian essayist amusing, more often than not unintentionally so.

Reuben had an old green book bag in which he carried his guidebooks.* He now pulled out Norwich's history and James Morris' *The World of Venice*. While he made notes, the pool area began to fill up. He recognized guests from past years (the September crowd at the Cipriani being a faithful one): the chic Austrian woman and her elderly male companion who arrived and departed separately, convincing Frost that their annual visit was a tryst; a young, outgoing American investment banker, who Frost was sure must be very successful, since the hotel was not exactly priced for the young, and his wife, a painter; a well-known British actor and his wife, she a Labour Member of Parliament; an American woman who owned a restaurant in San Diego, a boring chatterbox; and a peppy, dwarfish man who exercised by walking in quick-step around the pool, furiously smoking an especially obnoxious cigar almost as large as he was. The guests mostly seemed "acquainted with luxury," as one guide described the hotel's clientele. Or, as the local Tourist Board would call them, "elite" tourists, which meant simply that they stayed at least overnight, ate in restaurants and went shopping occasionally.

With the Baxter dinner in prospect, some new faces had gathered at poolside: a chummy group that Frost guessed were store buyers from the States; the wife of one New York leveraged-buyout artist and the ex-wife of another,

* See Appendix.

whom Reuben recognized; and (he was almost sure he remembered correctly) an editor of *Vogue*. All sat around idly, many reading trashy best-sellers; as was often the case, almost no one ventured into the pool.

A couple passed along the walk near where he was sitting and noticed him. It was the Spencers, Colin and Edith, from London. She taught mathematics at the University of London, he English literature at Oxford. (Cynthia called them the "brainy Brits".) They had been coming to the Cipriani as long as the Frosts for what they termed the "pricey part" of their annual holiday. After several years of nodding and smiling, the Spencers and the Frosts had become acquainted, at least to the extent of trading observations about changes in the hotel and hints about local restaurants. The Spencers shared Reuben and Cynthia's protective concern about the Cipriani and like them were leery of innovation; horror had struck, for example, the year they had found that the staff's uniforms had been changed from smart, nautical white to a dismal brown, looking like "something that wretched costume designer at your ballet company might have done" as Reuben had grumped to Cynthia at the time.

"What's new and different?" he asked the Spencers.

"Nothing, thank God," Edith Spencer said. "As far as we can see, everything's much the same. And the place looks wonderful, don't you think? The gardens seem especially lovely this year."

"I agree," Reuben said. "And I see that many of the old-timers are back."

"But what a lot of new ones," Colin said. "The place is absolutely full up, I'm told. Some Yank dressmaker is throwing a party tomorrow."

"The 'Yank dressmaker' is Gregg Baxter. Surely you've heard of him?" Reuben asked.

"Oh, indeed," Edith said. "Even in dowdy England we know that name. But is he really all that prominent in the States?"

"He's a very, very hot designer at the moment. Everyone from Mrs. Bush to Madonna wears his clothes. Cynthia tells me the showings last spring of his fall collection caused a sensation. He did something called the Malevich look, based on the work of the Russian constructivist, if you can believe it. The biggest success since St. Laurent was inspired by Mondrian, twenty-five years ago. He does men's clothes, too. Hasn't the 'gray look' reached London, Colin? Everything a different shade of gray—coat, trousers, shirt, socks, necktie."

"Good heavens," Colin said. "Sounds terribly somber to me. But, Reuben, why is an *American* giving a bash in Venice? Will you tell me?"

"You should really ask Cynthia, who knows all the details," Reuben said. "As I understand it, he's become interested in the work of a fabric designer here, named Cecilia Scamozzi. We know her a little bit, she's got one of those fancy local titles. La marchesa Scamozzi. Anyway, Baxter's announced that he's using her fabrics in his line for next spring, which he'll be displaying in New York in another month or so. This party is to drum up interest.

"If you care, the Paris *Tribune* says it's also a declaration of war on his European competition. Baxter's apparently determined to break into the market over here and challenge Paris and Milan. This party is the kickoff of a huge publicity campaign. And the Europeans are furious because it steals the thunder from their fall shows."

"So we're witnessing the first shots in an international trade war," Colin said. "Jolly exciting!"

"Are you going to the party?" Edith asked.

"In fact, we are."

"We've heard on the grapevine that Baxter is staying here," Edith said.

"So I understand. We met his assistant on the plane coming in from Paris."

"They say he and his friends have taken all the rooms up there on the second floor, looking down over the pool."

"That's bad news," Reuben said.

"Really? Why ever so?" Colin asked.

"Cynthia's a sometime customer of Baxter's. If he's stay-

ing up there, he's going to have to raise his prices to pay the
bill.''

Cynthia joined her husband for lunch at their usual table
on the terrace next to the pool. Finishing one meal, they
intensely discussed the next.

"I'm not quite ready to start the fish diet yet," Reuben
told his wife. "Let's try Da Arturo tonight."

"Suits me," she said.

Reuben made a reservation through the hotel's other Gianni, the concierge they had known the longest, and then set
off on a short excursion to start his quest for Doges' monuments. He had decided to visit San Francesco della Vigna,
which could be reached easily by the number five *circolare*,
the water-bus that stopped near the rear exit of the hotel. The
vessel was uncrowded when Reuben boarded. Being (basically) a good citizen, he purchased a ticket. For any lengthy
water-bus journey, Reuben did buy a ticket for the two
dollars-plus required; going a shorter distance, such as the
one-stop trip across to San Giorgio, he did not. It never
seemed to matter any more, since the single *marinaio* on each
boat, responsible for checking on fares, almost never did so.
Reuben was free to make up his own rules for paying.

At the Celestia stop he disembarked and walked the short
distance to the church, its white Palladian front tacked onto
a building designed by Jacopo Sansovino, the great
sixteenth-century architect and sculptor.

Doge Andrea Gritti (1523–38), whose severe portrait Reuben remembered from the lobby of the Gritti Palace Hotel,
had laid the cornerstone. It thus had seemed only fitting that
he should be buried there. Reuben found the tomb at the left
of the main altar without difficulty, recalling that the unfortunate Gritti had died, at age eighty-four, of eating too
many grilled eels on Christmas Eve. Though he was not yet
Gritti's age, Reuben vowed to watch his vacation diet.

The monument carried a Latin inscription that referred to
Gritti as a "most loved" leader; entirely appropriate, Reu-

ben thought, for the father of at least five illegitimate children. And, come to think of it, Gritti perhaps resembled Bruce Nevins, a Chase & Ward Executive Partner many years back, who had fathered a bastard (in the days when this was thought to be most dishonorable) and probably died of overindulgence of one sort or another, though not gorging on eels. And he, too, had been "much loved" (or as much loved as any Executive Partner ever is).

Reuben moved down the aisle, seeking the memorial busts of the Contarini, Doge Alvise (1676–84) and his ancestor Doge Francesco (1623–24). He was disappointed. The Contarini family chapel was boarded up, *in restauro*.

Thwarted, he strolled back to San Marco. Once in the Piazzetta beyond, he ran head-on into Edgar Filbert, a young partner at Chase & Ward, and Noreen, his wife. Reuben was surprised, since he had not known the couple was planning to be in Venice.

There were few people at the firm that Reuben did not like, but Edgar, and Noreen for that matter, were among them. Edgar, in or out of the office, had always seemed chronically incapable of hearing any voice other than his own or, if another's words did evoke a response, it was almost certain to be condescending. And Reuben found insufferable Noreen's smugness about her children, their home in Westchester and Edgar's model behavior as a husband.

Edgar was photographing his wife feeding the pigeons in front of the Marciana Library when Frost saw them. He thought first of fleeing as quickly as he could but Noreen, posing in her tan canvas skirt and a man's shirt, spied him. She quickly ran over, followed by her husband in his cerise trousers and a polo shirt that was too tight around his expanding middle.

After expressing mutual surprise at their chance meeting, Filbert asked Frost if his trip wasn't "awfully strenuous." "I mean, how does someone of your age manage to get around over here?"

Before Reuben could sputter out an answer, Noreen had joined in. "Do you spend most of your time at the hotel?" she asked.

It had never occurred to Reuben that he might be too decrepit to make the annual trip to Venice and he had, by God, been doing it for almost a quarter century. So, trying to conceal his rage, he mumbled quietly that "I do my best to see what I can." As he glanced toward the two huge columns that stood nearby, it occurred to him that in an earlier day the bodies of executed malefactors were hung from a rope tied between them. He could not resist the thought that such treatment would be appropriate for the Filberts.

Any notion of entertaining them disappeared as they asked their snide questions; the Frosts' schedule suddenly filled up with real and fancied engagements in case a get-together was proposed. It wasn't; the Filberts' conversation was confined to complaints. This was the second of two days in Venice (between Lake Como and Florence) and the results had not been good. It was too crowded. Too expensive. The shopping opportunities were overrated. The local fish wasn't fresh. And, without their Hertz car, Venice was too confining. Not a word about any site or object of artistic interest.

Reuben expressed the hope that the rest of their trip would be more to their liking and beat a hasty retreat. But not before Noreen had asked if Mrs. Frost was spending the afternoon "resting."

He hurried off toward the Cipriani's private dock and caught its *motoscafo* back to the Giudecca. As he looked out at the beautiful changing light reflected on the facades of the buildings bordering the *bacino* of San Marco, he reflected with satisfaction that the callow and unseasoned Filberts had been very wrong in their impertinent conclusions. And despite what he had said to them, he fervently hoped that their stay in Florence would be hot, sweaty, crowded and noisy.

*   *   *

That evening, back at the *centro storico*, the Frosts walked past the church of San Moisè and the Teatro la Fenice, the city's jewel box of an opera house. As the alleys narrowed, they reached Da Arturo.

They had never been clear why it was called that, since the genial proprietor was named Ernesto Ballarin. It was he who showed them to a booth in the vest-pocket restaurant, which was barely large enough to hold him, a young waiter and the chef.

"Ernesto, do you have spaghetti with Gorgonzola tonight?" Reuben asked. "I've been waiting a whole year to have it again."

"*Sì, sì. Spaghetti al Gorgonzola.* But let me make another suggestion. The *funghi alla Russa.*" He described the dish—mushrooms and potatoes in a cream sauce—and Reuben and Cynthia agreed to share one order of spaghetti, one of the mushrooms.

When it arrived, the pasta lived up to Reuben's memory of it. "Pretty good macaroni and cheese, what?" he said to Cynthia.

"Yes!" she said enthusiastically. But they agreed that the *funghi* were even better.

At Ernesto's urging, Reuben and Cynthia each ordered the *braciola alla Veneziana,* a pork cutlet marinated in vinegar, then breaded and baked. When their orders came, snaked down the narrow aisle by the deft owner, they agreed that he had guided them wisely to the *braciola,* which had an unusual piquant flavor.

"Have you seen Gregg Baxter?" Reuben asked his wife as they ate. "I expected a big show around the hotel, but there hasn't been any sign of him."

"I haven't seen him, either. He's probably spending all his time at the Palazzo Labia, getting it fixed up for the banquet."

They speculated how it would be decorated—apart from the Lhuillier dried flowers that Doris Medford had brought from Paris.

When their plates were clean, Ernesto asked the Frosts if they wanted dessert.

"This is one place where I break my rules," Reuben said. "I'll have the *tiramisù*."

"Not for me. Just some *fragole*, strawberries with lemon," Cynthia said.

"You don't know what you're missing," Reuben told her. "I'm not an expert on many things, but *tiramisù* is one of them and, as I've told you before, it's best right here. Ernesto's really is a 'pick-me-up' that deserves the name."

The owner spooned a portion of the quintessential Venetian dessert from a large bowl. His version was a soupy mixture of mocha and mascarpone cheese, different from the more solid varieties found elsewhere. It was outrageously delicious, and Ernesto could not resist smiling and looking satisfied as he watched Reuben eat. A second helping was offered but reluctantly declined.

Outside the restaurant, the narrow, dimly lit *calle* was deserted, so the Frosts walked along side by side.

"You know, I never can get over it, Cynthia," Reuben said, as she took his arm. "Being able to walk here at any hour of the day or night, drunk or sober, hearty or lame, and you feel perfectly safe. When you're used to being nervous at home about going around the corner to the Korean grocery, it's a marvelous sensation."

"You think the Venetians are less prone to crime than we are?" Cynthia asked. "I wonder."

"Maybe the difficulty in escaping from an island city is a deterrent. But then Manhattan's an island, too. . . ." Reuben's voice trailed off.

"God knows there's been plenty of violence in Venice's history," Reuben continued a moment later. "Take the street Da Arturo is on—the Calle degli Assassini. There has to be a violent history that goes with a name like that."

Once the Frosts reached the Campo San Fantin, they were no longer alone. Other pedestrians bustled about and there were drinkers in the Bar al Teatro. Looking up at the illuminated neoclassical facade of La Fenice, Reuben began quietly singing:

"La donna è mobile,
Qual piuma al vento. . . ."

"I knew you'd sing that when you got near the Fenice," Cynthia said. "You always do, especially after a little wine."

"And why not? It's one of the greatest arias ever written, and it was first sung right here. You know the story. . . ."

"On the day of *Rigoletto*'s premiere, Verdi held back the orchestra parts for *La donna è mobile* until late in the afternoon."

"He didn't want the gondoliers singing his masterpiece even before the first performance," Reuben said. "You want to hear more?"

"No, dear, and I don't want to hear *Questa o quella,* either."

PEACE AND QUIET: WEDNESDAY

WEDNESDAY MORNING FROST WAS DEEP INTO PLANNING his sightseeing when Cynthia joined him at the pool. "Where are you off to today?" she asked.

"I haven't decided yet. Most of the monuments I'm interested in turn out to be in San Zanipolo, but I'm going to save that for last."

"Oh, look what's happening here," Cynthia said, nodding toward the door of the hotel. A procession was coming down the sidewalk. In the lead, by himself, was Gregg Baxter. Barely forty, he was tall, thin and suntanned, with golden hair that had been bleached either by the sun or the contents of a dye bottle. He was wearing small, round steel-rimmed sunglasses, and, as befitted the creator of the "gray look," light gray shorts and a dark gray polo shirt.

Dan Abbott, his business partner, and Doris Medford followed at a respectful distance. Behind them was a stunning black couple. Reuben did not recognize them, but Cynthia pointed out that the man, Tony Garrison, was Baxter's up-and-coming design assistant—and lover, according to rumor—and that the woman was Baxter's favorite model, called simply Tabita.

Running ahead of the parade, which was moving at a stately pace, was a hotel functionary who frantically assembled five chaises at poolside, directly in front of the Frosts' semi-isolated enclave. Eventually the group reached its destination, but only after Baxter had stopped to embrace and kiss several women, including two wealthy customers from Fort Worth and New York recognizable from the pages of *W*.

Frost tried to recall the details of a *Time* cover story on Gregg Baxter that he had read a year earlier. He remembered that it had called Baxter the most gifted American designer since the young Halston and contained a wealth of biographical detail: Baxter had grown up in the Bronx, in New York City, and had attended the Bronx High School of Science before going off to Brown.

While at Brown, he had begun sketching at the Rhode Island School of Design in Providence. After college he had come to New York and signed on with Liz Claiborne, where he worked hard and learned the designing trade. By the end of the seventies, he was ready to try high fashion and go out on his own. He started his successful ascent almost at once, when the chief buyer for Bergdorf Goodman bought several of his creations.

Menswear followed in the mid-eighties, along with a more broadly distributed lower-priced women's line, which competed with the clothes of his old employer, Liz Claiborne.

The Frosts watched as Baxter, realizing how strong the sun was, sent Garrison back inside for a cap. The assistant was dressed from head to toe in black—a declaration of independence from the gray look?—starting with heavy shoes and moving up to a black felt baseball cap that said PADRES in yellow letters on the front. He came back with a second baseball cap that he handed to Baxter, this one for the New York Mets.

Baxter put on the cap and sent Garrison to find a waiter, who soon hustled over with cups of cappuccino. Then the young man was dispatched again to the hotel, from which he returned with a stack of Italian fashion magazines. Baxter immediately began tearing through them as if looking for a specific item.

He was jittery and nervous, to the point where it made Reuben jumpy simply to watch him. "You say that young black man is the great man's design assistant?" Reuben asked Cynthia. "I hate to say it, but Stepin Fetchit's more like it. The kid's done nothing except run his legs off since they came out here."

Cynthia did not have a chance to comment. Doris Medford had spotted the Frosts and was coming toward them. Reuben was sure she was around forty, though her swimsuit revealed that she had a well-shaped figure, free of the flab that so often comes with growing older. Her bright red lipstick would normally have made a pleasing contrast with her dark, black hair, but the effect was at least partially spoiled by her flushed, ruddy complexion.

"How's the flower girl?" Reuben asked. "They let you back in, I see."

"Oh yes. But I almost had to go back. We were going to be two hundred and fifty at our party. Then we decided to use a second room at the Palazzo Labia, so we can handle three-fifty. But that means another ten centerpieces. Thank God those stupid flowers I brought back could be subdivided without looking scrawny."

"That's a lot of people, three hundred-fifty," Cynthia said.

Medford covered her eyes with her hands. "You have no idea what a mess it is," she said. "Can you imagine . . . no, don't get me started. There are at least five hundred who want to come—all of Paris, Rome and Milan, it seems like. Gregg has intimate friends he didn't even know about. And now we have a war about who goes in the main room and who in the anteroom. It's something, that's all I can say."

As they chatted, Dan Abbott joined them.

"Do you know Dan Abbott?" Doris Medford asked.

Cynthia said no, and Medford made the introduction. Reuben reminded him that they had met "when you were at First Fiduciary."

"Jesus, that was a thousand years ago. In my other life. On days like this one I wish I'd never left."

Abbott was the oldest member of the Baxter entourage. Mid- to late fifties, Frost estimated. He was also the most unprepossessing, with a freckled face and a high-pitched voice. He had been going bald when Reuben first knew him, but now wore an obvious toupee. Observing it, Reuben could not help thinking of that emblem of the Watergate scandal, Howard Hunt's ill-fitting red wig. Not only was Abbott's hairpiece ill-fitting and red, it looked to be knitted of yarn, like the hair of a Raggedy Ann doll. It was so bad Reuben felt it must be a fashion statement, or antistatement, by its wearer.

"Is there anything we can do?" Cynthia asked.

"Maybe push a hundred people or so in the Grand Canal," Abbott said. "There's going to be a *riot* over there tonight."

"Dan, we'd better get back. Gregg's going to start feeling lonely and neglected," Medford said.

"Yes," Abbott said, sighing. "Along with everything else, let's not have him throwing one of his fits."

"Good luck to you both," Cynthia said. "We look forward to the party."

After Abbott and Medford had returned to their leader, Reuben noticed Medford whispering to Baxter. He looked around and stared at the Frosts, then got up and came over. He took off his sunglasses, which revealed piercing blue eyes. The kind of eyes, Cynthia later told Reuben, that could break a girl's heart if that had been Baxter's inclination, which they knew it was not.

"The Frosts, I believe," he said as he approached and, when invited, sat on the edge of Cynthia's chaise.

"I'm surprised to see you here by the pool," Reuben said.

"I came out to relax for half an hour and then it's back to work," Baxter replied. This prompted Reuben to reflect that if the frenetic behavior he had been observing was relaxation, he wondered what the designer was like when keyed up.

"Everything's ready for the party," Baxter said, "but I

expect it's going to take most of the day to finish the seating list.''

"That sounds like fun," Cynthia said.

"Not when you may offend your customers—and the prima donnas in the press. It's damned hard work.''

"Well, it's the party of the year," Cynthia said. "I know, because the *Tribune* said so."

"Pure hype," Baxter said, smiling.

"I hope it compares with *the* party that was held in Venice," Reuben said.

"When was that?" Baxter asked.

"Middle of the sixteenth century. I've just been reading about it. It was a banquet for Henry the Third of France. In the Doges' Palace for three thousand guests. All the women wore white and there were twelve hundred items on the menu. Plus trick napkins at each place sculpted out of sugar."

"We're operating on a more modest scale," Baxter said, smiling again. "Without any tricks."

"And of course there's the modern party that was held right where yours is going to be, at the Palazzo Labia," Cynthia said.

"Yeah, I've heard about that one. Some rich Mexican," Baxter said.

"Carlos de Beistegui," Cynthia said. "Charlie, I believe everyone called him. He spent a fortune buying and fixing up the Palazzo Labia and had a costume ball to end them all back in nineteen fifty-one."

"There are old ladies who still talk about it," Reuben said. "Though I think it's a little like the *Mayflower* and a good many more people say they were there than actually were."

"We're not quite up to Charlie's standards, either," Baxter said, as he stood up and tipped his Mets cap. "See you later."

"Oh dear," Cynthia said, when he had gone. "He seemed to leave in a huff. Did I make a mistake by mentioning the Beistegui party?"

"I don't think so. He'd heard about it. He said so."

Cynthia was mollified and again asked her husband whose tomb he was going to visit that day.

"Pasquale Cicogna."

"Never heard of him."

"Cicogna commissioned the Rialto Bridge. A wonderful example of bureaucracy at work. He held a competition and got entries from Michelangelo, Sansovino and Palladio, among others. But he picked a hack named Da Ponte—of all things—who had done some work for him on the Doges' Palace. The result is what we see over the Grand Canal. It reminds me of when Marty Lenmeade hired his shiftless, no-talent brother-in-law to redo the Chase & Ward offices."

"Where is Cicogna's monument?"

"In the Gesuiti. Why don't we have a late lunch at Harry's Dolci and I can sneak over there when the church reopens this afternoon?"

"Fine. I'd just as soon get out of here. With the party, there's bound to be lots of Euro-trash here at lunch."

It was exceptionally clear, with no clouds in the azure sky, and thus a perfect day to eat outside at the Dolci, the modest offshoot of Harry's Bar down the way on the Giudecca. The Frosts went out the back entrance of the Cipriani and strolled down past the Zitelle church, now wrapped like a mummy while *in restauro;* past the youth hostel, with a United Nations of young backpackers lunching outside; past the Redentore, Palladio's finest church.

At Harry's Dolci, they sat at a table fronting directly on the water. This created a unique immediacy with the heavy traffic in the Giudecca Canal: water-buses, tour boats, car ferries, tankers, barges, a Norwegian cruise ship. The world seemed just about perfect as they watched the passing traffic, drank Bellinis—that nectar of Prosecco, the sparkling white wine of the Veneto, and peach juice—and ate their club sandwiches, here formidable behatted structures that had to be attacked with knife and fork.

*   *   *

After lunch Cynthia walked back to the hotel alone and Reuben took the *circolare* from the Sant'Eufemia stop next to the Dolci around to the Fondamente Nuove. He paid the fare for the forty-minute trip.

He was happy to be returning to the Baroque church of the Gesuiti, or Santa Maria Assunta, which he regarded as the most idiosyncratic sight in all of Venice, its interior enveloped with green and white marble carving that looked like damask drapes. The sarcophagus of Cicogna (1585–95) framed the door to the sacristy. It was worth the trip, topped as it was by a delightful sculpted likeness of the reclining Cicogna, wearing his ceremonial regalia and *corno,* the traditional headdress of a Doge. His head rested comfortably for eternity on one elbow. The monument seemed splendidly irreverent and Reuben liked it.

Given the oppressive heat, which showed no signs of letting up, Reuben had planned to take another swim when he returned to the hotel but then decided against it. He didn't want to be tired for the evening ahead, which he was sure would be long. And hot.

A HOT NIGHT

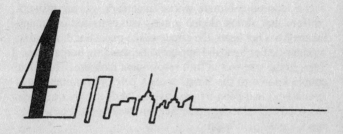

WITH AN EXPLETIVE OR TWO, REUBEN ASSEMBLED THE
components of his formal evening wear: studs and cuff
links, waistcoat, suspenders and black bow tie, white pocket
handkerchief and silk black stockings.

Cynthia, meanwhile, checked over her long dress. There
had been much discussion back in New York about which
of her gowns would be most suitable. It didn't *have* to be a
Baxter, she realized, but she had finally chosen a dark-green
silk of his. "It's two years old," she had said, "but everyone agrees his best designs are timeless, so it will do."

"All I can say is, this dinner better be good enough to
justify hauling a tuxedo all the way from New York," Reuben grumbled, as he struggled to put his gold studs into his
dress shirt.

Outside the front door of the Cipriani, an informal queue
began shaping up shortly before nine o'clock, waiting to
board the fleet of water-taxis massed in an aquatic traffic
jam in the lagoon. The unseasonable heat continued and two
of the formally dressed men at the head of the line took off
their jackets. This sent a signal back through the ranks and
a majority of the men eagerly followed their example.

Efficient as always, Virgilio directed the guests into the

waiting *motoscafi*, admonishing each in the appropriate language: *"Careful, sir," "Prenez-garde, madame," "Piano,
signore."* The Frosts shared a boat with six others, two
strangers and four they knew slightly from New York. One
was a Junoesque blonde whose trademark was an upswept
coiffure that almost defied gravity and extended out many
inches from her head; the effect was to make her diminutive
wheeler-dealer husband appear to be standing under a tree.
Tonight the tree was in full, resplendent blossom. The other
couple known to the Frosts were a pair of prominent fun-
lovers who had been hyperactive in the Kennedy era; their
wrinkled appearances made Reuben aware of just how long
ago Camelot had been.

The Frosts' *motoscafista* cut across to the Grand Canal
and sped down it, past the Salute and the Gritti, under the
Accademia and Rialto Bridges and then into the Cannaregio
Canal, off to the right. The boat waited its turn near the
pali, the blue-and-white striped poles in front of the Palazzo
Labia that matched the striped awnings over the twenty
windows on the two upper floors. Reuben observed with
awe the lighted *fiaccole* illuminating the palazzo and the
elaborately liveried figures helping passengers from the
boats.

A noisy collection of reporters and paparazzi was herded
behind a barrier a short distance from the entrance, but no
one on the Frosts' boat detonated an explosion of flash-
bulbs. The photographers were more interested in a jam of
demonstrators gathered on the Ponte delle Guglie, fifty
yards away. Apparently students, they screamed incomprehensible taunts and waved their arms as their pictures were
taken.

Once inside, those arriving encountered an assembly of
young women, dressed uniformly in black cocktail dresses
unquestionably by Gregg Baxter. There was also a crew of
young men with slicked-back hair, all in what appeared to
be black tuxedos but were probably Baxter charcoal gray.
Reuben thought that the effect was designed to make the
guests feel that they were among beautiful people (and

therefore must be beautiful themselves); but then, he realized, wasn't a purpose of fashion to make people feel beautiful or handsome?

One of the young women approached and softly asked Reuben's name. She went to a table at the side of the entry and returned with an envelope marked "Mr. and Mrs. Frost," which contained a slip showing their table assignment for dinner. The woman pointed them to an inner courtyard across a vast checkerboard floor of red and tan marble squares. Here a small army of waiters in white mess jackets with gold epaulets passed drinks and served a variety of canapés.

Although the building was wired for electricity, the ground floor was lit by candles. The effect created was exceedingly alluring—and exceedingly hot. Mercifully, the courtyard where drinks were being served was in the open air. Hoping for relief, the Frosts went outside, where they joined Emilio Caroldo, a local cardiologist, and his American wife, Erica Sherrill.

Dr. Sherrill, an art historian specializing in the early Renaissance, spent part of each year in New York, where she taught at the Institute of Fine Arts. The rest of the time she lived in Venice, where her husband practiced year round. Reuben and Cynthia had met the Caroldos in the course of the couple's tireless fund-raising efforts for Save Venice.

"Hot in the sun," Dr. Sherrill said, laughing. The Frosts just shook their heads. "It's such a pity. Gregg Baxter has obviously gone all out to make this a wonderful party, but the heat's going to overwhelm everyone."

While they were talking, a chamber orchestra began playing on the balcony above.

"Vivaldi," Dott. Caroldo said. "Very fitting. Venice's eighteenth-century answer to Cole Porter. By the way, Reuben, do you read the local newspapers while you're here?"

"I can't say that I do," Reuben answered.

"Too bad. *Il Gazzettino* has been filled with amusing stories about this dinner. This palazzo is now owned by the Italian state television network, R.A.I. The Milan designers

are making a *grande clamore* about the decision to rent it to
Baxter, to allow him to get publicity from a party in Venice.
Why should a national enterprise deal with one of their
foreign competitors, they've all been screaming. The answer, of course, is money. Your Baxter is paying very
much to use this splendid place.''

At this point, the male models originally hovering around
the entrance moved through the crowd and announced dinner.

"Where are you sitting?" Reuben asked.

"Nove," Dott. Caroldo said.

"Nine—splendid, so are we.''

Two of the decorative young men offered their arms to
Erica Sherrill and Cynthia, and led them up the two-tiered
marble stairway, carpeted for the evening with a rich, claret-
colored runner.

The ballroom, rightly called one of the most beautiful
interiors in Europe, was truly dazzling. The dried flowers
Doris Medford had brought back from Paris decorated each
of the round dining tables; they were superfluous in this
setting, which was dominated by Tiepolo's frescoes depict-
ing the story of Anthony and Cleopatra. The tables and
wooden banquet chairs were covered with a white silk fabric, which turned out to have been designed by la marchesa
Scamozzi. The discerning, among whom Reuben counted
himself, noted that the design picked up the one from the
gown of Cleopatra in one of the frescoes. The room was
illuminated by four magnificent chandeliers of Murano
glass; out of respect for the Tiepolos, there were no
candles—and no smoking.

Reuben found table nine easily. As he approached, he
saw Tabita, the model, switching a place card. He pre-
tended not to notice and introduced himself. She offered no
explanation or apology for what she had just done.

The Frosts, the Caroldos and Tabita—Tabita? Ms. Tabita? Frost decided on just plain Tabita, if you could call
"Tabita" plain—were soon joined by a well-dressed but
rather ordinary-looking woman roughly the same age as the

model. She turned out to be Priscilla Gordon, a free-lance reporter doing a piece for *Vanity Fair*. She had an American escort, judging by his accent. More Americans, this time a couple from Dallas, arrived, guided by Tony Garrison. They were the Radleys, Mildred and George.

Table nine was in a corner, under a fresco showing wine casks and revelers. Next to it was a door that opened to the anteroom that had been pressed into service to accommodate more guests. Reuben watched with amusement as the less fortunate scanned the ballroom for their table numbers before realizing that they had been banished. They walked through to the smaller room as if crossing the Bridge of Sighs from the Doges' Palace to the neighboring prison cells.

One determined matron, having confirmed the worst, returned to the ballroom, eyes ablaze, a trembling hand clutching the card with her table number on it. She looked around, presumably for someone to berate, but then shrugged her shoulders and resignedly returned to exile, her anger unassuaged.

Before sitting down, Reuben noted that Gregg Baxter was two tables away, flanked by la marchesa Scamozzi and Deidre Newville, the movie actress and probably the best-known celebrity present. Baxter was seated beneath Cleopatra, in the panel called *Cleopatra's Feast*, in which she is depicted imperially tossing a pearl into a glass as a puzzled Anthony and a cluster of admirers, including an attentive black servant, look on. By accident or design, the juxtaposition seemed fitting to Reuben; he wondered what Tony Garrison's opinion of the fresco might be.

Reuben had not seen Baxter earlier. There had been no receiving line downstairs and if he had been circulating in the crowd, Frost had certainly not noticed him. Now the designer did not look especially jubilant as he talked to la marchesa and Ms. Newville. The conversation must have been serious; smiles and laughter seemed absent.

Reuben thought wistfully of Deidre Newville as he realized that Mrs. Radley was to be his dinner partner. She was not unattractive, and was wearing a most becoming Baxter gown, but she did not have the allure-of the Hollywood actress. Oh well, Reuben consoled himself, he would at least be looking across the table at Tabita, and Erica Sherrill, on his other side, was always good company. Now that everyone was seated, he figured out that Tabita had switched her place card with Ms. Gordon's, separating the reporter from her escort and putting herself next to Tony Garrison.

The first course was delicious *granzeola*, the local spider crab, the succulent meat cooked and returned to the shell. While the guests were eating, a small phalanx of photographers circulated about, snapping pictures. They disappeared as the waiters cleared the plates and prepared for the next course.

Observing the noisy retreat, Dr. Sherrill remarked to Reuben that it was "like the St. Stephen's Day banquets."

"I don't follow you," Reuben said.

"No reason why you should. During the heyday of the Republic, the Doge had an elaborate banquet on the feast of San Stefano, the day after Christmas. The custom was to admit the citizens to the Doges' Palace to observe the guests eating the first course, after which they were required to leave. Just like the photographers here."

"Why didn't the masses riot?" Reuben asked.

"It was thought to be a warm and considerate gesture by the Doge."

"Hmn. Why don't we try that in New York sometime, Erica?"

"Old Beistegui also did something like that," she went on. "When he had his famous masked ball—right here in this room, for heaven's sake—he had another orchestra outside in the *campo* so the people could celebrate, too."

While they were talking, the entree, veal with white truffles, was brought in.

"The first truffles of the season," Dr. Sherrill said.

"You like them?"

"My dear Reuben, truffles are the reason I don't teach the first semester in New York. That and not wanting to be away too long from Emilio, of course. I simply must be here in the fall for the truffles and the *funghi,* the mushrooms that are in season as well.''

"*Tartufi* and *funghi* do help to make living worthwhile, don't they? And this wine is good robust stuff,'' Reuben said, referring to the red Campo Fiorin '79 being served. Its dry and fresh taste blended nicely with the veal, which was succulent and moist even though it had been prepared for three hundred and fifty.

Reuben's happy concentration on the meal was interrupted by Mildred Radley, on his right. ''Which one is your wife?'' she asked bluntly. ''My husband's over there,'' she added, pointing him out next to Dr. Sherrill.

Startled, Reuben nodded across toward Cynthia.

''Nice-looking lady,'' Mrs. Radley observed. ''She's wearing a Baxter. Is she a good customer?''

''A modest one I would say, Mrs. Radley. How about you? Have you helped to make Gregg Baxter rich?''

''We're not here because of our wit and charm, Mr. Frost. Gregg does all my clothes. I love them.''

''You're a lucky woman,'' Frost said. He had already concluded that she must be an important Baxter client, seated as she was next to a very attentive Tony Garrison.

''There are some advantages to being well fixed,'' came the pithy reply. Then, to Reuben's dismay, he got a severe dose of right-wing politics, centering on the sins of Big Government in discriminating against—and oppressively taxing—the rich. It was not what Reuben had bargained for, sitting amid the splendors of the Tiepolos; he was tempted to point out to her that the income tax had been invented in Venice, but restrained himself. Even more appalling, Mrs. Radley launched into a spirited defense of Jesse Helms and his crusade against ''government-sponsored smut.'' He was glad that Cynthia, now the chairman of arts grants for the Brigham Foundation in New York, could not hear. She had been active in the bitter fight with Helms over the funding of the National Endowment for the Arts, and would not have appreciated Mrs. Radley's harangue one bit.

"America can be thankful for Jesse Helms. And for George Bush, who supported him. You've got to hand it to my fellow Texan, Bush. He knows who to support and who to oppose. Like that Arab psycho, Saddam Hussein."

Reuben listened without comment. Then when Mrs. Radley asked, "What do you think of him?" Reuben could stand it no longer. Aggravated by both the intolerable physical heat in the room and the ideological fire emanating from his neighbor, he opened up.

"I think he should have been stopped the first time he opened his mouth. He's a bully, but he would have understood strength."

"I'm glad we agree. Bush should have started bombing Baghdad the day Saddam invaded Kuwait."

"Who are we talking about?" said Reuben, in confusion. "I was referring to Jesse Helms."

"Oh. I thought you meant Saddam Hussein," Mrs. Radley replied, in a suddenly chilly voice. When the dessert—complicated balls of chocolate surrounded by frozen vanilla *sorbetto*—was served, she wasted no time in resuming an earlier conversation with Tony Garrison.

Frost had observed Baxter's young assistant during Mrs. Radley's lecture. The light-skinned young man was exceptionally handsome, with warm, friendly eyes, now unobscured by his PADRES cap. To Frost's surprise, he had been speaking to Dott. Caroldo in Italian. He dismissed the twinge of conscience that struck him—that it was racist to wonder at his command of Italian—but nonetheless concluded that it *was* at least mildly intriguing that a young American dress designer from New York should be fluent in Italian, whatever his color. His ruminations were interrupted by Erica Sherrill's laughter beside him.

"St. Lucy's eyes," she said, looking at the two iced globes that were her dessert.

"What?"

"Santa Lucia's eyes! Her symbol is a pair of eyes on a plate. So, *eccoli*, there they are, right in front of you, even though they're about to melt. I'm sure nobody in this room is aware of it, but poor Santa Lucia's bones are right next door, in San Geremia.''

"Ah, yes. That's what that big sign is all about, on the side of the church facing the Grand Canal," Reuben said. "A Renaissance billboard, in Latin, that tells you her relics are in there. It never occurred to me, but that's what it is. A billboard!"

While they were talking, Priscilla Gordon, the reporter, quickly ate her dessert and then excused herself, saying that she had "work to do." She pulled a small notebook and a pen from her purse and left the table, presumably in quest of printable comments on the evening's dinner (or perhaps unprintable ones on the temperature). Mrs. Radley took advantage of the opening to move across and sit next to her husband, undoubtedly to give a whispered report on Reuben's remarks about Senator Helms. Tony Garrison also got up and began greeting people at other tables.

All the movement gave Reuben an opportunity to move next to the gorgeous Tabita, an opening he did not let slip by.

"That's a handsome dress you're wearing. I've been admiring it all evening," Frost told her. He was not exaggerating and had, indeed, regarded the woman's gown with the greatest pleasure. It was a rich, deep purple in color, with an intricate gold pattern superimposed upon it.

"Thank you. It's an experiment," she said, pleased at the compliment.

"How do you mean?"

"Tony, Tony Garrison? Who was sitting here? He designed it for me."

"It's a very unusual fabric."

"It's one of Ceil Scamozzi's. It's based on an old Venetian design. Isn't it beautiful?"

"Yes, it certainly is."

"You know that Gregg's spring line is going to be heavy on Ceil's—the marchesa's—fabrics."

"That's one reason for this party, isn't it?"

"Correct. I shouldn't say this, but you're not a reporter, right? And not in the business, right?"

"I'm just an innocent bystander," Reuben said.

"Well, it was really Tony who had the inspiration to use Ceil's fabrics. The dress I'm wearing is the one he created to convince Gregg."

"I can see why it worked."

"Gregg didn't like it much that I wanted to wear it tonight. He was afraid it would give too much away about next spring's clothes."

"I think Mr. Garrison is to be commended. I was surprised, incidentally, to hear him speaking Italian before."

Tabita smiled slyly. "Othello spoke Italian, Mr. Frost."

"I didn't mean . . ."

"I'm sure you didn't. And I agree with you that hearing a black man speak Italian doesn't happen every day. But you should know that Tony *is* Italian. Half, anyway. His father was an American G.I. stationed in Livorno, where his mother lived. Tony was born there and only came to New York when his father was discharged."

"I see," Reuben said.

"Yes, Tony's a man of the world," Tabita said. "He comes to Venice every chance he gets. He's the one who found the marchesa. Then, when Gregg was at Lake Como buying fabrics last year, Tony persuaded him to detour over here and look at her work. The rest is history. Or will be after next month's show."

"I assume you say that because you've seen what Baxter's created?" Reuben said.

"Ha! Gregg designs right up to the last minute. Or maybe I should say *at* the last minute. The business is all so crazy. Right now he's looking at new fabrics here in Italy for next fall—a year from now. Then he has to go back and concentrate on the spring collection, which he'll unveil next month. Of course Tony's already done a lot of sketching—" Tabita stopped suddenly, her guilty look indicating that she was afraid she had been indiscreet.

"How about you? Where are you from?" Reuben asked.

"Am I an exotic creature like Tony, you mean? The answer's no. I'm a little hard-shell Baptist from the Mississippi Delta—God-fearing and innocent." She gave Reuben a look that appeared anything but innocent. But who knows, Reuben thought, with her phenomenally sexy aura, maybe this is the closest to a modest look that she can achieve.

Tony Garrison returned from his glad-handing and Reuben started to get up so that he could reclaim his chair.

"No, no," he said, putting his hand on Frost's shoulder. "I'll sit over here. What's your name again?"

"Reuben. Reuben Frost."

"Mind if I call you Reuben?"

"Not at all."

Garrison started drumming a tattoo on the table and grinned when he saw that Reuben was watching. "We going out on the town later, Rubes?" he asked.

Frost could not decide whether he was more shocked at the invitation or the monniker "Rubes"—a new one. And perhaps even worse than the short-lived "Frosty" that he had squelched years ago as an undergraduate at Princeton.

"I doubt it," he said. "I don't think this is much of a town for night life."

"Stick with me, Rubes. You might be surprised."

Frost had to admit to himself that the handsome young man's easy cheekiness had an appeal, abhorrent as "Rubes" might be.

While Garrison was issuing his invitation, the waiters had circulated and filled the flutes at each place with Prosecco. Reuben expected, and was sure others did as well, that Baxter would give a toast. Or, perhaps, that someone would salute Baxter, their generous host. This did not happen.

Reuben had noticed that Baxter had remained fixed at his place—possibly mesmerized by Deidre Newville—and, unlike his gregarious assistant, had not circulated among the guests, even to soothe the dented egos in the adjoin room. This had seemed most odd, given the prom nature of the party, but the host still did not m espresso and liqueurs were served. To the c up and left the room, with Doris Medfo him. Dan Abbott, when he saw what was happening, abruptly left a nearby table and joined the retreating party.

Baxter looked sullen and did not acknowledge anyone along his path to the stairs. Why was he angry? Was he upset at the uncomfortable heat? Did he think it had ruined his party? Reuben decided to ask Tabita what might be wrong.

"I see your boss is leaving," he said. "You suppose he doesn't like the company?"

She rolled her eyes and gently moved her head from side to side. Another "innocent" gesture. "Beats me. You have to understand that Gregg Baxter is very complicated. And very unpredictable."

Those who had seen Baxter leave had soon passed the word to those who had not, and the partygoers began drifting toward the front entrance. Soon there was a crowd backed all the way up the staircase, while the flotilla of water-taxis outside began loading. Those who made up the crowd were not the sort used to standing in line. Their boiling points already elevated by the heat, they were in a grumbling, ungrateful mood, not the grandly festive one that should have prevailed. It was as if Gregg Baxter had inconvenienced them terribly by inviting them for an uncomfortable evening.

Four of the efficient women who had been so evident before dinner passed out souvenir shopping bags, red ones for the women and, of course, gray ones for the men. The recipients eagerly dug into the tissue-paper wrapped contents, much like children at Christmas in the orphanage, and discovered, among the miscellany within, women's scarves and men's pocket squares in fabrics bearing Gregg Baxter's signature and, in tinier script, la marchesa Scamozzi's as well.

Then the traffic flow was stopped entirely as a guest, already outside, pushed her way back in. It was the same wiry matron Reuben had seen earlier, the one who had ___ made a scene about her exile from the ballroom. ___ she frantically sought out one of the women with the bags of party favors; hers had fallen into the water as she boarded her *motoscafo* and she had now returned, determined to get a replacement. She was given one and went outside again, allowing departures to resume.

The Frosts were with the Caroldos, who had said they would go back to the Cipriani with them and take the number eight water-bus from the Zitelle to the Zattere, where their apartment was located.

"Does it run at this hour?" Reuben asked, it then being after midnight.

"Oh yes," Emilio said. "Only on the half hour, but it operates all night. The other alternative is to get our *motoscafista* to go around the back way so he can leave us off on the Zattere."

The chief traffic director put the Frosts and the Caroldos in a boat with four other couples. Again the paparazzi, still on duty, held their fire. The chanting students had not left the Ponte delle Guglie, but their taunts could not be heard clearly. Probably a good thing, Reuben thought.

Emilio Caroldo did persuade the operator of their boat to go around to the Giudecca Canal. The Frosts and the Caroldos managed to sit together, ignoring the others, whom they did not know.

"L'abia o non l'abia, sarò sempre Labia," Erica Sherrill declaimed as they passed the Piazzale Roma.

"I'll bite," Cynthia said. "What does that mean?"

"It's a pun, and roughly translated means, 'Whether I have it or don't have it, I'll always be a Labia.' It was supposedly said by one of the family's disreputable ancestors after a banquet, when he was drunk and throwing the gold dinner service out the window into the canal."

"The only thing that went into the water tonight was that poor woman's gift pack," Reuben said.

"See you Tuesday night," Erica said when they got t~ the Zattere, referring to a dinner invitation she had ext~ earlier in the evening.

As they continued the trip back, the Frosts c~ hearing the chatter around them, all in Engl~

with complaints about the heat and, for one couple, the outrageous seating arrangements. One of the women regretted that there had not been dancing, in a tone implying that Baxter had been chintzy not to have a band.

At the Cipriani, the *motoscafista* backed their boat alongside the landing stage at the rear of the swimming pool; the one in front was customarily closed after ten-thirty to cut engine noise in the bedrooms. The Frosts clambered up the steps with the others. They decided to have a nightcap in the bar adjacent to the pool and ordered Scotches from Walter, the barman.

"I know Gregg Baxter will get his publicity," Cynthia said. "But I do feel sorry for him, with all those ingrates as guests. I've never heard such griping and whining. He couldn't control the weather, though somebody might have warned him about all those candles."

"And whoever advised him about using that second room should be fired," Reuben added. "He should have been smart enough to realize you can't divide your guests into an obvious 'A' list and 'B' list. It's a shame, because otherwise it was a beautifully planned party. The work involved must have been incredible, to say nothing of the cost. I'm also sure he sensed everybody's discomfort."

"Do you think that's why he left so quickly?" Cynthia asked.

"That's my guess. But he wasn't being very hospitable even before that. As far as I could tell, he didn't circulate at all. Is he shy, do you think?"

"Good heavens, no," Cynthia said. "I've been to his shows in New York and he's very much the social butterfly. And you've seen him at parties. He's very outgoing, especially if there's a good-looking boy to flirt with."

Massimo, the bar pianist, returned from his break while they were talking. Spotting the Frosts, he broke into "New York, New York." He gave them a grin and they smiled back.

"Good heavens, there's Doris Medford," Cynthia said, _____ring toward the door. Reuben called to her as she came by their table, seemingly oblivious of all those around her. She started when she recognized the Frosts.

"Won't you join us?" Reuben asked.

"No, I'm just going to the bar and celebrate my talent as a weatherman. Weatherperson."

"What do you mean?"

"What I mean is, Gregg Baxter has just fired me because tonight's party was, as he put it, a 'major, major disaster.' And it was all my fault. Up to and including the weather."

"I'm very sorry, Doris."

"Forget it. That's what I'm going to do. Have a drink or two or three at the bar and forget it. Please excuse me for not joining you. . . ."

"We understand, my dear," Cynthia said. "And we really *are* sorry. *We* had a terrific evening."

"Thanks," Medford said as she walked away.

"That's terrible," Cynthia said to Reuben. "Even if you did say the person who came up with the 'A' room and the 'B' room should be fired."

"It's too bad, but I'm not going to get involved in Gregg Baxter's employee relations," Reuben said.

"You know who I didn't see there tonight?" Cynthia asked. "Eric Werth and the Irish sumo wrestler."

"Neither did I, come to think of it. Very odd. They most likely were smart and went to an air-conditioned restaurant."

"Now don't be another ingrate, dear. The evening was hot and ever so uncomfortable, but I wouldn't have missed it for the world."

5

CYNTHIA HAD ANNOUNCED WEDNESDAY NIGHT THAT, DE-
spite staying up so late, she was going to Murano the next
morning to shop for "replacements for all the things you've
broken." At home the Frosts had a modest collection of
hand-blown Venetian glasses, all of attractive modern designs but so delicate they often broke.

"I see. I thought perhaps you might be going to buy a
glass flamingo," Reuben had retorted. "Just don't wake me
if you're getting up early."

She now crept around the bedroom so as not to disturb
her husband. Her precaution proved futile as the telephone
rang on the dot of nine o'clock. It was Dan Abbott, full of
apologies for the early call but asking Frost if they could
meet for breakfast.

"When?" Reuben asked.

"As soon as you can," Abbott replied.

"What's this about?"

"I'd rather tell you in person. It's somewhat touchy."

Reuben was intrigued, so he told Abbott he would meet
him in fifteen minutes.

"I've got a suite, or a junior suite, or whatever the hell
they call it. I'd prefer to meet there if you don't mind. Num-

44

ber 42, over by the pool. It's the first door when you come up the stairs to the second floor." Abbott asked Frost what he would like to eat and said he would place the order.

Reuben described the call to Cynthia. "What do you suppose he wants?"

"Maybe he needs advice about where to buy a new wig."

"Very funny. If it's one thing I don't know anything about it's wigs. My hair may not be as thick as it once was—it's thinning out at an appalling rate, if the truth be known—but I'm not in the wig business. At least not quite yet."

"I know, dear. Besides, I hope when you are you'll have the courage to go around bald."

"Hmn."

Dan Abbott was dressed in khaki Bermuda shorts and a blue polo shirt—wig in place—when he opened the door to his suite after Reuben's knock.

"Thanks for coming over, Mr. Frost," he said. "Breakfast just arrived." A waiter was arranging the order on the table outside on the balcony. There was a tomato omelet for Reuben (a dish he regarded as one of the greatest delights of the Cipriani kitchen) and a simple *caffè completo* for Abbott, resting under metal warming covers.

"Come sit under my big magic umbrella," Abbott said.

"Why 'magic'?"

"Well, every morning when I get up this umbrella is open, although it was closed the night before. I'm sure nobody's walked through my room to open it, so it must be magic."

"Probably a very agile houseboy, who climbs along the edge of the balcony," Reuben said.

"That's what I think, too. Have a seat," Abbott said. Then, with a deep sigh, he added, "It seems like mid-afternoon already."

"Why so?"

"Doris Medford. I had to get up at dawn and help her move to the Bauer Grunwald. Gregg fired her last night and she had to get out of here."

"Why didn't she go to the Gritti?" Reuben asked. He had never especially liked what he had seen of the Bauer Grunwald.

"Absolutely full."

"We saw Ms. Medford late last night and she told us the bad news. I gather they had a falling out over the party."

"It's more complicated than that, but too tiresome to go into so early in the morning." It was clear the subject was closed. Abbott told Reuben that he had "a pretty good reputation as a detective around New York." Then he added, "Different than working on First Fiduciary loans."

Reuben laughed. "You're right about the banking part. But you're not very accurate about my reputation. I'm just a retired lawyer who's had the bad luck on occasion to be in the wrong place at the wrong time."

"You're too modest. I'm an old friend of Grace Mann, who told me about your part in solving David Rowan's murder."

"Yes, I did have a hand in that. But, tell me, how did I earn this breakfast?"

"I need your expertise. Or more precisely, Gregg Baxter does."

"Mr. Abbott, I can't possibly respond to that until I know what it is you're talking about."

"It's very simple. Gregg Baxter thinks someone tried to poison him yesterday."

Abruptly Frost realized that the designer's odd behavior at his own dinner might have had a deeper cause than the weather.

"What happened?" Reuben asked.

"I'm sure he'll want to tell you himself."

"What am I supposed to do? Find the poisoner?"

"The first thing I need is assistance in trying to calm him down. He's got all kinds of work to do. This poison thing has to be cleared up if he's going to concentrate properly. Needless to say, we'll pay you whatever fee you think appropriate."

"Mr. Abbott, I'm not a licensed detective, nor do I care

to be one. I couldn't possibly charge you. And, anyway, I'm here on vacation, not looking for detective work, legal work or any other kind of work.''

"I understand. But I'd consider it a great favor if you'd hear what Gregg has to say and offer him whatever advice you can. I'm sorry I mentioned pay. That was crass. But if you can get to the bottom of this weirdness perhaps we can do something for Mrs. Frost. Christ, if you succeed, we'll keep her as well dressed as Mildred Radley for the rest of her life.''

"I couldn't go along with that, either. And for your own sake and mine, I suggest you not pass that proposal on to her.''

"Gregg's at the other end of the hall,'' Abbott explained, when they had finished their breakfast. ''We're all happy campers here in the compound. Come with me.''

Number 45 was unlocked and Abbott went in without knocking. Baxter was sitting on the private balcony outside the room, wearing an ornate dressing gown, drinking coffee and looking woebegone.

"Hi,'' he said to Reuben. Then he ordered Abbott to pour him another cup of coffee. Abbott was about to do so when the designer barked, ''Wash the cup out first. Otherwise it will taste like shit. You know that.''

Abbott dutifully went inside to the bathroom and returned with a rinsed cup. He poured coffee and warm milk from the pitchers on the table and handed the cup back to Baxter. Never in the process was there even a muttered ''thanks.''

"Did you tell him?'' Baxter asked Abbott.

"I told him the problem, yes,'' Abbott replied. ''I figured you'd want to give him the details.''

"It was your idea to get him involved. You tell him.''

"I'd like to hear your version,'' Frost said, taking a seat opposite Baxter.

"Oh, okay, okay. The story is this. I'm a diabetic. I take insulin twice a day—by injection—once first thing in the morning, the second time before dinner. Yesterday, I decided to take my shot here before going off to the party. It meant I'd have it a little earlier than I should—it's supposed to be just before you eat—but it seemed less of a hassle than taking all the damn paraphernalia over to the palazzo.

"I've been keeping my insulin in my minibar refrigerator," he continued. "I had two bottles with me. I finished one yesterday morning and threw it away. Then, last night, I took out the other one and found that it had already been unsealed. I knew I hadn't opened it, and when I took off the top there was a funny smell. Like garlic, for Christ's sake. That was definitely wrong and all I could think of was that someone was trying to poison me."

"Let me ask you a couple of questions," Frost said. "First of all, where's the bottle?"

"In the room safe, inside."

"Good. Now, you seem very certain that your second bottle of insulin hadn't been opened by you. Are you *sure* of that? Isn't it possible you opened it when the first one ran out yesterday morning?"

"Not a chance, Mr. Frost. I'll tell you why. I'm not too careful about many things in my life, but I don't fool around with my shots. Since my diabetes was first diagnosed a few years back, at different times I've had both hyperglycemia and insulin shock—too much blood sugar and too little—because I didn't pay enough attention to measuring my dosages. My doctor convinced me—scared me—that I could kill myself if I wasn't more careful. So I'm both fussy and finicky when it comes to insulin. Besides, even if I wasn't uncertain about when I opened the bottle, I sure as hell wouldn't have injected myself when the stuff smelled like garlic."

"What do you suppose the garlic smell means?" Abbott asked.

"Christ alone knows," Baxter replied. "But I wasn't about to find out."

"I don't know anything about diabetes," Reuben said, "but I've always understood that you must take your shots regularly."

"That's right," Baxter said. "If you miss even one, you risk hyperglycemia."

"So what did you do last night when you decided your insulin was contaminated?" Reuben asked.

"I sent Dan over across to town to buy some more. You don't need a prescription for insulin, you know. Just the needles—for obvious reasons."

"There was a *farmacia* in back of St. Mark's that was still open," Abbott explained.

"You may have noticed I wasn't exactly the life of my own party last night," Baxter said.

"I did," Reuben answered.

"So what do you suggest, Mr. Frost?" Abbott said.

"The first thing is to have that insulin bottle analyzed. I think we should get Cavallaro from the front office up here. He should be able to help you find a laboratory. Unless, of course, you want to go to the police."

"I don't think there's any point in involving the police," Baxter said. "I'm supposed to be here to get publicity. I don't need the sob sisters clucking over who tried to poison me. You disagree, Dan?"

"Not at all."

"I'm not a sob sister, Mr. Baxter, but who *do* you think might have tried to poison you? Assuming there's poison in that bottle," Reuben said.

"Valerie Steifel," Abbott said.

"Not amusing, Dan," Baxter said.

"Who is Valerie Steifel?" Frost asked.

"The head buyer for Saks Fifth Avenue," Abbott explained. "She was here for the party and Gregg took the occasion to tell her he's pulling out of his Saks boutique unless she remodels it."

"And remodels it like *I* want it," Baxter added. "The place looks like a Kmart."

"She was ready to kill you after you gave her the bad news," Abbott said.

"I assume you're not serious," Frost said.

"Mr. Frost, the rag trade is cutthroat. Probably even

worse than the legal profession,'' Abbott said. ''If I've learned one thing, it's never to be surprised at what happens in this business. And to the people in it.''

''No, he's not serious,'' Baxter said. ''Valerie was leaked off as hell, but she's not about to murder me.''

''Any other candidates?'' Reuben asked.

''Probably one of the blackies. They're always ready to kill me over something.''

''Gregg, if that's all you can say, shut up,'' Abbott said angrily. ''To talk like that is childish. Tabita and Tony are completely loyal to you and you know it.''

Baxter smiled, seeming pleased that he had upset his partner. ''I guess that leaves only you, Dan,'' Baxter continued. ''A pretty drastic way of taking over Baxter Fashions, wouldn't you say? But I guess you're desperate to get your hands on it.''

There was a definite edge to his voice, even though he kept smiling. Abbott looked hurt but did not reply; Frost guessed that he was accustomed to Baxter's abuse.

Frost was curious at the conspicuous omission of Doris Medford and decided to ask about it. If he was going to be involved in this strange imbroglio, there was no point in holding questions back.

''Medford?'' Baxter said, when Reuben had asked his question. ''That drunken bitch? I doubt it. She screwed up my dinner, but she's not the murdering type. You agree, Dan?''

''Basically, yes,'' Abbott said. ''Though when she's on one of her rampages, it's best to watch out. Booze fuels her up like a NASA rocket.''

''Surely with all the party preparations she wasn't drunk yesterday,'' Reuben said. ''At least until late last night.''

''Quite right, quite right,'' Abbott said. ''I was making a general observation that isn't relevant here. I'm sorry.''

''Let's call Cavallaro,'' Frost said. ''But before we do, let me just say one thing. If I'm involved, and we find out that your insulin bottle had poison in it, Mr. Baxter, I'm going to try my damndest to find out who put it there. As far as I'm concerned, the chips can fall where they may. Is that clear?''

"We wouldn't want it any other way," Abbott said.

"I hear you Mr. Frost," Baxter said. "Our objectives are the same—I'm going to find out who tried to poison me if it kills me."

Alfred Cavallaro appeared at Baxter's suite, his facial expression a mix of concern and apprehension.

"What we've been hoping, Alfredo," Frost said, once the problem had been presented, "is that you can direct us to a laboratory that can find out quickly whether Mr. Baxter's suspicion is justified."

"Yes. That is possible. I have an old friend in Mestre who runs a commercial *laboratorio*. I'll try to call her. I have her number in the office."

"Excellent," Reuben said. "Meanwhile, Mr. Baxter, why don't you retrieve the insulin bottle from your safe. I take it no one has handled it except you?"

"As far as I know," Baxter said.

"And no one else has the combination?" Frost asked. Lesser rooms, like his own, did not have such fancy appurtenances.

"No. I set it myself. It's one of those gizmos where the guest picks the numbers."

"I don't think there's much else we can do right now, once we get the bottle off to Mestre," Reuben said.

"Let me ring my friend," Cavallaro said.

"And I guess I'll go down to Ceil's," Baxter said. "If someone's trying to do me in, I'd better try to get my work done fast." Reuben was going to warn him to be careful, but when he noticed a vein pounding in Baxter's temple, he decided that a warning was not necessary.

ANTICA BESSETA

6

CYNTHIA FROST RETURNED TO THE CIPRIANI ABOUT SIX, after a busy day of shopping, first on Murano and then in the shops of the Mercerie behind San Marco. She was laden with bundles when she came into Room 201.

"Looks like you bought out the town," Reuben said.

"Not quite, dear," she replied, sitting down heavily on her bed, plainly tired.

"Did you get to Murano?" Reuben asked. He was bursting to tell her about Gregg Baxter's insulin bottle, but had decided it would be more fun to surprise her after she had described her own day.

"Yes, first thing this morning. And you'll be happy to know they said at Salviati we can get replacements for our broken glasses by Christmas."

"Just goes to show that money can do anything."

"They *are* expensive, God knows. But beautiful and worth it. You do agree, don't you?"

"Of course," Reuben said. "Where did you have lunch?"

"A trat on the canal in Murano. My big discovery was the glass museum. Have you ever been there? I never had."

"No."

"A lot of what they have is appalling junk—"

"Did that surprise you? There are only about six patterns of Venetian glass that are tolerable. Including our glasses, I hasten to add. The rest is rubbish."

"It *was* interesting. Did you know, Reuben, there's a legend that the glass-blowers used to produce drinking glasses so fine that they would shatter if the slightest bit of poison were put in them?"

"Hmn. I know someone who could use one of those."

"What do you mean?"

"Just that while you were out buying up Venice, I was being consulted about an attempted murder."

"What on earth are you talking about?"

Frost told his wife about his morning meeting with Baxter and Abbott.

"So they still don't know whether there was poison in Baxter's medicine," Cynthia said, when he had finished. "Maybe it's his imagination."

"It could be. We should know tomorrow."

"Any shrewd guesses about who might have been playing with his insulin?" Cynthia asked.

"If anybody was, that is. No, I don't, really. I suppose it could be any of the people around him—Doris Medford, Dan Abbott, that knockout model, young Garrison."

"Well, let's hope the lab report is negative. This is our vacation, after all."

"*È vero.*"

"What did you do later?" Cynthia asked.

"I had a typical afternoon of Venetian sightseeing," Reuben said. "I tramped around to three churches—all of them closed. *Chiuso*. I forgot to say a prayer to the patron saint of Venetian tourists—Santa Maria delle Chiusure. Saint Mary of the Closings, pray for us."

"And don't forget San Giovanni in Restauro. He should get a few prayers, too."

An hour later, Reuben was at last able to reach Dan Abbott in his room. The business manager had nothing to report but said "thank God" Baxter had kept busy during the afternoon at Ceil Scamozzi's workrooms, which had taken his mind off the poisoned insulin bottle. Reuben, in turn, reported a conversation with Cavallaro, in which he said he'd been promised a lab report not later than tomorrow.

"I guess we just have to sit tight till then," Abbott replied. "Any suggestions?"

"Yes. I'd keep an eye on my partner. If there's a poisoner out there, he may just try again."

"Don't worry, I intend to," Abbott replied.

Reuben and Cynthia stopped downstairs for a drink before setting out for the Antica Besseta, their culinary target for the evening. They noticed that the hotel seemed overrun with formally dressed couples, with even more debarking from water-taxis.

"It looks like there's a blow-out here almost as big as Gregg Baxter's," Cynthia observed.

"What's going on?" Reuben asked Bianco, the bar waiter.

"A dinner. Americans. Bankers."

Frost now recalled that they had been told this when they first checked in. "Do you know where from?" he asked.

"No, sir, I don't."

Having finished their drinks, the Frosts got up to leave. It never ceased to amaze Reuben that the elaborate bookkeeping and chit signing so intrusive and bothersome in the average hotel was almost completely absent here. If the bartender knew a guest, he looked up the room number himself; if the guest was a stranger, he asked the room number just once. That was the extent of the red tape. (Not that one did not pay, God knows, for every drop consumed.)

Outside, they ran into two acquaintances, Ted and Sandra Demetrios from New York. He was a partner in Hughes & Company, an old-line investment banking firm. His father, "old" Ted, had been a classmate of Reuben's at Princeton, and the latter had followed, though not closely, the upward progress of "young" Ted (now a mere forty-five). Demetrios was wearing black tie, his wife a long yellow evening dress (a Baxter, at that).

Questioning revealed that the Hughes partners from around the world were gathered for a "retreat" that had begun in Milan and had moved to Venice that morning for three days of socializing, including the black-tie dinner for the bankers and their spouses that was about to begin.

"We've been held prisoner all week in Milan. It sure is good to get out," Demetrios said.

Reuben learned that they were staying at the Gritti, and that the Hughes group was divided between the Gritti and the Cipriani.

"Business can't be bad if you're having a formal dinner here," Reuben said.

"No, it's not, thank God. But the black-tie part's a pain in the neck."

"All due to Suzie Benedict," Sandra Demetrios whispered, referring to the wife of Hughes' senior partner. "If there's a chance to be pretentious, she'll find it."

Reuben and Cynthia joined in the conspiratorial laughter and then went off.

By the time they had negotiated the lengthy trip to the Riva di Biasio at the bottom of the Grand Canal, both were hungry and looked forward to putting themselves into the capable hands of the Volpes, Nereo and Maurizia, the owners of Antica Besseta. The modest trattoria had been recommended to them years before by a knowing New York restaurateur who had pronounced it "without question" the best in Venice.

Nothing ever changed about the place, except the occasional addition of a work of art to the cheerful miscellany on the walls (including a painting by Peter Begley, a young American artist living in Rome they had known for some years). In many restaurants, the heart sank when one encountered modern stereo systems and other latter-day "improvements." There was never such a danger at the Antica Besseta.

The Frosts were greeted ebulliently by the Volpes, Nereo

rushing from the dining room, kissing Cynthia's hand, embracing Reuben, and calling to his wife, who appeared at once from the kitchen. They were quickly paraded to a corner table and without delay were drinking the house Pinot Bianco. There was a large and jolly party of locals; otherwise the room was filled with foreigners including, Reuben was startled to discover as he looked around, Doris Medford, Eric Werth and Jim Cavanaugh. The Frosts waved, deciding to postpone a more personal greeting until the others had finished dining.

Reuben's and Nereo's respective deficiencies in the other's language did not inhibit a spirited discussion of both the fortunes of the Volpe family and the evening's menu. With confidence, knowing that Nereo bought his fish from the *Mercato del Pesce al Minuto*—literally, the market of fish of the minute—below the Rialto at four o'clock each morning, they ordered the *antipasto di pesce*, a wonderful assortment of fresh seafood, both familiar and (quite often) not so familiar.

"Fancy seeing our friends here," Cynthia said.

"Not so surprising. After all I told them on the plane that it was our favorite restaurant. Nereo should pay me a commission."

Cynthia was silent for a while and then burst out, as if it had been troubling her, "I can't believe you're going to get mixed up in another escapade, Reuben."

"I'm sure I won't," he replied. "If I'm lucky, Baxter's problem will turn out to be a false alarm."

"But if that insulin *was* poisoned?"

"There's still not much I can do, as far as I can see. Question all the pharmacists in Venice? That's a job for the police. I'm very confident our vacation's not going to be interrupted. As confident as I am that these tiny *gamberetti* will be delicious." He pointed to the minuscule "shrimplets" on the diverse and vivid plate of marine life Nereo Volpe had brought each of them.

Cynthia, always adventuresome, attacked a boiled *polpo*, a small octopus. "I agree, there doesn't seem to be much that you could do. Which makes me wonder why they consulted you at all.''

"Dan Abbott said my reputation was considerable. I can't believe that's true—though it's nice flattery—but he had heard about the Rowan case from Grace Mann. Anyway, to answer your question, if I were in a foreign country and saw my meal ticket threatened, I'd try to get help any place I could. He's got a pretty good motive for keeping Gregg Baxter alive and well.''

Despite their animated conversation, the Frosts' plates were soon empty—even the most peculiar and least known creatures had been eaten—and were quickly replaced by steaming bowls of *spaghetti alle vongole,* perfectly cooked spaghetti with clams in their shells.

"If the worst happens, and we're dealing with a case of poisoning,'' Reuben continued, "about all I can do is advise Mr. Baxter to get the hell out of here.''

"If I were he, I'd have left already,'' Cynthia said.

"He's got work that has to be done with Ceil Scamozzi. If he flees, he'll have to come back later, or so Abbott told me.''

"Isn't he frightened? I would be.''

"I'm sure you're right. There were little signs this morning that he was. Like a throbbing vein in his forehead.''

"Reuben, aren't these *vongole* the best dish in the whole world?'' Cynthia asked.

"No.''

"No?''

"No. Maurizia's grilled sole, which you're about to have, is the best thing in the whole world.''

"It's a close call,'' Cynthia said. As she spoke, Nereo Volpe presented with a flourish the *sogliole alla griglia* his wife had prepared, then took them back for deboning.

"This sole *is* delicious, Reuben,'' Cynthia said, once she had sampled it. "I'd forgotten how fantastic it is here.''

"Better than the *vongole?*''

"Yes. But what a choice!''

"*È andato bene?*" the proprietor asked as he stopped at the Frosts' table when they had finished their sole.

"*Sì, Nereo. Era proprio squisito,*" Reuben said, meaning it: their most delicious meal had indeed gone well. Cynthia and Reuben declined dessert, pleading that they were absolutely stuffed. Then Jim Cavanaugh, who must have been watching their progress, came over and asked them to join him and his friends "for a *digestivo,* as they say."

"I'm not sure I'm up to that, but we'll be happy to join you for coffee," Reuben said. After a shuffling of chairs, they arranged themselves in a semicircle around Cavanaugh's table.

"This was a good recommendation, Mr. Frost," Eric Werth said. "This place was a new one on me and I thank you."

Sig. Volpe returned with a bottle of homemade grappa, complete with its label showing an old woman money changer, the namesake *antica besseta.* Cynthia, Reuben and Eric Werth declined—with profuse thanks—but Cavanaugh and Medford did not.

"Have you been having a good time, Mr. Cavanaugh?" Reuben asked, genuinely curious.

"I can't say as I have," the lawyer said. "This place is a joke—no cars, no street signs that mean anything, dirty water. And prices you wouldn't believe. And the dog crap! Nobody warned me about the dog crap! It's everywhere!"

Reuben laughed. "A couple of years ago they passed a 'scooper' law here, like the one in New York, but didn't bother to enforce it. Now I'm told they are and you can be fined two hundred thousand lire—almost two hundred dollars—if you don't clean up after your dog."

"If they call what they're doing enforcement, I'd like to know how they handle serious crimes," Cavanaugh said.

"I'm sorry you're disappointed with Venice," Cynthia said. "I hope your business has been successful."

"Negative," Cavanaugh said. "We haven't had any luck in that department at all."

"Gregg Baxter won't even see us," Werth added. "We fly all the way over here, and *he won't even see us!*"

"That seems peculiar," Reuben said.

"We've been trying to talk turkey with Gregg Baxter for two years," Werth said. "He's so big right now that if we could get a license to use his name on a line of perfume, we'd have a money machine like you've never seen. But will he cooperate? Not on his life. Says all he really wants to do is high-line fashion, that's enough for him. *Coo-toor.* The fancy stuff."

Werth's reference to "coo-toor" drew an exuberant laugh from Medford. "Hail, hail," she said, as she reached for the grappa bottle and poured herself and Cavanaugh generous refills. "Have some more of this diesel fuel, honey," she said to the lawyer, patting him affectionately on the back of his head.

"Baxter looks down on us," Werth went on. "We're beneath him. He won't license us or anybody else to do anything. Why, Dan Abbott said it was all he could do to get Baxter to do a line of better dresses."

"Better dresses?" Reuben asked.

"Yes, better dresses," Werth said. "The stuff between high fashion and what's mass produced. They should be called 'worse' dresses, I suppose, but the trade calls them 'better.' "

"Do you know Dan Abbott?" Cavanaugh asked.

"Yes," Frost said.

"Good solid fellow. He's been trying to talk Baxter into making a deal. He's the one who got us to make this trip. As I told you the other day, he thought Baxter might sit down and talk when he's relaxed, when he's out of New York. Fat chance. We even got uninvited to Baxter's party."

"*Un*invited?" Cynthia asked, incredulous.

"That's right," Werth said. "We'd received engraved invitations back in New York, but once we got here Abbott called us at the Gritti and said that Baxter not only wouldn't see us, he didn't want us at his party. So we wasted good time and money to get here for nothing. Temperamental son of a bitch. I could kill him!''

You and a party unknown, Reuben thought. ''I'm afraid we have to be going,'' he said, then asked Nereo for the *contecini*.

The owner smiled at Reuben's use of the local slang expression for a bill—not a word for a small *conto*, or check, as Reuben had mistakenly thought the first time he had heard it, but a reference to the late Count Cini, an openhanded local philanthropist but apparently a legendary avoider of paying when he dined out with others.

''We'll come with you,'' Werth said. ''We had a helluva time finding this place and I'd hate to get lost going back.''

Cavanaugh, who had already paid, and Medford each had another grappa while Reuben counted out the lire to pay his bill.

''I should leave something for all these drinks we've been having,'' Cavanaugh said.

''Don't worry, I'll take care of it,'' Reuben said, adding another bank note to the pile in front of him.

Their new companions waited awkwardly at the front of the restaurant while the Frosts said goodbye to Nereo. Maurizia Volpe, as she often did, had already slipped away home. So now the leave-taking consisted of a flurry of embraces with Nereo, kisses, vows of lifelong esteem, paeans of compliments to la signora and her cooking and a firm promise by the Frosts to return *presto*.

Arm in arm, Reuben and Cynthia led the others back to the Riva di Biasio. Never mind that the Riva was named for a medieval innkeeper who allegedly killed and stewed small boys to make his *squazzetto;* after their delightful meal and generous draughts of wine, it would take more than this ancient tale to disturb their sense of well-being.

They did not have to wait long for a *vaporetto*. Like all *vaporetti* it was misnamed, powered as it was not by steam but by diesel; doubly misnamed in this case for, although called *l'accelerato*, it made every stop along the Grand Canal.

The slow pace was quite all right with Reuben and Cynthia. They had agreed, many years ago, that the two-mile passage up the Grand Canal late at night was the most thrillingly beautiful journey one could imagine. Reuben even sought out the *marinaio* to pay the fare, then joined his wife in an outdoor seat to take in the exquisite palazzi that lined the route, some receding into the shadowy darkness, others with brilliantly illuminated rooms visible from the water. Even Jim Cavanaugh seemed impressed.

"What's our stop?" Eric Werth asked, after they had passed under the Rialto Bridge.

"Santa Maria del Giglio," Reuben told him. "We'll get off there, too. After that dinner, we can use the walk to San Marco."

As they went up the Canal, Reuben was surprised to see Jim Cavanaugh unobtrusively holding Doris Medford's hand. An Adriatic romance? he wondered.

Once ashore, Cavanaugh said he would walk to the Bauer Grunwald with Medford. Eric Werth, at the prospect of being alone, said he would go to the Square with the Frosts. "We've got time," he said. "It's only ten thirty-five."

"That's about eleven hours till we have to leave for the airport," Cavanaugh said.

"You're going home tomorrow?" Reuben said.

"Unless some new twist develops," Werth said.

Reuben wondered what "new twist" there could possibly be at the late hour, but refrained from pressing the point. At the Bauer Grunwald, Medford begged off from walking on to San Marco and announced that she was going to bed. Cavanaugh said he would see her to the elevator. After observing the hand-holding on the *vaporetto*, Frost thought this might be the last they saw of him. But in a few minutes he came back and they started walking east toward the Piazza.

"This way—that's a dead end," Reuben instructed, as Cavanaugh veered off toward the right of the church of San Moisè, straight ahead of them. Frost got everyone heading leftward, and in five minutes they had reached the Square.

When they had walked to the center of the Piazza, Eric Werth asked Reuben if he knew "the story of those horses," pointing to the four bronze statues mounted on the facade of the basilica. "Didn't they come from Constantinople? That's about all I know about them."

"You're right," Reuben said. "The Venetians captured Constantinople in one of the Crusades, and brought them back as booty. They're not Byzantine, you know. It's thought they originally came from Rome. Napoleon took them to Paris when the Republic collapsed, but they were returned in 1815."

"They've done a fair amount of traveling," Cavanaugh said.

"Yes, they have. At least one of them was sent to museums around the world a few years ago," Reuben said. "Of course I hate to disappoint you, but what you're looking at are reproductions. The originals are in an inside room, away from the outdoor air pollution."

"I have a feeling everything in this place is a reproduction," Cavanaugh said.

"You mean Venice is some sort of Renaissance Disneyland?" Frost asked. "I'm afraid I have to disagree with you. There's really very little that's not real. Restored, yes."

Cavanaugh looked up at the Campanile, the Piazza's bell tower, and then turned to Reuben. "You say this place isn't full of fakes. How about that?" he said. "I bought a postcard this morning that shows a pile of bricks over there, where the original tower fell down. So the one we're looking at's a replica."

"Touché, Mr. Cavanaugh," Frost said. "The original campanile stood there for a thousand years and then collapsed back around 1900. The Venetians decided to rebuild it just like it was. So, you're right, it's a replica."

"This whole damn square's one big copy. Those horses, that tower . . . It's Alitalia back to New York for me. Shall we head for the hotel, Eric?"

The two men bade farewell to the Frosts and doubled

back through the Square. Reuben and Cynthia walked on to the Piazzetta and then to the Cipriani dock.

"This place looks like a convention," Reuben muttered, when he and Cynthia arrived back at the hotel shortly before eleven-fifteen. Getting off the Cipriani *motoscafo,* they had been all but bowled over by rousingly happy—perhaps even drunk—guests from the Hughes & Co. dinner, eager to cross to the San Marco side. One of their number, with at least a smattering of Italian, was shouting, *"Avanti al Campiello!"* Frost assumed the reference was to a late-night bar he had heard about but never visited.

Moving on to their own bar, the Frosts took one look and decided to forgo a nightcap. The room was crowded almost to overflowing with still more formally dressed couples.

"Poor Dan Abbott," Reuben said, as he looked at the scene from the door. He pointed toward the Baxter Fashions executive sitting at the small bar, amid all the revelers. While the Frosts watched, Abbott tossed down a drink from a shot glass, followed by a large gulp of water, and ordered another.

"It's too noisy to join him," Reuben said to Cynthia, as they went back outside. "I've never seen this place so jammed. It's a madhouse."

"Not the place for us," Cynthia said.

"Agreed."

MURDER

"WHERE TO TODAY?" CYNTHIA ASKED FRIDAY MORNING, as Reuben opened the window shutters to bright sunshine.

"The Frari. I can knock off three Doges in one visit," he said. "Want to come along?"

"No. I feel like a good swim, and then Giorgione beckons. I'm going to the Accademia to see *The Tempest*."

"Who knows, maybe you'll figure out what that painting's about."

"Sex, I think," Cynthia said.

At breakfast, the Frosts ran into Dan Abbott, eating by himself. They stopped at his table.

"How's everything?" Reuben asked, though really meaning, "Is Gregg Baxter still all right?"

"Fine, thanks. A little apprehension in our merry band about what that laboratory's going to report, but we'll just have to wait that one out."

"Baxter's okay, I assume?" Reuben said, deciding to ask the question directly.

"Far as I know. He was gone when I came to breakfast. Already on his way to la marchesa's, I imagine. He wants to finish and get the hell out of here."

"Can't blame him for that," Reuben said.

"Let me know if Cavallaro is heard from," Abbott said. "I just stopped at the desk to check and he hadn't learned anything yet," Reuben answered.

After breakfast, Reuben said goodbye to Cynthia and went across in the hotel boat. Then he rode the number thirty-four *diretto* down the Grand Canal to San Tomà, from where he walked to Santa Maria Gloriosa dei Frari. He approached the campanile, second in height only to the one in the Piazza (with the added virtue that it had never collapsed in its 600-year history), and the massive Gothic redbrick church itself.

It was the only active church in Venice to charge admission to tourists, so he queued up and paid the 1,000-lire fee. The first monument he wanted to see was built around the door through which he had entered, the Baroque tomb of Doge Giovanni Pesaro (1658–59). It was most eccentric, held up by four straining Moors, each at least twenty feet high. The massive structure was covered with carved *putti* and allegorical statues, including two grotesque skeletons, that were not identified in any guidebook Reuben had consulted.

Taking *The Stones of Venice* out of his green bag, he found that John Ruskin had dismissed the monument as "a huge accumulation of theatrical scenery in marble." Ruskin fumed that "here sculpture has lost its taste and learning. It seems impossible for false taste and base feeling to sink lower."

Reuben felt that Ruskin had been excessively harsh, though he was amused to recall that Doge Pesaro supposedly had no teeth, a fact not evident from his marble likeness, in which his "arms expanded, like an actor courting applause, under a huge canopy of metal, like the roof of a bed." And Reuben did have to admit that the *Madonna di Ca' Pesaro*, the adjoining Titian masterpiece commissioned by a member of the family in 1519, was a surpassingly more interesting work of art.

Moving toward the sanctuary, Reuben sought out the

tombs of Doges Francesco Foscari (1423–57) and Nicolò Tron (1471–73), which flanked the high altar and the even greater Titian work above it, *The Assumption of Mary*.

Stopping to admire the monks' choir in the center of the church, he was startled when he heard Cynthia's voice. He turned to see her rushing toward him.

"I thought you were going to the Accademia," he said when she had caught up to him.

"Thank God you're here. They got him. Gregg Baxter has been killed."

"What!"

"Stabbed to death."

"Where, for God's sake?"

"I don't know the details. Somewhere near the Bauer Grunwald. They found him very early this morning."

"So someone was trying to kill him after all! How did you find out?"

"I was in the pool when Dan Abbott came and started shouting at me. I swam over to the side and he told me the police had called the hotel with the news, that Baxter's body had been discovered. He'd been killed sometime in the night."

"Let's go outside. We shouldn't be talking in here," Reuben said, as he led the way out to the Campo San Rocco. "It was a stabbing?" he asked.

"That's what the police told him."

"And behind Doris Medford's hotel."

"I know. I thought of that."

"Do the police have any idea who might have done it?"

"If they do, I don't believe they said."

"What about Abbott? What does he think?"

"He's completely shocked. Dumbfounded, I guess would be the word."

"Rats," Reuben said, after a long pause. "Remember the year, before I retired, when I was on the phone most of the time we were here? Talking to New York about a damn fool merger that ended up never taking place? I can see this may be the same thing—total interruption of our vacation."

"Well, dear, you do have a knack for being around when murder happens."

"What exactly am I supposed to do?" he asked testily.

"Dan has gone to see the police. He wants you to meet him there."

"Where is 'there'? I haven't the faintest idea."

"I asked Gianni at the concierge's desk and he said it would be the Questura, the headquarters of the P.S., as he called it. La Pubblica Sicurezza. It's at the Fondamenta di San Lorenzo."

"It's not the Carabinieri?"

"Apparently not."

"I'm not quite sure where San Lorenzo is," Reuben said irritably.

"Gianni showed me on the map. Here, let me see yours." Reuben pulled his map of the city out of his green bag and unfolded it.

"Here we are," Cynthia said, moving closer. "Looks like you take the *vaporetto* to San Zaccaria."

"He really wants me there?"

"He *begged* me to find you."

The Frosts walked to the landing stage.

"You'd better go ahead and have lunch without me," Reuben said, when they reached San Marco, where he handed her his green bag to take back to the hotel. "God knows how long I'll be tied up."

"You poor dear. Good luck. And be careful." She kissed her husband on the cheek and left the boat.

Reuben, remaining aboard, felt put-upon. It wasn't fair that murder should blight this beautiful day in La Serenissima.

Bells throughout the city were ringing the noon Angelus when Reuben got off at San Zaccaria. He headed inland past the perilously leaning campanile of San Giorgio dei Greci, then along the Fondamenta di San Lorenzo to the austere entrance to the Questura. It was a reddish-brown building with four stories by an American's count, three by an Italian's.

Once he arrived, he paused outside. He did not know quite what to do. What should he say? Whom should he ask for? What if no one spoke English? His dilemma was solved when he saw Dan Abbott and, unexpectedly, Doris Medford come out of the second building further down on the Fondamenta. Medford was sobbing and Abbott had his arm around her. He looked stricken and frightened, hardly the sturdy pillar that Medford unquestionably needed.

When she saw Reuben, she stopped crying. "Oh, Mr. Frost, thank God you're here," she said.

"I came as soon as I heard," Reuben said. It seemed plain to him that some strong coffee might do the distraught pair some good, so he suggested that they go to a *caffè* where they could sit while they briefed him.

Medford and Abbott agreed, so they walked back to the Caffè ai Greci and settled down at an outdoor table at water's edge next to a row of pots of vivid red geraniums. Reuben ordered espresso, and Medford and Abbott cappuccino.

"Tell me what happened."

"After you saw me at breakfast, I went to my room to get my wallet," Abbott began. "I was planning to go to Ceil's. As I told you, I hadn't seen Gregg since last night, but assumed he'd already gone down to her workshop. When I got back to the room the phone rang. It was Cavallaro who said he must come by, that he had some bad news.

"I figured he was going to confirm Gregg's suspicions about his insulin, but then he laid it on me that they'd found Gregg's body. A guy coming to work at the Bauer Grunwald came across it near the service entrance to the hotel. It was in a temporary rubbish bin that had been set up for a construction job at the church next door.

"The police recovered his wallet—they don't think it was a robbery—and were calling hotels when they found he'd been registered at the Cipriani. Once Cavallaro gave me the news, I got hold of Doris and came over here. Oh, yes, and I also told your wife." Abbott took a large gulp of his coffee when he had finished his account.

"They sent us to see a detective named Valier. Jacopo Valier—"

"*Commissario* Valier," Medford interrupted. Her voice was hoarse and she cleared her throat.

"He's the one that wanted to see us," Abbott explained.

"What does he think happened?" Reuben asked.

"It's very strange. Gregg was stabbed with a glass dagger," Abbott said.

"How do they know that?" Reuben asked.

"It broke off in his gut. The glass blade was inside him, with the handle broken off."

"That's a new one," Reuben said.

"Valier said it was a blade as sharp as a razor."

Abbott's narrative prompted more tears from Doris Medford. He stopped talking, pulled out a large white handkerchief and handed it to her. Then he waited until she had composed herself before going on.

"Valier says such daggers can be bought at some of the fancier glass places. They're an old Venetian tradition, he says."

"So anybody could've gotten hold of one."

"Correct."

"Any idea who it might have been?" Frost asked.

"None. But I'm not really thinking very lucidly right now."

"What do we know about Baxter's whereabouts last night?" Reuben asked.

"He was with me," Abbott said. "We'd gone to a place called Fior, something like that."

"Da Fiore?" Reuben said.

"That's it."

"Just the two of you?"

"No, Tony Garrison and Tabita were there, and Ceil Scamozzi and her boyfriend, Luigi Regillo."

"When did you leave?"

"Early. A little after ten. Tony and Tabita had already left. The rest of us walked over to the *vaporetto*. Ceil looked at the timetable posted on the wall and said there'd be a boat at ten-seventeen. I remember looking at my watch and it was ten-ten.''

"Where would that be? San Tomà?" Reuben asked, referring to the stop he had so recently left.

"That sounds right," Abbott said. "Ceil and Luigi got off after two stops. They said they would walk across and take the boat to the Giudecca on the other side. That's a shortcut that avoids St. Mark's, apparently.''

"Okay, so then what happened?" Reuben asked, simultaneously motioning to the waiter, who had come into view for the first time in several minutes. They all ordered more coffee.

"The boat went across the Grand Canal to—"

"—Santa Maria del Giglio," Reuben interrupted, suddenly realizing that he and his party had been tracing Baxter's path practically at the same time he was.

"I think so," Abbott said. "Gregg announced that he was getting off. There's a bar he was going to."

"Haig's? Across from the Gritti?" Reuben asked.

"That's the one."

"It's a gay bar, isn't it? That's what I've always been told," Reuben said.

"Not necessarily. Mixed is more like it," Abbott replied. "Doris here has been there with us. Most times women are around. It's open late. Gregg had been there every night since we arrived, except after the big dinner."

"That's the night he got his kicks out of firing me," Medford interrupted.

"Anyway," Abbott continued, "I'd gone with him a couple of times, but he always outlasted me."

"Baxter *was* gay, was he not?" Reuben asked.

"Yes," Abbott said.

"Did he try to make pickups in Haig's?"

"Not while I was there," Abbott said. "But I'm sure he did when I wasn't."

"Successfully?"

"I have no way of knowing. I never discussed Gregg's sex life with him if I could help it."

"If you don't mind my asking, I assume you're not gay," Reuben said.

"Your assumption's correct, unless you mean it in the sense of 'gay young bachelor,' " Abbott said sardonically. "I've been very expensively divorced twice."

"So what happened? Did Baxter get off the boat?" Frost asked.

"I urged him not to. With the poison mystery hanging over him, I figured he ought to play it a little cool, like you said last night. There might be someone out there waiting to get him. Unfortunately, I was right. I told him he was a damn fool, that he was risking his life. But it didn't do any good."

"Why didn't you go along to protect him?" Reuben asked.

"I tried to, but he refused to have me. And if he was on the prowl, as I'm sure he was, there wouldn't have been a helluva lot I could have done if he picked somebody up. I couldn't exactly go along as a chaperone."

"I see your point. So what did you do?"

"I stayed on the *vaporetto* to San Marco and then took the boat back to the hotel."

"What about Garrison and Tabita?"

"I don't know about them. They bugged out early from the restaurant. And they'd already gone out when I looked for them this morning," Abbott explained.

"Are they an 'item,' as they say?" Reuben asked.

He saw Abbott and Medford make eye contact. "The answer is yes," Medford said.

"My wife and I sat with them at your dinner. That was our impression," Reuben said. "Even though I'd understood Baxter and Garrison were lovers."

"A thing of the past," Abbott told him.

"What about you, Ms. Medford?" Reuben asked. "I believe it was a little after ten-thirty, maybe ten-forty, when we said goodnight to you at your hotel. What happened after that?"

Medford's face became even redder than usual. "This is

a terrible thing to say, Mr. Frost and I'm embarrassed. I have no recollection of the evening after I left you. The last thing I remember is going up in the elevator at the Bauer Grunwald.''

"So you, um, passed out?" Frost asked.

"I'm ashamed to say it, but I'm afraid that's the answer."

"Let me ask another question," Frost said. "Were Baxter and la marchesa Scamozzi getting along?"

"Famously, I'd say," Medford said, palpably relieved to be talking about someone other than herself. "No problem there at all."

"Then who is there, here in Venice, with a reason for murdering Gregg Baxter? How about Eric Werth? Or his lawyer?"

"Eric Werth? What's he have to do with anything?" Abbott asked nervously.

"Just speculating," Reuben said. "He did come to Venice to see Baxter."

"How do you know that?" Abbott demanded.

"We met him and his lawyer on the plane from Paris and have been running into them ever since. Everywhere except at your party."

Abbott now seemed even more nervous. "That couldn't be helped. Gregg wouldn't have them there."

"Why not?"

"They were a nuisance. He didn't want to do business with them."

The tables set in front of the *caffè* had begun to fill up as they talked. There were now two waiters bustling about, getting ready for the lunch trade. Theirs came by and asked if they wished to eat, *"Volete mangiare?"* They declined, so he asked if they wanted anything else, the implication being they should give up their table if not.

"We'll only be a few minutes," Abbott told him.

"Where do we go from here, Mr. Abbott?" Reuben asked.

"I hate to be callous about it, but my first concern is to

call every buyer Doris and I can get hold of to tell them
Baxter Fashions is going to back Tony Garrison and go right‘
on producing. Thank God New York is six hours behind us.
Then, after that, I guess we have to worry about getting
Gregg's body back to New York.''

''Does he have family?''

''Only a sister. His parents are dead.''

''What about your Commissario friend?''

''I was sort of hoping you'd give us a hand there.''

''How do you mean?'' Reuben said.

''This guy Valier was very stiff. He wants us back at
three o'clock to make formal statements. He didn't exactly
treat us like suspects, but he was pretty cold. You're an
outsider. There's no logical way you can be linked to the
murder. I think you'll be able to get on with him better than
we can.''

''I'm not so sure,'' Reuben said. ''A professional police-
man being asked to cooperate with an amateur detective,
and a foreigner at that . . .''

''I took the liberty of telling him you were Baxter's lawyer.''

''But that's not true,'' Reuben protested.

''It is, sort of. You are a lawyer and Gregg asked you to
help him yesterday.''

''It's stretching things,'' Frost said, not entirely happy
with what he was hearing. Still, he couldn't deny that he
was curious about Baxter's murder, and if this was the way
to get him involved, despite all his grumbling protests, perhaps no great harm had been done.

''We told him you might come by to see him and he said
that would be fine with him.''

''So you think I should talk to him?''

''We'd both appreciate it,'' Abbott said.

''Will he be there now?'' Frost asked.

''He said he'd be in all afternoon. He's in that smaller
building down from the Questura, incidentally.''

''Where I saw you come out?''

''Yes.''

"Then I'll go pay a call," Reuben said, realizing that he was inexorably changing the character of his vacation. But then, the Doges' monuments would still be there another year; the chance to participate in a murder investigation in exotic Venice might not be. And he could even end up with a tale or two to astound the Filberts when he next saw them.

"Commissario Jacopo Valier. Do I have the name right?"

VALIER

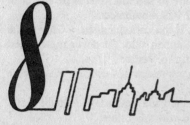

REUBEN WAITED ON THE FONDAMENTA DI SAN LORENZO until Abbott and Medford disappeared. They were on their way back to the Bauer Grunwald; Abbott had again volunteered to help Medford move, this time back to the Cipriani.

Frost walked quickly to the entrance of a building with the austerely forbidding sign SQUADRA MOBILE. If he were lucky, he would catch the Commissario before he went to lunch. Taking a deep breath, he went inside.

"Prego?" An immensely tall figure had materialized. Unsmiling and unshaven, he wore a dark navy uniform jacket and blue-gray trousers with a narrow red stripe. Rudimentary English met rudimentary Italian, but Reuben soon was face to face with Commissario Jacopo Valier in his plain but spacious office.

In contrast to the doorkeeper, Valier was short, though he stood almost militarily erect as he shook hands. He had carefully barbered salt-and-pepper hair and, though his face was unlined and tan, Reuben took him for perhaps sixty. He was wearing a single-breasted light brown suit, of a thick, rough fabric that must have been uncomfortable on the warm September day.

"You are here about Mr. Baxter," Valier said, as he and Frost sat facing each other across a spare wooden desk,

Valier behind an antique typewriter. Reuben had seen computer terminals in other offices he had passed, but there was not one here.

"Mr. Baxter's friend, Mr., ah, I have it here, Mr. Abbott, said you would come to see me. You were the dead man's lawyer, I believe? His mouthpiece."

Frost was taken aback at the colloquialism. "Only in the most technical sense," Reuben said. "I never represented Mr. Baxter before this trip to Venice."

"You mean then you represent his estate? When were you hired? This morning?"

"No, Mr. Baxter retained me yesterday. I doubt that I shall have anything to do with his estate."

"Which will be big, yes?" Valier asked.

"I have no idea, but it's safe to say Baxter was very rich. He's been an extremely successful fashion designer in the States."

"In other words, we may have set a record."

"How do you mean?" Reuben asked.

"Mr. Baxter may have been the richest man ever murdered in Venice," Valier said.

"Surely that can't be true?" Reuben said. "The Doges who were assassinated . . ."

"No, no. There were four Doges assassinated—that we know about—but they had all fallen on hard times when they were killed. Until now, the wealthiest victim we ever had was il conte Lanza, the very rich owner of the Palazzo Dario. He was killed twenty years ago and I regret to say his murderer has never been found. But your Mr. Baxter sounds even better off than Lanza."

"Interesting," Reuben said.

"May I ask why Mr. Baxter hired you now, at this time? I assume you are here on vacation, not business?"

"You're right about why I'm here. As for why he hired me, it had to do with the poison episode."

"Poison episode?" Valier asked, looking perplexed.

"Mr. Abbott didn't tell you?"

"I recall no mention of poison, pal."

Reuben found this odd, but did not let on to the Commissario. "The late Gregg Baxter was a diabetic. *Diabetico.* Two nights ago, Wednesday, he was about to take his insulin shot—just before the big dinner he gave—when he thought the medicine bottle had been tampered with. He also said the liquid inside smelled odd. He was sure it had been poisoned. They called me in Thursday morning and we arranged to have it sent out for testing at a laboratory in Mestre. We're still waiting for the results."

"If you'll excuse me, Avvocato Frost, why did they call you? It doesn't sound like a job for a lawyer."

"I agree with you. I think Baxter, or perhaps his man Abbott, foresaw a situation that might become complicated and wanted to bring in an outsider." Reuben did not think it timely to mention his experience with other homicides.

"Seems odd to me. But what's the name of the laboratory?"

"I don't know. Il signor Cavallaro, at the Cipriani, made the arrangements."

Valier picked up the phone on his desk and called a number from memory. It turned out to be the Cipriani and Alfredo Cavallaro was soon on the other end. Reuben tried to understand the side of the conversation he could hear, but the Commissario's Venetian dialect seemed almost impenetrable. Deliberately so, Reuben suspected.

The call was not short. Valier swiveled away from Reuben and put his feet up on the edge of a shelf behind him as he talked. Reuben could not help but notice the man's well-shod but small feet. And the large poster on the stark white wall for *Via Col Vento,* starring Clark Gable and Vivien Leigh.

The conversation ended soon after Valier had written a name and number on the pad in front of him. Glancing at it, he dialed again, without a word to Frost. This time the call consisted of questions by Valier, which grew more excited as the conversation progressed.

"Arsenico," he said when he had replaced the receiver. "What do you say? *Arsenic and Old Lace*?" He gave Reu-

ben a hint of a smile. *"The gentleman died because he drank some wine with poison in it,"* he said, mimicking a female voice.

Frost was baffled at what he guessed to be a line from the movie or the play of *Arsenic and Old Lace*, but the message seemed clear that Baxter's insulin had been poisoned. "So it was poison," he said.

"That's what la signorina Preti, the chemist, told me. The fluid in the bottle she was given contained arsenic. Which doesn't assist the theory of Mr. Abbott."

"Which is?"

"That Mr. Baxter picked somebody up at Haig's Bar and had a fairies' quarrel with him. A fatal fairies' quarrel."

"Can I ask you what did happen, as far as you know?" Frost said.

"Baxter's body was found early this morning in an alley not far from the bar. In a trash bin in the Calle dei Tredici Martiri. He had been dead several hours."

"Several hours? Wasn't the body right out in the open?" Reuben asked.

"Not exactly. The trash bin I made reference to was there for a construction job. It is very large and about four feet high. So it is possible people went by without seeing the body. Sadly, I do not believe it. There must have been those who saw the corpse—those coming to work at the Bauer Grunwald, for example—and simply went along their way, not wanting to get entangled. Regrettably, this happens."

"The phenomenon occurs in my city, too, Commissario," Reuben said.

"The cause of death was a single stab wound in the *sterno*—I'm sorry, I don't know the English—that went through to the *ventricolo sinistro* of the heart. At least that's the preliminary conclusion of the Polizia Scientifica. There was no sign of a struggle. It looks like Baxter was taken by surprise and didn't put up a fight. There is one strange thing, however. Perhaps Mr. Abbott told you. The murder weapon was a glass dagger. The handle broke off and the blade was left inside him."

"Yes, Mr. Abbott did tell me. It sounds bizarre," Reuben said.

"It's very Venetian," Valier said. "You know our city well, Avvocato Frost?"

"Reasonably. My wife and I have been coming here for twenty-odd years now."

"The Tourist Bureau would be delighted to hear that. But back to the glass dagger. You most likely know that glassware is one of the few things that through our history was *made* in Venice. As opposed to goods that were merely traded. From at least the twelfth century to the seventeenth, Venice tried to maintain a monopoly on glassmaking in Europe, which is one reason the industry was moved to Murano in the thirteenth century—to keep it from prying eyes.

"Any glassmaker who committed the treason of leaving the Republic to go into business elsewhere was condemned to death—a sentence carried out by the enforcers of the Republic with a *pugnale di Venezia*, a razor-sharp dagger made of glass."

"Abbott said one could easily obtain such a weapon."

"Yes and no. Not in every souvenir stand that sells glass beads, but in some of the fancier shops. Probably one dealing in antique glass. It's something my men will cover. Let's hope someone remembers selling a *pugnale*—and the person who bought it."

"Sounds difficult."

"No, more bothersome than difficult. We are a small town, Avvocato Frost. Seventy-five thousand souls today. Only three million of us ever. There's a store selling glass every two meters, but the kind we're talking about is much fewer. So, as I say, bothersome but not difficult. I told Mr. Abbott that it would be just as well to keep the detail of the glass dagger quiet for the moment, not least because it would create a sensation in the press. But also, so we might have at least one concealed ace up the sleeve."

"The secret's safe with me," Reuben said. "But one question. What did you say the name of the street was where Baxter was killed? I may go take a look."

"The Calle dei Tredici Martiri—the street of the thirteen martyrs."

"Which makes Baxter the fourteenth martyr?"

"Not quite. The *tredici martiri* were patriots killed by the Fascists in 1944. Ca' Giustinian, which is on one side of the Calle, was the headquarters of the Gestapo."

"I see," Reuben said quietly, and then, after a pause, asked how he could be helpful.

Valier did not reply right away, but stood up from the desk and went to the window and looked out on the dark facade of the abandoned church of San Lorenzo. He stroked his already flawlessly combed hair, then plunged his hands into his pants pockets.

"Mr. Frost, do you know what a *bocca di leone* is?" he asked finally, turning back to Reuben.

"Vaguely. It means the mouth of the lion, doesn't it? It was the name for a container, like a mailbox, where a citizen of the Republic could deposit an anonymous denunciation."

"Very good. You are well informed on our history, I see. Anyway, I predict, before this process is finished, that once your interest in Mr. Baxter's murder becomes known, you will become a sort of walking *bocca di leone*."

"That sounds farfetched to me," Reuben said.

"We shall see, my friend," Valier said. "You're from New York, I understand."

"Yes."

"New Yorkers are tough and clever, is that not true? And if you're a lawyer there, you must also be intelligent. We can use your brains on this one. Everybody's going to be on our backs to solve it. And to solve it *subito*. People sometimes forget a murder that is solved, but they don't forget one that's not, especially when the victim is as celebrated as Mr. Baxter was. Or as rich as he was. For God's sake, let's not tell anyone about his being the richest corpse in our history. Let's not make the journalists' headlines for them.

"Right now, the tourist trade here has quite enough difficulties. Down the hall there you will see the offices of my colleagues in the terrorism squad, who are trying to prevent even the *suggestion* of a terrorist threat. So we did not need this murder. Nor do we need every rich and fashionable woman in the world saying 'Oh yes, murdered in Venice, poor thing,' every time Gregg Baxter is mentioned or someone recognizes one of his dresses. Or worse, as I'm sure some of them would say, 'Oh yes, Venice, the city where they killed Gregg Baxter.' " Valier gave a small shudder as he contemplated his own dire imaginings.

"Everyone's going to be interested in this one. The Questore—that's our police chief. My bosses, the Vice Questore and the Commissario Capo. The magistrate in charge—the Procuratore della Repubblica—majestic title, heh? And the fellow looking right over my shoulder, the Sostituto Procuratore. Not to mention the journals, the television, the foreign office. Or your consul general in Milan."

"I sympathize," Reuben said, dazed at the bureaucratic structure Valier had outlined.

"*Dunque*, if you want to be helpful, the first thing you can do is tell me what you know about Mr. Abbott, Miss Medford and the others in Mr. Baxter's group."

Reuben informed the Commissario of all that he knew. Valier took meticulous notes in a small, fine hand, asking Frost to slow down at one point. After discussing Abbott and Medford—including what details he knew about her firing—Reuben said that "the only others in Baxter's immediate party were Tony Garrison, his design assistant, and Tabita, his favorite model."

"Tony. Anthony. Antonio. Italian?" Valier asked.

"Ah . . . in part, yes. His father was a black American soldier, but his mother was Italian."

"And Tabita. What kind of name is that? Negro?"

"Black, yes."

"Beautiful, I'll bet."

"Yes again."

"That's it?"

"Well, there's la marchesa Scamozzi. Baxter was working with her to develop fabrics for his line."

"Cecilia."

"You know her?"

"Avvocato Frost, as I said, this is a very small town. I've known her all my life."

"You come from Venice, then?"

Valier nodded. "I hope Mr. Baxter's death will not keep Cecilia from doing a good business. She can use the money."

"A marchesa needing money?"

"A title doesn't guarantee money in Venice. The only money you can be sure of was the amount paid to the Austrians, back in those unspeakable years when they occupied us, to buy the titles the blackguards were selling.

"I'm pretty sure Cecilia is what you Americans call landpoor. She has a home and studio on the Giudecca. But her husband flew the coop years ago. So she has to worry about the upkeep of the house—and of Luigi Regillo, who is a man of expensive tastes."

"How does he fit in? Is he a gigolo?" Reuben asked.

"Not precisely. Do you know the term *cicisbeo*?"

"Vaguely."

"In the dying days of the Republic, every wealthy woman in Venice had a *cicisbeo*, a beautiful young man constantly at her side. He may have been taking her to bed, maybe not. The term *cicisbeo* doesn't tell you. Luigi is a modern version—Ceil's companion, but I don't think her lover. Which isn't to say he doesn't cost her much money."

"Interesting."

"Is there anyone else I should know about, Avvocato Frost?"

Reuben told Valier about Eric Werth and Cavanaugh.

"We should talk to them. Where are they staying?" Valier asked.

"They were at the Gritti, but they left this morning."

"For New York?"

"Yes."

"So we have two men, angry with Mr. Baxter, at a hotel very near where he was killed. I'm sorry they got away.

When are the others leaving, do you know? I don't want to lose them.''

"They haven't told me, but I had the impression even before Baxter's death that they were eager to get back to the States.''

"I'll have to see to that. It would be most unfortunate if they left now. I must inform them.''

"Are you saying they're not free to leave?''

"Until our investigation becomes clarified, it would be prudent for them not to.''

"In other words, they're under house arrest?''

"Mr. Frost, I merely said it would be prudent for the interested parties to remain. *Per prudenza.* I did not use the term *arresti domiciliari.* Can we leave it at that?''

"As you wish,'' Frost said. "But I have another question. What about Baxter's body?''

"The Polizia Scientifica released it at the scene and it has been taken to the Ospedale Santi Giovanni e Paolo. You know it?''

"Yes. Next to San Zanipolo.''

"Correct. Not far from here. What we call a *medico legale* will do an autopsy and then the body can be released.''

"Good. Mr. Abbott was concerned.''

"I already told him not to worry. We aren't going to keep it. We have no extra room for bodies here in Venice.''

"Thank you.''

"Now. Haig's Bar should be opening soon. I think I'll go have a talk with the bartender. Can I drop you at San Marco?''

"That would be very kind.''

"Good, I'll call the boat. Just give me a minute. There are some papers I must sign.'' Valier made the call and then took out his half-glasses to scan documents from the box on his desk. Reuben watched him as he did so, and listened to him whistle softly. Frost did not quite believe what he heard and finally could not resist satisfying his curiosity.

"May I ask you something?'' he said.

"Yes?" Valier said, looking up from his reading.

"You were just whistling. Am I wrong in thinking the tune was what we call 'Don't Sit Under the Apple Tree'? A song I don't think I've heard since I was in the Navy during the War?"

Valier laughed softly. "You are right," he said, then sang the first lines, in English:

> *"Don't sit under the apple tree,*
> *With anyone else but me,*
> *Anyone else but me. . . .*

"The Andrews Sisters. Patty, Laverne and Maxine."

"I didn't know their reputation had spread to Italy," Reuben said, puzzled at the almost surreal occurrence.

"I heard them when I was a guest in your country," Valier said.

"During the War?"

"You've trapped me, Avvocato Frost. I was, as they used to say, a 'P.W.' An eighteen-year-old *caporale* captured in the Battle of Palermo, in Sicily, in 1943. July twenty-two, I'll never forget. Your General Patton and the Seventh Army. They put us on a troopship returning home to Hampton Roads, Virginia. Then by train to Monticello, Arkansas."

The source of the Commissario's disconcerting Americanisms now became clear to Frost; they had been learned in Arkansas, of all places.

"They put us to work in a sawmill and lumberyard," Valier went on. "My job was to count the boards as they came out of the mill. Not very demanding, but I believe they did not want me to sabotage the American war effort. They did not want us dangerous Italians sacking Atlanta like your General Sherman." He smiled, turning toward his *Gone With the Wind* poster.

"The good part was that I listened to the radio all day long—your Young Men's Christians had given us several—and fell in love with the Andrews Sisters. And learned a little English, though my English today is truly *pessimo.*''

"Not at all," Reuben said, without adding that there was a certain time-warp to the Commissario's idioms.

"Not long after we arrived in Arkansas, Mussolini was thrown out and arrested and Italy surrendered. Suddenly we became not the enemy but what the Allies were pleased to call a 'co-belligerent.' Your Army had no idea what to do with us. Italy was occupied by the Germans, so we couldn't be sent back. Yet it wasn't quite right to keep us as P.W.s, now that we were on your side. So they took away the uniforms with the big P-Ws on them and gave us new ones that said I-T-A-L-Y—and kept us working in the lumber-yard. They did raise our 'pay' from eight dollars a month as prisoners to twenty-four dollars as your co-belligerents.

"Many of us wanted to stay in your country, but fifty thousand Italian P.W.s was not what your immigration had in mind. After we were given more freedom, we desperately tried to meet local girls, thinking if we married them we wouldn't have to come back. But your Army was too smart for that. They forbidded us to marry—even when the girls became pregnant. Not, I assure you, that I tried that *stratagemma.*

"So . . . after V-E day in 1945, I came back here to Venice and joined the P.S., where I've been ever since. I was sixty-five two months ago, so I retire at the end of this year. Unless, of course, I'm fired before that for failing to find Mr. Baxter's killer."

"That's quite a tale, Commissario—"

"Please, Avvocato Frost. Jack, if you will, for old time's sake. That's what they made of Jacopo in Arkansas. Jack Valley-yare. Come on, I'll give you a lift, as you Yanks say. Or used to, at least."

WHEN REUBEN PICKED UP HIS ROOM KEY AT THE HOTEL, Gigi, the concierge on duty, told him that Cynthia had already eaten and gone across to San Marco. He decided to have lunch by himself at the outside snack bar, which he hoped would mean that he could avoid the whirlwind of gossip he was sure would be swirling among the guests. Yet even in the comparative isolation of the snack bar, Reuben overheard one woman ask another, "What about the *murder*?" The second woman became flightily upset, until assured that the deed had taken place "in town."

"Who was it?" she asked.

"Some queer dress designer I've never heard of named Baxter." Gregg Baxter's international reputation had apparently not traveled to the outlying reaches of America where the first woman was from. Judging by the leopard-patterned culottes and high-heeled pink shoes she wore, Reuben saw no reason to doubt her ignorance.

"They say a boy picked him up and killed him," the first woman said, evoking a scandalized cluck from her companion.

Reuben ate his hamburger and wondered where the leopard-skin lady had heard about Baxter picking up a boy. It was one thing for Commissario Valier, who knew of the dead man's movements the previous evening, to speculate about homosexual murder, quite another for a total stranger, presumably without any of the facts, to do so.

As Frost mulled over this puzzle, Alfredo Cavallaro came strolling by his table.

"You've heard about Mr. Baxter?" Cavallaro said.

"Yes."

"And the laboratory test?"

"Yes, yes. I was with Commissario Valier when he called you."

"It is very, very sad."

"Do you have any thoughts on who might have killed him?" Frost asked. "If you've seen or heard anything unusual around here, I'd like to know it."

"All I'm aware of is what Mr. Abbott said, that they think an *omosessuale* killed Mr. Baxter," Cavallaro said. "But I will most surely inform you if anything comes to my attention." He bowed and moved off.

After lunch, Reuben stopped to make a reservation for dinner that evening. He had already decided that it might be interesting to go to Da Fiore, where Gregg Baxter had eaten his last meal.

Gigi said he would make the reservation and wrote down Reuben's request in his book. Seeing this gave Frost a sudden idea.

"Gigi, does your book show the reservations you made yesterday?"

"It shows the ones we've made for the whole year."

"Then let me ask you this. Did you make any bookings for Da Fiore last night?"

The concierge flipped back in the bound volume. "Yes. Il signor Baxter and his party . . ."

". . . I know about that. . . ."

"Then the Madreaus. They're from Paris and went home today. And, yes, I forgot. La signora Morrison and la signorina Cochran went there last night."

Frost thanked the concierge and went into the adjoining room to write Augusta Morrison a note, inviting her and her companion, Sarah Cochran, to tea at five-thirty. Mrs. Morrison, a vigorous, energetic and rich widow of eighty-nine from Philadelphia, had been coming to the Cipriani for the month of September every year since the hotel had opened in 1958. She was both flamboyant and amiable, and well known to the September crowd. They all assumed she would outlive her protector, Ms. Cochran, who, indeed, had broken her ankle and been temporarily replaced on the trip the year before. Neither woman ever missed a detail of what went on around them; the chances that they might have something to report to Reuben were excellent.

Meanwhile, Frost went back to San Marco to have a look at the spot where Gregg Baxter had been killed. He got off the Cipriani boat and walked to the church of San Moisè. At one side of its heavy facade was the major pedestrian thoroughfare that brought one from St. Mark's to such familiar landmarks as the Gritti and the Accademia Bridge. On the other was a short passage between the church and the Hotel Bauer Grunwald.

Reuben went down this passage, which led into the Calle dei Tredici Martiri. The bar of the hotel, with opaque windows, was on his right, and what he took to be the rectory of the church on his left. Walking along, he came to the service entrance of the hotel, then doubled back and examined more carefully the makeshift trash receptacle where the body had been found. It was now filled with plaster fragments, topped by a Fanta bottle and an empty cigarette pack. There were no bloodstains and no evidence at all that a homicide had taken place a few hours earlier; someone had cleaned up thoroughly.

Except for the open service entrance to the Bauer Grunwald, the Calle dei Tredici Martiri seemed a convenient spot for murder. The short street ran to a dead end at the Grand Canal, so that it was not heavily used; in the fifteen or so minutes Reuben spent nosing around, he did not encounter another person. There were two doors that appeared to lead to residential apartments, but all their windows were shuttered.

In an odd twist, the Ca' Giustinian, the erstwhile headquarters of the Gestapo that faced the water at the end of the Calle, was now a local tourist office, the Assessorato al Turismo; Baxter's murder must have delighted the promoters of tourism inside, Reuben guessed. He walked up and down the Tredici Martiri and the surrounding streets several times, during which he noticed the plaque commemorating the thirteen martyrs, *Trucidati dai Fascisti,* slaughtered by the Fascists, on July 28, 1944.

He could not figure out what the light pattern in the Calle would be like at night, so he returned to the Campo San Moisè. He went up the steps of the bridge over the Rio San Moisè and looked across at the front of the church. If one were coming from the Gritti—or Haig's Bar—and heading for the Cipriani boat, it was necessary to veer to the left to avoid the facade and then turn right at the second street beyond it, the Calle Valleresso. For someone who did not know the route well it would seem more logical to favor the right side of the church closer to the Grand Canal, and to head down the Calle dei Tredici Martiri, just as Jim Cavanaugh had started to do the night before.

All this was evident to Reuben as he surveyed the Campo from the elevation of the bridge. Had the killer enticed Gregg Baxter into the deserted Calle, perhaps falsely suggesting that it was the route home? Or had Baxter become lost on his own, an accident of fate that had brought murderer and victim together in the isolated street?

Satisfied that there was not anything more he could learn, Frost decided to continue his Doges project with a brief visit to the Basilica di San Marco, close at hand.

At the basilica, he was almost swept aside by a small army of Slavic pilgrims, in an eager frenzy to see the treasures inside. They were speaking what Reuben made out to be Hungarian or Czech, were carrying brown bags that looked as if they might contain lunch and, unlike more affluent tour groups, were not laden down with cameras.

Reuben recalled a conversation with Dott. Caroldo at the Baxter dinner. "The Hungarians humiliated us back in the

Quattrocento, when we were forced to give them all of Dalmatia," he had said. "Yet the Magyars were never able to invade Venice itself. But look at what's happening now. After the upheavals in Eastern Europe, the Hungarians and the Czechs are free to travel for the first time in forty years. So are the Poles.

"Where do they want to go? Venice, of course," he had continued. "The only problem is the poor souls have almost no money. Some *piccolo imprenditore* from their town herds them into a bus and they ride all night to get here. They can't afford the *vaporetti*, so they walk from the Piazzale Roma to San Marco, where they sprawl out and eat the lunch they've brought from home. They do a little *giretto* around the Piazza and the basilica and then trek back to their bus.

"As you can imagine, the merchants love it—love having the city filled with tourists who spend maybe three thousand lire apiece. It does not appeal to the rapacity of the Venetian soul, I can tell you."

Reuben was now witnessing what Dott. Caroldo had been describing. He stood aside until the throng had passed. Then he entered and, aided by the diagram in his Lorenzetti Guide, tried to locate the baptistry, to seek out the tomb of Doge Giovanni Soranzo (1312–28). It was *in restauro*, completely closed off.

Reuben was disappointed. On vacation, the figure of Doge Soranzo appealed to him. Historians had concluded that the most exciting event of his sixteen-year reign was the birth of three cubs to a pair of lions that he had been given by the King of Sicily. (The only possible rival event was the conception of the cubs, which allegedly had taken place at the Doges' Palace before a large crowd.)

As he walked under the cupolas of the atrium, Frost remembered how much time he had spent there on the two vacations when he had been studying the basilica's mosaics. The cupolas and lunettes above told the story of Joseph, and he was pleased that he remembered to look for the depiction of Reuben, the first son of Jacob, searching for Joseph, his younger sibling.

Fighting to the exit—this time through an onslaught of Germans—with some relief he went back to the Giudecca, where he made a turn around the pool to see who might be there. Tony Garrison and Tabita were sitting on the stretch of grass in front of the Baxter suites. They called to Reuben as he passed and he went to join them.

"I'm glad we caught you," Garrison, wearing a Madonna T-shirt and his omnipresent PADRES cap, told Frost. "We were just going to change so we could go over to town. We have to be at the police station at four o'clock. Dan Abbott and Doris are there now.

"It's on the Fondamenta San Lorenzo?" Garrison asked. "I know this old *città* pretty well but I'm a little soft on police stations."

"That's right," Reuben said.

"*Sempre diritto*, as the natives like to say," Garrison observed. "Straight ahead—which of course it never is."

"Just remember it's not the Questura itself you want but the headquarters of the Squadra Mobile two buildings further down. It's marked."

"Do you know how to get there or not?" Tabita demanded to know.

"I do, babes, I do," Garrison told her and then, turning to Frost, said, "Rubes, Dan Abbott said you were the expert in how to handle the police and would help us."

"Mr. Abbott seems very free in giving me a role in this mess," Reuben said, with some annoyance at Abbott's matter-of-fact assumption, not to mention Garrison's insistence on calling him "Rubes." "I would be the wrong person to advise you about dealing with the American police, let alone the Italian ones."

"Do they have any idea who killed Gregg?" Tabita asked.

"I don't believe so," Reuben answered. "I talked with Commissario Valier, who's the detective in charge of the case. He's completely in the dark, I'd say. How about you? Any theories?''

"None," Tabita said. "That's what's so scary. There's a murderer out there and nobody knows who he is, or why he killed. And we don't know if he was only after Gregg or if he's after his friends, too. Like us."

"Somebody must really have wanted to get the poor bastard," Garrison said. "First trying to poison him, then tracking him down at midnight."

"You two know about the poison attempt then?"

"Yes," Tabita replied, shuddering.

"What do the police want with us?" Garrison asked.

"I presume you'll be talking to Commissario Valier and that he'll want to ask the same thing I did—if you have any helpful ideas. He'll also want to know where you were last night."

"That's easy. We had dinner with Gregg and Dan at Da Fiore. Tabita and I left early and ended up back here around one in the morning. I was supposed to spend today working with Ceil Scamozzi—she and her friend Luigi also were with us last night—finalizing our selection of fabric designs. I knew it would be a rough day, so I wanted to get to bed at a decent hour. I didn't know how rough. . . ." Garrison stopped and swallowed hard.

"I'm interested in your saying you wanted to get to bed 'at a decent hour.' Yet you said you didn't get back here until one o'clock," Reuben said.

Garrison smiled broadly. "Diff'rint strokes for diff'rint folks."

"Tony has funny ideas about time, Mr. Frost," Tabita said. "He's a night person if there ever was one."

"What did you do after you left the restaurant?"

"Just walked around. Two lovers in the moonlight," Garrison said sardonically.

"Once you got back here, did you hear or see Dan Abbott? He's in an adjoining suite, isn't he?"

"That's right. He's on one side and Doris Medford's on the other—or at least she was until she moved out yesterday. The last time I saw Dan, or Doris for that matter, was at the restaurant. I didn't hear or see them back here."

"Actually, Tony, we did hear Dan Abbott's TV, remember?" Tabita said. "It was very low, so it didn't bother us. It sounded like he was watching a movie."

"You're right, I forgot that," Garrison said.

"When did you find out about Baxter's death?"

"This morning, like everybody else," Garrison said. "We'd already gone to Ceil's workshop, when Dan called and told us."

Frost started to leave, but told them as he did so that "perhaps I should clarify my role in this."

"What I told Mr. Abbott the other day was that I would be willing to lend a hand to try and identify Baxter's murderer, or attempted murderer, as it was then. I'm a naturally curious person and the killing of one of the greatest dress designers in the world intrigues me. So, if you have any bright insights, I hope you'll share them with me."

Garrison and Tabita readily agreed and went inside. Frost decided it was time for a nap. When he went to pick up his room key, he was pleased to see that there was a note from Augusta Morrison, accepting his invitation for tea.

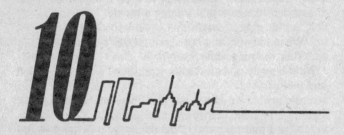

LATER THAT AFTERNOON, REUBEN ASKED CYNTHIA IF SHE wanted to join his tea party.

"Of course," she said. "That woman is pushing ninety, but I wouldn't trust her alone with you for anything."

Augusta Morrison, who insisted on being called Gussie, was a welcome face on the Frosts' trips to Venice. The very first time they had stayed at the Cipriani, Gussie and her nurse-companion, Sarah Cochran, had invited the Frosts to join them one evening when they were all sitting in the bar, and they had been friends ever since.

Gussie's long-dead husband had made a fortune in the machine-tool business in Philadelphia, sold out to an aggressive conglomerate in a booming market, and promptly died, leaving his widow with an amply overstuffed bank account and two adult sons. By her own admission bored with life as a Main Line matron, she was always determined to enjoy her annual Venetian furlough to the maximum.

Her given name was apt, for she had an august and grand presence. She was Massimo's biggest fan in the bar, listening to his renditions of the classic show tunes while smoking her king-sized cigarette and savoring the one Sambuca she permitted herself after dinner. (Gussie was withering to anyone who suggested that she was endangering her health with tobacco or alcohol. "Booze and cigarettes have made me happy and, I'm certain, prolonged my life. Besides, there's no point in going teetotal now," she would say.)

The sharp-tongued and witty woman was thoroughly likeable, armed as she invariably was with the latest gossip and information about the guests currently present, recently departed or about to arrive.

Morrison's devoted companion, Sarah Cochran, was a wise woman in her own right, capable of both shrewd observation and wry humor. One of Gussie's sons was an internist and had demanded many years before, when his mother was a mere seventy, that she be accompanied on her junkets abroad. Ms. Cochran, a former army nurse, had been available, and the two tough-minded and independent women, perhaps to their own surprise, had hit it off and genuinely enjoyed each other's company.

For Sarah Cochran, her annual working trip to Venice was a welcome break in her routine as a private-duty nurse. Gussie Morrison was much healthier than the patients she saw during the rest of the year. The only real tasks she had were to see that Gussie took her various pills regularly; to traipse about the city with her on sightseeing jaunts and visits to her favorite restaurants; to keep her company in the bar for a long stretch each evening (the most difficult of her chores); and to take care that she never herself stole the limelight from her employer.

Reuben was fond of both of them. Sarah Cochran was in her late sixties, but she continued working; he admired this. And Gussie, more than ten years his senior, gave him hope that there were future trips in store for him and that, at seventy-seven, life was not yet quite over.

Given the small number of restaurants on the circuit followed by experienced visitors to Venice, it was never surprising to run into other guests from the Cipriani on an evening out. But it was still fortuitous that the Philadelphia ladies had been at Da Fiore when the Baxter entourage was there; it would be even better luck if they had been in proximity at the restaurant, in which case no detail would have escaped them.

Reuben and Cynthia went to sit outside just before five-thirty. Gussie Morrison, walking jauntily and unassisted, arrived precisely at the appointed hour.

"What a nice idea!" she said to Reuben, as she took a seat beside Cynthia. "Sarah will be along in a minute." Then, lowering her voice, she said, "You know I'm a little worried about her. She's never been quite the same since she broke her ankle last year. She just doesn't get around the way she used to." Gussie had neatly reversed the roles of kept and keeper—not for the first time.

"I have so many people to look after and to worry about," she went on. "Did I tell you the other night that my son George has retired?" She was referring to her son the internist in Chicago. "He's sixty-eight and said it was time to give up his practice. I couldn't for the life of me see why—he enjoys it, he's in excellent health. Why not go on? I would have, and so would you, Reuben."

"Maybe he wants to travel, like his mother," Cynthia suggested.

"He's never been interested in travel, ever. He'd rather stay in Chicago and see patients. Ask his ex-wife."

Sarah Cochran arrived, apologizing for being late, just as Reuben was asking Gussie what she wanted to drink.

"Do you want tea, Gussie?"

"Oh dear, I really don't," she replied. "Tea gives me gas. Is it too early for a martini? Surely the sun is over the yardarm by now."

"No, it's not too early, and I'll join you," Reuben said, not at all displeased with the turn of events. "What do you think, Gussie, is it the air here that makes them seem so good?"

"I thought it was the gin," she replied.

Cynthia and Sarah, more circumspect, each ordered Campari and soda.

"Now, I want to know all about this fellow Baxter's

murder," Gussie said. From past conversations, she knew of Reuben's skill as a detective.

"I was hoping to get the inside story from you, Gussie," Reuben said.

"All I know is what they were saying around here at lunchtime. *Salute*."

"What were they saying?" Reuben asked, after a mutual toast was finished.

"That Gregg Baxter's body was found this morning over near the Bauer Grunwald. That he'd been stabbed."

"No rumors about a killer?"

"Oh yes, they all say it was a gay Baxter picked up. But I've got a different theory."

"You do? Let's hear it," Reuben said.

"I suppose you're mixed up in it," Morrison said.

"I'll admit I've talked to Baxter's partner."

"We saw Baxter last night," Sarah Cochran said. "At Da Fiore."

"That's what I wanted to talk to you about," Reuben said.

"You're involved, just as I thought," Morrison said. "Well then, put *this* olive in your martini."

"I'm listening," Reuben said.

"Baxter and his crowd were at Da Fiore, as you already seem to know. Sarah and I were there, too, sitting on the other side of the dining room, but with a perfect view of their table."

"*You* had the view, not me," Cochran said.

"Be that as it may. I could see and hear everything. Baxter was in command. He was doing all the talking, in a voice loud enough to hear up and down his table, and even across at ours. It was like the time we saw Frank Sinatra and his hangers-on at a restaurant in Palm Springs—he did the talking, the others the laughing. Appreciative laughing. Baxter was also putting the wine away, let me tell you."

"What was he holding forth about?" Reuben asked.

"He was being awful, truly awful. I've never heard anything like it. Maybe it was creative genius at work, but if that's what it was, I'm glad I'm just a country simpleton. He was baiting everybody, starting with la marchesa Scamozzi. He said he needed her fabrics to make dresses for beautiful, rich women and it was only too bad most of her designs were only good for upholstery.''

"Everyone laughed," Cochran added. "Including the marchesa.''

"It was unbelievably humiliating," Gussie continued. "But she just sat there and smiled with the rest of them.''

"What about her boyfriend?" Cynthia asked. "Luigi Regillo?''

"If he's the one I think he is—slippery-looking—he laughed, too," Gussie said. "Business is business, I suppose.''

"No sign of anger?" Reuben asked.

"Not that you could see," Gussie said. "But if I'd been that woman, I'd've been furious.''

"Ceil wasn't the only one he picked on, is that right?''

"Lord, no," Morrison replied. "When he was through with her, he started in on that black model of his.''

"Tabita.''

"If you say so. By now Baxter was getting drunker and talking even more loudly. Fortunately, those near his table were Italians who didn't appear to speak English, so I don't think they understood how obnoxious he was becoming. 'You better watch out with him, Tabita,' Baxter told the model. 'You don't know who he's been sleeping with,' he said, pointing his finger at the black boy in the party—''

"—Tony Garrison," Reuben interjected.

" 'That's very dangerous these days,' Baxter said. 'Look at me. Who'd have guessed I was HIV-positive? But that's what the test showed last week.' I didn't know what 'HIV-positive' meant, but Sarah here, being a nurse, did. Do you think Gregg Baxter really did have AIDS?''

"It's not AIDS, Gussie," Cochran explained. "It's what they call a precondition to it.''

"Call it what you like. It's not a good thing to have. And

after Baxter said that, the handsome black boy got up and left the restaurant and took the model with him.''

"What did he say?" Reuben asked.

"Something original, like 'I don't have to take this shit!' He didn't argue, he just grabbed the girl and left.''

"Did anybody chase after them?"

"Negative. The next thing that happened was that the other man in the party, that I've seen around here with Baxter—''

"That would be Dan Abbott, his partner," Reuben said.

"He moved next to Baxter and said it was time to go. Baxter said he'd leave when he was good and ready and ordered another carafe of wine. Abbott conferred with the waiter, and he brought coffee all around instead. 'First you run my business and now you plan my dinner,' Baxter yelled. It was something. Then he started shouting even more—I'll try to get this straight. 'St. Laurent has Pierre Bergé, Valentino has Giancarlo Giammetti, what do I have? A freckle-faced, bald-headed creep like you. You should have stayed at the bank. You'd probably be a teller by now!' Is that about right, Sarah?''

"A masterful performance, Gussie. That's pretty much how I remember it. I couldn't see but I heard all the goings-on," Cochran said. "I'm surprised someone hadn't killed that man long before last night.''

"And then?" Reuben asked.

"Baxter calmed down, his partner paid the check, and the four of them left.''

"Four—Baxter, Abbott, Ceil Scamozzi and Luigi Regillo," Frost double-checked.

"Yes," Gussie said. "The two blacks had already left, as I told you.''

"This has been very interesting, Gussie.''

"I've earned my martini?" she said.

"Absolutely. If we weren't already committed for dinner, I'd say you'd sung for your supper, too.''

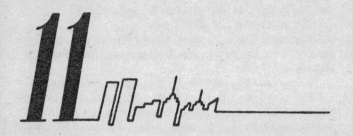

"SHE'S REALLY AMAZING, ISN'T SHE?" CYNTHIA SAID to Reuben after they had left Gussie Morrison and headed back upstairs.

"Yes, but she's got a shirker son. Imagine wanting to retire when you're only sixty-eight!"

"I thought Sarah Cochran looked pale," Cynthia said.

"You would, too, if you had to keep up with Gussie."

"What do you make of what she told us?"

Reuben declined to answer until they were inside their room.

"I want to know more about Baxter and Garrison," Reuben said. "They used to be lovers. But now it looks to me as if Tabita has turned Garrison around. Given the way he acts with her, he has to be bisexual at least. There may be a lovers' quarrel at the root of everything."

"Don't forget the AIDS angle," Cynthia said. "When Baxter started ranting about being HIV-positive he probably scared Garrison and Tabita."

"More likely *enraged* them."

"Garrison could have killed Baxter for exposing him to AIDS. Or Tabita could have killed him for starting the chain that exposed *her*."

"Possibly," Reuben answered. "You know, if Gussie

got the picture correct, Baxter was in a foul mood and managed to pick a fight with everybody. I'd like to hear what Dan Abbott has to say about what went on. I'm going to call him.''

Frost rang Abbott's room. Not getting an answer, he reclined on his bed and turned on the television to the Cable News Network. A few minutes later, CNN began a segment on Gregg Baxter. A moderator interviewed Priscilla Gordon, the reporter the Frosts had sat with at the Wednesday dinner, and two other fashion writers. All agreed that Baxter had been one of the most exciting and influential figures ever to appear in American fashion. Gordon said the designer's plans for tackling the European market promised to be "the most successful invasion since D-Day." The montage of dresses and men's clothes that followed, distilled from ten years' creations, underscored the extravagant praise and showed Baxter's unquestioned originality.

The fashion show over, the scene switched to Venice where Jacopo Valier was interviewed by a local TV reporter. The Commissario's vernacular contrasted with the halting English of his questioner. He would not comment on whether there were suspects, but said an investigation was being conducted "strictly according to Hoyle."

"According to?" the newsman asked.

"According to our established procedures," Valier replied.

Just as CNN turned to a new subject, Valier called. Having just seen the detective on television (even if on tape), talking to him so immediately gave Reuben an odd feeling. Valier, all business, asked if he could come and see Frost, "to turn some stones." This puzzled him, until the Commissario declared that "we must leave no stone unturned." Reuben said that he and Cynthia were about to leave for dinner and then, impulsively, asked Valier if he would like to join them at Da Fiore. He accepted with alacrity.

"Should I change the reservation to three?" Reuben asked.

"Avvocato Frost, with the rotten tourist season we've

been having, I assure you it's not necessary. But if you would feel more comfortable, let me call and change the booking.''

Reuben almost said he thought that would be according to Hoyle, but refrained.

A half hour later, heading down the walk to get the Cipriani *motoscafo*, the Frosts met Dan Abbott and Doris Medford, who were just arriving from San Marco. Reuben wanted to talk with both of them—preferably separately—but there was no practical way of getting them aside, especially if he and Cynthia wanted to be on time for dinner. The best he could do was to ask Abbott and Medford if they wanted to eat with them.

"We're going to Da Fiore," Frost said.

"I couldn't face it," Abbott said.

"I'm exhausted," Medford added. "But thank you anyway."

Frost resigned himself to pursuing them later.

Maurizio Martin, the young owner of Da Fiore, greeted the Frosts genially, seeming to remember them from earlier visits. They were placed at a table at the back of the pleasant dining room, with its soft lights and yellow-and-white striped wallpaper. It would be easier to talk here; Reuben wondered if Valier had arranged this.

"I think you'll like Jacopo Valier—Jack, as he wants to be called," Reuben said to Cynthia.

"He's coming now," Cynthia said, recognizing him from his CNN appearance.

Commissario Valier made his way slowly through the dining room. He was quite evidently a local celebrity, stopping at several tables, working the room like a politician. He introduced himself to Cynthia before Reuben could do so.

"Good evening, Avvocato Frost," he said to Reuben. "You were holding out on me."

Reuben did not understand what Valier was getting at, and said so.

"I was talking to the police in New York—the NYPD, I believe you call them—to make a routine check on the late Mr. Baxter and his friends. I included you among them, and my old contact reported that you are quite well known as a detective in New York. An amateur, of course, but a very successful one."

"My reputation is terribly overblown," Frost said.

Maurizio Martin reappeared and Commissario Valier engaged him in vigorous conversation, in Italian too rapid for Reuben to understand.

"Excuse me, I was just asking Maurizio what he recommended to start with tonight," Valier explained. "Of course we must begin with these." He pointed to the plate of deep-fried *schie,* tiny shrimp, a specialty that a waiter had brought. Reuben remembered their delicious sweet taste from other meals at the restaurant.

"Why don't you order for all of us," he said; the dialogue he had been unable to follow had sounded authoritative.

"You want to put your lives in my hands?"

"With pleasure, Commissario," Cynthia said.

More rapid-fire conversation followed and the owner hurried off.

As they enthusiastically consumed the plate of *schie,* they drank the fresh, fruity, straw-colored Breganze Vespaiolo that Valier, urged on by Reuben, had selected.

"We saw you on television," Reuben told the Commissario. "The CNN broadcast."

"Ah yes. Death in Venice, if I may dare to use that phrase. Wonderful publicity for us."

"You seemed confident that Baxter's killer will be caught," Reuben said.

"One must bluster the press," Valier said.

"I've been curious," Cynthia asked. "How frequent are murders here in Venice? I'd never heard of one before."

"We have more than you imagine," Valier said. "Maybe four or five a year. Mostly one criminal killing another, especially over drugs, or sometimes a jealous husband."

Reuben did a quick calculation. "If Venice has a population of seventy-five thousand, five murders a year is a rate of one per fifteen thousand."

"How does that compare with New York?" Valier asked.

"We average about six a day, or something over two thousand a year. With a population of eight million that's, let's see, one per four thousand. Your record is better."

A waiter served up three dishes of tagliolini, with a sauce of minced shellfish and cheese covering the pasta.

"Venetians seldom serve fish and cheese together," Valier explained. "But you'll like this."

After a taste, Reuben and Cynthia expressed immediate approval.

His pasta selection commended, Valier called the owner over to discuss the next course.

"You wanted to see us, Jack," Reuben said, when the ordering was completed.

"Yes. I'd like to see what we know and what we don't know about Mr. Baxter's murder. We now have statements from Mr. Garrison, Miss Tabita, Mr. Abbott and Miss Medford. And, of course, there is the information you first gave me, about the poisoning attempt. I have talked to the barman at Haig's Bar and I've had two *ispettori* asking questions around Santa Maria del Giglio.

"From this, we know the following. *Primo*. Someone unsuccessfully tried to poison Gregg Baxter on Wednesday. *Secondo*. Baxter had dinner last night with his colleagues and la marchesa Scamozzi and her gentleman friend, right here, at this restaurant. *Terzo*. Baxter separated from his companions at Santa Maria del Giglio at approximately ten-twenty-five and went to Haig's Bar. *Quarto*. An hour or so later Baxter left Haig's with a young man named Nicolò Pandini, then returned to the bar alone after another hour had gone by. *Quinto*. Baxter had one drink of Scotch and left the bar again, by himself. This was at approximately one o'clock. And, finally, *sesto*, Baxter was killed in the Calle dei Tredici Martiri, sometime between one and three A.M., or so they concluded from the *autopsia*."

At this point the waiter brought the largest plate yet, containing a giant *branzino*, or sea bass, which had been prepared *bollito*, boiled in white wine.

"This is very healthy for you," Valier explained. "No heavy sauces, which I believe you Americans no longer eat."

The simple fish was delectable, and the Frosts again congratulated the Commissario for choosing it. He smiled and quickly returned to the subject of Baxter.

"Now, let us see what we don't know. *Primo*. Who placed the poison in Baxter's insulin? *Secondo*. Where did Baxter and Pandini go when they left Haig's Bar together? *Terzo*. How did Baxter get from Haig's to the Calle dei Tredici Martiri? Alone? With his murderer? And *finalmente*, the jackpot question, who was that murderer?"

"You have facts we didn't know before," Reuben said. "Pandini, for instance. Who is he?"

"He is *un uomo che si prostituisce*, a male prostitute, a hustler. Or, as we say in Venice, a *recio*. He's a bad egg who preys on queer tourists. He's smart enough not to rob them, but he charges a fancy price and we suspect is not above blackmail if the opportunity comes along. We've had an eye on him for a long time. He's good-looking and friendly, so he makes out well."

"Let me see if I have this straight. He met Baxter in Haig's, went outside somewhere with him and then Baxter came back into the bar alone."

"Yes. That's what the bartender says."

"But Pandini could have met up with Baxter again later, after he left the bar?"

"Of course."

"What does this Pandini say?"

"He's disappeared," Valier said. "We haven't been able to find him."

"And what about the neighbors? You said your men had questioned them."

"Nothing," Valier said. "Usually, no matter where you are in Venice, or what hour of the day or night it is, there is at least one grandmother, *una nonna*, peering out a window, or at least listening to the sounds. Unfortunately, there are not that many apartments along the Calle where Baxter was killed.''

"I know, I went there this afternoon," Reuben said.

"Anyway, no one heard a thing or saw a thing. Or so they all claim."

"What about the workers in the hotel?" Reuben asked. "This afternoon the service entrance was open and one could see and hear people moving about inside."

"The door is closed at night. My *ispettore* asked the same question. Right now, I would say young Pandini is a likely suspect, wouldn't you?"

"There's only one difficulty with that," Cynthia said. "If we assume the person who tried to poison Gregg Baxter was the same one who murdered him, it seems improbable that Pandini was the poisoner. As far as we know, he met Baxter for the first time last night."

"That is true, Mrs. Frost. So let us put Pandini to one side for a moment. There is another intriguing fact I did not include in my enumeration, because I don't know what it means. We have taken the *deposizione* of la signorina Medford. She claims to have no memory of what happened after she returned last night to her hotel."

"I told you, Jack, about her being fired," Reuben said.

"Yes. That is why we were especially interested in her statement."

"What I didn't tell you is that we saw Ms. Medford last night," Reuben said. "She was with Eric Werth, the perfume manufacturer I mentioned, and Jim Cavanaugh, his lawyer, at the Antica Besseta. They came back with us and we left Medford at the Bauer Grunwald."

"What time?"

"Around ten-forty, I'd say."

"Was she drunk—*ubriaca?*"

"She seemed all right when we left her," Reuben said. But then he thought of the quantity of grappa she had put away. And her wine consumption on the plane, Baxter's reference to her as a "drunken bitch" and her perpetually red face. She was probably a two-fisted drinker. "If she was drunk, she would hardly have been in shape to kill Baxter."

"She may have stayed sober long enough to kill him and then done some serious drinking afterward," Cynthia observed. "Wiping out her memory of the murder in the process."

"That's true," Valier said. "In fact, Mrs. Frost, you have made a very good point. I shall have my men do some more checking at the Bauer Grunwald."

"Jack, not to jump around, but are you aware of the quarreling that went on here at Da Fiore?" Reuben asked.

Valier looked surprised. "Quarreling? What do you mean?"

"What I mean is that Cynthia and I have heard that Gregg Baxter picked fights with most of his party during dinner."

Together, the Frosts reported what they had been told by Gussie Morrison and Sarah Cochran.

"I am very surprised," Valier said, when they had finished. "Neither Garrison nor the model mentioned trouble to me, and neither did Mr. Abbott."

"Nor to me," Reuben added.

"You say it was an old lady who told you this?" Valier continued. "Perhaps she was confused."

"Our source may be old, but I've yet to find her confused," Reuben said.

"We can settle this pretty easily," Valier said. He motioned to Maurizio Martin, who came over to the table. The crowd had thinned out and the dining room staff was less harried than it had been earlier; the owner had time to sit and chat, and did so.

"Maurizio, you've heard about the murder of the American?" Valier asked.

"Yes. The fashion person. It was unbelievable. He was here for dinner last night," Martin said, speaking in English.

"We know that," Valier said. "And we've been told that Baxter, the dead man, was quarreling with his group."

"He talked much."

"What was he saying?"

"I could not hear. It was very busy and I was moving around. He must have said something *sgradevole*, something disagreeable, because two of the people he was with, the two *negri*, got up and left."

"And you didn't hear anything that was said?" the Commissario pressed.

"No."

"What happened after the black couple left?"

"Il signor Baxter started shouting at one of the men with him. Not Luigi Regillo but the other one."

"Dan Abbott," Frost said.

"Then they took off."

"What time?"

"I would say around ten. A little after, perhaps."

"Maurizio, thank you."

After Martin had left them, Valier said over coffee that he wanted to talk to Baxter's colleagues again.

"An *ispettore* has gone to the Cipriani this evening to speak with the employees who were on duty last night," he continued. "I'm going to try to reach him now to ask him to make questions at the Bauer Grunwald as well. First thing tomorrow morning, I'll find out what he's learned and then call the famous New York detective." Valier smiled and looked at Cynthia.

Reuben ignored the taunt. Their business done but their coffee unfinished, he asked Valier if he were a native Venetian.

"Oh yes. I've spent my whole life here, except for my short stay in Sicily and then my enforced vacation in your country. I always refused to leave Venice to serve in the P.S. elsewhere, which is why I'm a mere Commissario and not the Questore of, say, some booming metropolis like Salerno. I took care of my mother for very many years, you see, so could not leave. Which was all right. Valiers should be in Venice. It is an old Venetian name. The family had two Doges in the seventeenth century, Bertucci and Silvestro. Poor Bertucci was sick the whole time and died within two years. Silvestro, his son, lasted longer, but was stricken with apoplexy after a fight with the Dogaressa, his wife.''

''Are there monuments to the Valiers?'' Frost asked, after explaining his vacation project.

''There is only one—a huge mausoleum in San Zanipolo.''

''Ah yes. I remember reading about it now.''

''It is the tomb of both Bertucci and Silvestro. And Silvestro's wife, the Dogaressa Elisabetta Querini. The legend is that she felt so guilty about quarreling with her husband, and causing his death, that she had the grandest possible monument built to ease her conscience.''

''A touching story,'' Cynthia said, an amused edge to her voice.

''I have to make an assault on San Zanipolo soon,'' Reuben said.

''Right now I have to make an assault on the bed,'' Valier said. ''It is sack time. Let me call you in the morning. And, Avvocato Frost, thank you for the information you supplied. I think in this *processo* two gray heads—ours—may be better than one.''

SATURDAY MORNING, REUBEN WENT TO THE POOL EARLIER than usual. He knew that it was invaded on weekends by rich Milanese and their families. More precisely, the pool area became crowded early in the day with mothers, children and nannies: the children scampered about, the nannies looked bored and the young mothers, uncovering and greasing their bodies, sought desperately to absorb the last sunshine of the season. The Italian surgeon general, if there was such, had clearly not warned his constituents of the dangers of sunbathing—or of smoking, for that matter. The young matrons in their bikinis puffed assiduously on their Marlboros.

Reuben was dismayed to find a family group camped near his favorite spot. He reclined there on a chaise all the same, hoping that the three infants uncomfortably close by would behave. He was disappointed. The two girls and a boy rousingly chased each other around and around.

To his relief, an Italian-speaking termagant finally shouted, *"Basta! Tornatevene dalla mammina!"* The nanny's stern imprecation, coupled with a severe look, had a positive effect and the chastised noisemakers did return to their mother, settling down in wiggly silence beside her.

Later, emerging from his morning swim, he lay back and looked up at the suites occupied by the Baxter party. There was no sign of anyone on the balconies, though the anonymous and limber member of the staff had done his climbing act that morning and opened the large umbrellas. Then, just as he closed his eyes, a porter approached with the message that Commissario Valier wanted him to call.

Frost put on his robe and went to an outdoor telephone near the landing stage. Once on the line, the Commissario proposed that Reuben meet him early in the afternoon at his office. "We put things together so well last night, I'd like to try again today," he told Frost. "I have some new information to be fitted into the puzzle."

Valier was no more forthcoming, so it was plain to Reuben that making the trip to the Squadra Mobile was the price of learning what the "new information" might be. He agreed to be there at two.

That afternoon, the Commissario was dressed in suit and tie; Reuben was tieless and wore a blue blazer. Perhaps as a concession to it being Saturday, Valier's suit was a pale tan, lighter than his own complexion, and he wore two-toned brown shoes on his tiny feet. Again Reuben noted that his erect bearing made him appear taller.

"You have news?" Frost asked.

"Yes, I do. Hot off the press. My assistants have been busy. While we were having our very good dinner last night—for which I thank you once more—one of them questioned the *motoscafista* of the Cipriani boat who was working Thursday night and the watchman who guards the rear door at the hotel. Also the second watchman who patrols the property. Also the concierge on duty. The result of these interrogations is this. *Primo.* Mr. Abbott returned to the hotel around eleven, according to the boatman."

"That fits with my having seen him in the bar later."

"Yes. He said he was in the bar until just before midnight, when he rented a movie from the concierge and watched it on his VCR. A film with your Mr. De Niro—or maybe he's ours—called *Midnight Run*. Not that the name matters.

"Then, *secondo*, Mr. Garrison and Miss Tabita came back later, the boatman says about twelve forty-five, though the concierge thinks it was more like one-thirty when they picked up their room key. There were so many revelers from a party of Americans that no one seems quite sure of anything."

"I know. I was there," Reuben said. "Perhaps they returned and had a drink in the bar before going to pick up their key."

"Unlikely. The bar *did* stay open to accommodate all the drinkers, but neither the bartender nor the waiter saw Garrison and Tabita."

"Isn't it possible they could have missed them in the crowd?"

"They are a pretty distinctive-looking couple, Avvocato Frost."

"Point taken," Reuben said.

"So I think we have to realize that there may be a discrepancy between what the boatman says and what the concierge says."

"What do *they* say?" Reuben asked.

"They split the difference. Their *deposizioni* both state that they got back around one o'clock and went straight to their suite, after picking up their key.

"Now let me turn to what my other *ispettore* learned," Valier continued. "Point *terzo*, which I find intriguing. The records at the Bauer Grunwald show that three miniature bottles of vodka and two miniature bottles of Scotch were consumed out of Miss Medford's minibar between the time she checked in Thursday and when the bar was checked and restocked Friday afternoon. Thus there is possible support for the theory offered by your wife last night that Medford may have killed Baxter and drowned her sorrows afterward."

"Both Scotch and vodka were drunk, you say. That could mean she drank vodka at one time and Scotch at another—

not necessarily the binge you pictured. Or she may have been drinking with someone else."

"Or she drank all the vodka and then started on the Scotch," Valier said. "The hotel only includes three bottles of vodka in each minibar."

"Hmn," Reuben said.

"So *terzo* is ambiguous. Which brings me to the deceased. As I told you at Da Fiore, Baxter came to Haig's Bar around ten twenty-five or ten-thirty Thursday night, picked up Nicolò Pandini, left the bar for an hour or so and then came back. He departed the second time about one A.M., after which he was killed."

"So what do you have to add to the story today, Jack?" Reuben asked.

"*Quarto* is what I have to add. We have found out what Baxter and Pandini were doing," he said, then paused. "They went for a gondola ride."

"Gondola ride! That's preposterous!"

"Is it, really? Making love in a gondola is not unheard of, you know. Read your Casanova. Including two men going at it, I should think. Maybe not buggery, but there are other themes and variations that would have been possible. In the dark, under a blanket, no one would ever know. Including the gondolier, unless he's a voyeur."

"You've talked to the gondolier? What does he say?" Frost asked.

"His name is Viscusi and he works at the gondola station right there between the Gritti and Haig's."

"Yes, I know where you mean."

"Viscusi says Pandini, whom he knew, and another man—he later identified him, so we're satisfied it was Baxter—hired him at eleven forty-five for one hour. They discussed a price and decided to go up the Rio Barcaroli— not too far from where they were—and back. Viscusi says he's sure of the time, because he was to quit at midnight and had been looking at his watch repeatedly. He took the job and finished where he'd started at twelve thirty-five."

"That's only fifty minutes."

"To a gondolier, that's an hour."

"Just like an American psychiatrist," Reuben grumbled. "What did the gondolier say was going on?"

"Gondoliers do not make a habit of being talkative with the police, Avvocato Frost. He saw nothing, or so he claims."

"And I take it Mr. Pandini has still not been found?"

"Correct."

"That leaves la marchesa Scamozzi and her friend—what about them?" Reuben asked.

"My men found out that they were on the number five, the *circolare sinistra,* that went from the Zattere to Sant-'Eufemia, over on the Giudecca near where la marchesa lives, at ten forty-five. Both the crew members on duty remembered seeing them. The trip across takes only two minutes, so they were on their way home at ten forty-seven."

"Unless one or both of them doubled back to the murder site," Reuben said.

"We've checked every boat that might have stopped at the Giudecca—the *circolare,* the number eight, the nine, the number thirty-four. No one working on them saw Scamozzi or Regillo leave the island. And there's no record of a water-taxi being ordered. So, unless they swam across, there is not any way they could have been at the Tredici Martiri at the crucial time."

"La marchesa doesn't have a boat of her own, I assume?" Reuben asked.

"You are very suspicious, Avvocato Frost. But the answer is no."

The two were silent for an instant and then Valier asked Frost what he made "of all this."

"Let's go through the list," Frost said. "You just eliminated Ceil Scamozzi and Regillo, or apparently so. Dan Abbott's alibi seems to check out, too. Back to the Cipriani before the time of the murder, a nightcap or two in the bar, then a rented movie in his room.

"I'd like to think the murderer was your young punk,

Pandini. But I still have the problem Cynthia mentioned last night—how could he have been linked to the attempted poisoning?"

"That is a good riddle your wife brought up."

"On the other hand, his running away doesn't exactly help his case."

"I'm with you."

"Then we have Tony Garrison and Tabita—and uncertainty about their whereabouts in the early morning hours. And finally we have Doris Medford, whose amnesia is either a put-on or was genuinely induced by alcohol. When did she have those drinks from the minibar?

"Then I can't quite forget my perfumer friends, Werth and Cavanaugh. They were still here Thursday night, remember, and were staying at the Gritti, right near the crime scene."

"I wish we had a stronger case against one of these people—any one of them, or any combination of them," Valier said. "It's most unfortunate that so much is *nebbioso*. But right now, I'm afraid I'd have to say, *'Ricordatevi del povero fornaretto!'* "

"That's beyond me," Reuben said.

"Remember the poor baker-boy!" Valier replied, smiling. "It's an old legend told by the gondoliers. There was a baker-boy who one day found the sheath for a dagger on the street. The dagger itself had been used to kill a nobleman and when the baker-boy was discovered with the sheath on his person, he was executed for the murder.

"Years later, a criminal in Padova, on his deathbed, confessed to the crime. After that, as long as the Republic existed, the Council of Ten never again pronounced a death sentence until they had been solemnly warned, 'Remember the poor baker-boy!' We have to watch out that we don't end up with a poor *fornaretto*."

"Or *fornaretta*," Reuben added.

"Yes. Or *fornaretta*."

13

WALKING DOWN THE RIVA DEGLI SCHIAVONI—A PERILOUS undertaking amid the legions of tourists converging on San Marco on a Saturday afternoon—Frost reflected on his meeting with Valier.

As he almost literally pushed against the sweeping human tides heading toward him, his thoughts turned again to Eric Werth and Cavanaugh. He wanted to bring them into better focus. As he reached the Molo, which was even more densely packed than the Riva, he had the sudden inspiration to contact Ted Demetrios; he was sure that, in their brief encounter at the Cipriani, the banker had said that he and his wife would be around at least through the weekend.

He decided to walk to the Gritti Palace and check. Demetrios could easily get a line on Werth's business; the information might be useful. Avoiding the Piazza San Marco, Reuben strode along the water's edge in front of the Giardinetti Reali, though the area was scarcely less crowded than the Piazza itself.

Within ten minutes, he was in the lobby of the Gritti, which he was appalled to find had been redecorated in a style more appropriate to the eccentricities of the Gesuiti than to a hotel. A heavy marble reception desk, resembling an altar, was forbidding; those approaching it resembled supplicants, not welcome guests. Here he was told that Mr. and Mrs. Demetrios were still registered but were out at the moment. He decided to linger for a bit and went to sit on the almost deserted deck, outside the bar. It was far too early in the afternoon to resume drinking, so he ordered a mineral water to keep his franchise.

The view of the Grand Canal and the Salute across the way was breathtaking; as far as he was concerned, it was the finest spot at the Gritti and, indeed, one of the most exciting vistas in the entire city. Noting the complete absence of clouds, he recalled the observation—he thought it was William Dean Howells'—that the sky was "never so tenderly blue over any other spot of earth" than in Venice.

Reuben sipped at his San Pellegrino as his attention was drawn to the noisy gondoliers at the station next to the hotel. Suddenly he realized that it was here that Gregg Baxter had embarked on his odd midnight ride with Nicolò Pandini.

He considered going over to interview the striped-shirted gondoliers; Viscusi, the one who had taken Baxter and Pandini on their trip, was probably on duty. Then he had to admit that this would most likely be unproductive. His Italian was simply not good enough to conduct an interrogation with masters of the nearly incomprehensible Venetian dialect. Instead he went inside and left a note for the absent Demetrios.

Back at the Cipriani, Frost tried to reach Dan Abbott, but he was also out. Gianni told him that he "thought" Abbott, Medford, Garrison and Tabita had gone to explore the Lido. At least Abbott had questioned him closely about the Casino there, and had asked him to make a dinner reservation for four at the Hotel Excelsior.

Frost gave up and stretched out on his bed waiting for Ted Demetrios to call him back. When the banker did so, just before six o'clock, he said that he was leaving for the States the next day, Sunday, and that he would be back in his office "at dawn" Monday morning. "I get to work early. Have to make the rent, you know, with an early call to Japan."

Frost put forward his request, for whatever information could be gathered regarding the House of Werth, and Demetrios said he would see what he could find out. A bad joke about getting out of Venice before they were murdered ended the conversation.

That evening Sandro Scarpe, the proprietor of the Caffè Orientale, led the Frosts to the small balcony of the restaurant, overlooking the tiny Rio Marin. The half-dozen outside tables were much prized, and they considered themselves fortunate to have captured one on a Saturday night.

"I hope you have your *risotto ai frutti di mare* tonight," Reuben said to the owner once he and Cynthia were seated—and had expressed pleasure over their placement outside.

"For you, always. We do. We have."

"That's what I want. I've been thinking about it all week."

"And to start, Signor Frost?"

"How about the *sardine in saor?*"

"You are in luck this night. We have made them."

"Good! Your pickled sardines, if I can call them that, are the best in town."

"*Grazie,* signore. But we are neglecting la signora."

"That's all right, I'm still pondering," Cynthia said. "I feel like something simple. What do you have that's grilled?"

"Ah. San Pietro."

While his wife was deciding, Reuben considered the total mystery of why "San Pietro" was never translated into English as "St. Peter," but instead as "John Dory," a name that meant absolutely nothing to Reuben or to any other English speaker he had ever asked about it. When fresh, as it was sure to be here, the white fish was succulent, whatever it was called. Cynthia decided to have it.

"And for you, signora, to start?" Sandro asked.

"Gamberetti?"

"Sì, sì. With sauce?"

"Just lemon, Sandro, please."

The owner bowed and hastened off to the kitchen. The waiter, meanwhile, brought a bottle of Tocai Friulano; the white wine had an almost erotic taste in the soft, cool evening.

As Cynthia and Reuben drank, a procession of gondolas passed beneath the balcony. The gondoliers rowed without a sound, though the passage of the graceful vessels was heralded by a stentorian tenor, standing upright in the first boat and singing a vigorous rendition of "Santa Lucia" to accordion accompaniment.

The tenor's captive audience was Japanese. As the small fleet passed the restaurant, most of the men in the party snapped pictures of the diners on the balcony, one of their number almost falling into the Rio Marin as he stood up to get a better shot.

"I wish I had a camera," Reuben said to Cynthia.

"Why?"

"So I could take a picture of them taking pictures of us. It would be one of the weirdest photographs since Man Ray."

"Eat your *sardine,* dear," Cynthia said, anxious to distract her husband. He was a fair-minded, tolerant and compassionate man, but as a Navy veteran of World War II in the South Pacific, he could occasionally be heard to mutter less than flattering remarks about the erstwhile enemy.

Before leaving the hotel, Reuben had told his wife about his meeting with Commissario Valier. He had also aired his new, and totally unfounded, suspicion of Eric Werth and Jim Cavanaugh. Cynthia brought this up as they waited for their entrees.

"You know, Reuben, I was thinking on the way over here about Eric Werth and what you said earlier. You may be entirely right, but I think you have the same problem pointing the finger at Werth or Cavanaugh as you did with Pandini—there doesn't seem to be any connection between them and the poison attempt. They couldn't even get to see

Baxter, for heaven's sake. How could they have been in a position to tamper with medicine in his bedroom? You think about it while I make a pig of myself with this San Pietro.''

Reuben, for his part, attacked his risotto. He motioned for a new bottle of wine. When Sandro Scarpe returned with it, he was shaking his head.

"You Americans,'' he said.

"What have we done now?'' Reuben asked.

"Six of your *compatrioti* came in just now and asked if we served Chinese food. Can you imagine?''

"Did they think that 'Orientale' implied Chinese?'' Cynthia inquired.

"I suppose so,'' Sandro said.

"What did you do?''

"I sent them to La Grande Muraglia, over in the Castello.''

"The Great Wall. I've never eaten there,'' Reuben said. "But you made a great mistake, Sandro. Six customers wanting Chinese food. You should have told them you have it.''

"But I couldn't.''

"Of course you could. You have spaghetti, don't you? Didn't Marco Polo bring spaghetti back here from China?''

"That's the story,'' Sandro said. "I should have thought of that. You sure you don't want to go into business with me, Signor Frost?''

Once Sandro turned his attention elsewhere, Reuben pondered what Cynthia had said earlier and reluctantly conceded that she was probably right, as she usually was, about Werth and Cavanaugh. He asked her where she thought that left the situation.

"I hate to say it, since I know she's a fan of mine, but isn't Doris Medford the most likely murderer? Not to dwell on it, but her alibi—'I don't remember'—seems pretty weak. She also had free access to Baxter's room, and to his insulin. And his shabby treatment of her may have been enough to motivate her to kill him. God knows how much time and emotional energy she had invested in that dinner of his, for which her reward was getting fired.''

"You could say the same for Garrison and Tabita, alone or together," Reuben said. "A soft alibi, access to the dead man's insulin and a motive. With Baxter dead, Garrison stood to become the creative force running one of the most successful fashion houses in America, if not the world. And Tabita would have become even more famous, as well as the wife—or at least the girlfriend—of a very wealthy man.

"There are a couple of other things to put on the scales, too. The AIDS business—very possibly a life-or-death matter for them. Surely enough to give them a motive, or to buttress one they already had. And going along with that, there's their failure to tell me or the police about Baxter's provocative mention of AIDS Thursday night.

"A final point. We have no idea where the damned glass dagger came from. But let's not forget that Garrison knows Venice well and speaks Italian—both helpful qualities when in the market for such an oddity, I should think."

"Sounds like a stalemate to me, dear," Cynthia said. "So why don't you try to relax for one evening?"

While they had been talking, Reuben had been following a developing scene out of the corner of his eye. He had earlier noticed an empty gondola moored next to the iron gate separating the restaurant from the water. Then he realized that the absent gondolier must surely be the darkly good-looking youth in a boldly striped gondolier's shirt sitting with an equally attractive girl at the small table across the way.

From what he could overhear, Reuben figured out that the girl was an American, a student about to take up residence for the fall in Bologna, staying temporarily at the youth hostel on the Giudecca. Her companion was a voluble talker, with a better grip on English than she had on Italian. Though they were holding hands and rubbing each other's arms, it was also quite evident that they were getting acquainted as well, in a confused mixture of flirtation and foreplay.

Reuben lowered his voice and described his guesswork to Cynthia. Then, while the Frosts were drinking their espresso, the dashing sailor paid the check, opened the gate, escorted his Yankee prize to a seat in the gondola, leaped onto the prow and rowed off.

"That's the damndest thing I've ever seen!" Reuben said, laughing aloud. "It must be the wind. What the Brits here call the *scirocco*. It makes people do odd things in Venice, from seduction to murder. Since I don't have my gondola here, shall we start walking?"

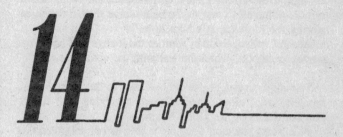

ONCE THE *VAPORETTO* HAD BROUGHT REUBEN AND CYN-thia to San Marco, they decided to walk through the Piazza. Many in the Saturday night crowd were couples, some hold-ing hands. A few stopped to listen to the orchestra outside Florian's play (inevitably) the theme from "Dr. Zhivago." The lights along the sides, the Procuratie Vecchie and the Procuratie Nuove, glowed and seemed to warm the crisp September air.

Thinking of the ardent gondolier and his pretty compan-ion, Reuben took Cynthia by the arm as they walked slowly toward the shadowy magic of the basilica; there was no reason the young should have a monopoly on romance.

Later, going back to the hotel, Reuben described a strat-agem he had been working out since leaving the Orientale. His plan was to invite Abbott and Medford to go the next day to Torcello.

"It's a humane thing to do, since they're stuck here and can't leave," Reuben told his wife.

"Dear, I doubt that humaneness is your real motive," Cynthia chided him.

"Okay, it's to get them talking as well. Gregg Baxter's still a puzzle. Something of interest might come out during some relaxed sightseeing, or over a good lunch. Besides,

123

we haven't been to Torcello in years and I'd like to go at least once more before I die."

"Don't be morbid, dear. Your disingenuousness is quite enough. But seriously, it's a splendid idea. And, you're right, we haven't been to Torcello since they finished restoring the mosaics. It's high time."

At the Cipriani Reuben went to the lounge and wrote out a note to Abbott, which he left with the concierge.

Sunday morning, the telephone rang in the Frosts' room moments after nine. It was Abbott, accepting their invitation but declining for Doris Medford.

"I'm sorry she won't be able to join us but delighted that you will be," Reuben told him. "Let's leave from downstairs a little after ten. It takes about an hour, and we want to be there in time to see the church before lunch. There's supposed to be an excellent new restaurant—new to us anyway—and I'll make a reservation."

"Medford's not coming," he told Cynthia. "That could be just as well. We may do better zeroing in on Abbott alone. One thing, dear. I hope you won't be offended if we break away from you at some point."

"To talk man-to-man, you mean."

"Something like that."

"Why should I? It's a good cause. The sooner the murder gets solved, the sooner I can get you to relax again."

"Fine. Let's leave it like this. If I mention last night's romantic gondolier, that's the signal for you to—"

"—get lost."

"Yes."

The Frosts met Abbott in the lobby, as arranged.

"Do I need a jacket?" Abbott asked. He was wearing olive slacks and a blue polo shirt, a Shetland sweater tied loosely around his waist.

Reuben, who was wearing a wheat-colored linen jacket, assured him that his attire was fine and there was no need to dress up any more than he was.

"The easiest way to get there is to take the number five out the back door here. We have to go around to the Fondamente Nuove and change to a number twelve. We could, of course, order a water-taxi, but it's more expensive and less colorful."

"You're the boss."

Once aboard the *circolare*, Abbott seemed distracted and oblivious to either the sights or the sunny weather. "I haven't had a chance to ask you, but when do you think we can leave this place, Mr. Frost? I appreciate taking this excursion today, I really do. Or spending the day at the Lido, like we did yesterday. Even if I dropped a bundle at the craps table. But I've got a business to run. I can't reassure our customers well enough on the overseas telephone. They need some personal stroking. And Tony Garrison has to get to work finishing the spring collection—by himself.

"Our biggest emergency is with Doris Medford. She's *got* to get to Milan to finalize some details on a huge fabric purchase for next spring's better line. We run the risk of losing out if she can't pull out of here soon."

"It's been Commissario Valier's strong advice that all of you stay in Venice," Reuben said. "But as long as Ms. Medford doesn't leave the country, he may not object. I'll ask him when I talk to him."

"What if we all just took off?"

"Legally, you probably could. But I wouldn't make any bets against the P.S. finding a way to stop you."

"What do they think's going to happen?"

"I'm not sure they know."

"Christ, we may be here forever."

Cynthia, curious, asked Abbott if Tony Garrison really could continue the business.

"Oh, absolutely," Abbott said. "The kid's got a million ideas a minute. He's a natural, the same way Gregg was. And now that he's stable, now that he's got Tabita, he's going to be even more dependable."

Frost was sorry to have the conversation interrupted by

arrival at the Fondamente Nuove. He was also not happy to
see the size of the Sunday crowd, mostly locals, waiting for
the number twelve. After a short wait, they boarded the
two-decked *motonave* and were able to sit together on the
upper deck.

"Mr. Abbott—"

"—Dan—"

"Dan, how did you get hooked up with Gregg Baxter in
the first place?" Reuben asked, when they had staked their
claim.

Abbott laughed. "Fate," he said.

"I'd be interested to hear the story."

"It's not very exciting, but sure, I'll be glad to tell you.
I had a very conventional upbringing, up in Westchester,
then went off to the Wharton School at Penn.

"When I got out, I went to work for First Fiduciary
Bank, where you and I first met. Eventually I was assigned
to commercial lending and, in particular, the group that
made loans to Seventh Avenue.

"I really got to know the garment industry. The garmen-
tos liked me—I was their goy friend in the big bank. That's
where I met Gregg, when he broke away from Liz Claiborne and wanted to borrow money to get started on his
own. I liked his ideas, even if he didn't have much of a
business plan. We made the loan, Bergdorf's made its first
buy the next year and he was on a roll. That's when he
asked me to join him. 'You had faith enough to lend me
money, why don't you have guts enough to be my partner?'
he said.

"I knew he needed practical business help. And I was
getting restless. Watching other people get rich with the
loans I was making was getting to me. Why wasn't I becoming rich, too? So I took him up on his offer."

"I know this is a rather private question," Reuben said.
"But I have an idea the more I know about Baxter and his
business the more intelligent I'm going to be in helping to
find who murdered him."

"Hell, I don't mind. What's your question?"

"How big a percentage of the business do you own?"

"Now, or back then?"

"Now."

"A third. I began at twenty-five percent, but Gregg let me buy a bigger share as we went along."

"What about Tony Garrison?"

"Ten percent, with a promise of more to come."

"An option?"

"No, there was nothing in writing. Just Gregg's word."

"What about Ms. Medford?"

"Zilch. She's on salary. A damned good one, but no points. The only owners are Gregg—were Gregg—Tony and me. Tony argued for giving her a piece, but Gregg never did. She drinks too much, you know. She's a very valuable person and balanced Gregg nicely right from the beginning, but she's got a real problem with the bottle. Sometimes she goes crazy when she drinks. Tony's always been willing to overlook it, but Gregg was more cautious about bringing her in. I'm sorry to mention this, but you asked."

Their boat stopped at Murano as Abbott was explaining the ownership of Baxter Fashions. Here there was another large influx of Sunday trippers, mostly families, but Abbott paid no attention to them.

"What happens to Baxter's share now?" Reuben pressed, as they headed off again.

"There's a right to buy out Gregg's interest from his estate. Luckily we had a key-man insurance policy on him, so with some borrowing from my old friends at First Fiduciary, we should be okay and Tony and I can take over."

"You'll have to increase Garrison's percentage won't you?"

"Sure. But I'm damned certain I'm going to put a pair of golden handcuffs on him so he isn't tempted to wander off."

"And you think he can go on by himself?" Cynthia asked.

"Absolutely. I'm not going to jump on Gregg's grave,

but Tony's steady, reliable and smart. And he has a fresh eye, which is worth everything in our business."

"Will you continue the Baxter name?"

"Oh, sure. That's worth millions. Maybe someday we'll put Tony's name out there, but not now. You look skeptical, Mrs. Frost. But look at other houses. Chanel's been dead how long? Twenty years? And Dior even longer. They survived with other designers—did better than ever, in fact. Or take Perry Ellis. They had a bad time when he died, but they're doing fine today. I'm very confident we can do the same."

"There's Torcello," Reuben interrupted, pointing to the small island, with its lonely and ancient cathedral tower. "Do you know about its history, Dan?"

"I'm afraid I'm very ignorant when it comes to that."

"The original settlement in the lagoon was here, in the early part of the seventh century. People fleeing the barbarians sought a safe hiding place off the mainland. I read that the population at one point got up to twenty thousand."

"Looks to me like it has gone down since then."

"Yes. There're about a hundred people living here now," Reuben said, as their boat was tied up. He looked around to get his bearings and then followed the crowd to a narrow footpath along an interior waterway.

Ten minutes later, Reuben, Cynthia and Dan were in what remained of the Piazzetta in front of Santa Maria Assunta. Reuben sat down on a bench to refresh his memory of Torcello with the help of his Lorenzetti Guide.

"Let's go inside," he said, after some quick reading. Standing in the nave, he noted that the cathedral had first been used in 639. "It was *rebuilt,* for God's sake, in 863 and again in 1008!" he told Cynthia and Dan.

Like all visitors to the church, Dan Abbott was drawn by the mosaic of the weeping Virgin in the center of the gold-encrusted domed arch over the main altar.

"The guidebook says that's thirteenth century," Reuben explained, "and the apostles down below the Virgin are twelfth. Now," he directed, "turn around and look at the mosaic on the opposite wall." Abbott did as he was told and looked up at the extraordinary *Apotheosis of Christ and the Last Judgment* on the inner facade, a truly terrifying work from the twelfth to thirteenth centuries, showing at the bottom the wicked being consigned to the fires of hell and the tortures of the damned. If Abbott has any scruples of conscience at all, Reuben thought, he'll play it straight with me after looking at *that* for a few minutes!

"I've worked up an appetite," Cynthia said as they emerged into the sunshine. "When is our reservation?"

"I'm sure we can show up anytime. I've reserved at the Osteria al Ponte del Diavolo, which translates rather vividly, if I've got it right, as the Inn at the Bridge of the Devil," he told Abbott. "The alternative is the Locanda Cipriani, which is charming and has a beautiful garden. We can peek in there when we go by. But I was curious about the Diavolo. We've never been there. Besides, a small rest from the Cipriani heritage may be good for us."

"Reuben, I like the thought you put into everything," Abbott said. "It all sounds fine to me."

The restaurant, a fisherman's cottage turned into a small inn, was surrounded by outdoor tables, which were beginning to fill up, the larger ones with families spanning three generations and, in one case, what appeared to be four.

Sitting outside was perfect, as the temperature was mild, and Reuben enthusiastically ordered a *grande caraffa* of the house white wine, a Cabernet from Friuli. He was surprised when Abbott declined a glass.

"I'm afraid I'm your original spoilsport," Abbott explained. "I gave it up when I was married to my first wife. I thought if I quit, she might, too." Abbott hesitated, perhaps embarrassed at having stumbled into such a personal matter, then continued. "She didn't. Instead she drank for both of us. After we were divorced, I never went back to the stuff. I figured you couldn't be both a workaholic and an alcoholic. Sorry to get so personal, but I usually feel I have to explain. Then there's the situation at Baxter Fashions, too. With Doris. Jack Spratt and Mrs. Spratt, Gregg called us once. With Doris licking the bottle clean.''

"In my opinion, drinking is a private matter," Reuben said. "If I went on a mineral-water regimen, I'm sure it would be better for me."

"Not a very likely prospect," Cynthia said.

"I'll ignore that," Reuben said, turning his attention to the menu. Following Cynthia's lead from the night before, Reuben ordered filetto di San Pietro, while she opted for the restaurant's version of grilled sole, *sogliola ai ferri*. Abbott sided with Reuben, though all three agreed to start with *spaghetti con seppie*. Reuben decided to bear in on Abbott once they had ordered.

"Dan," he began, "I'd like to bring up a difficult subject, and one that you may not want to discuss."

"Try me."

"Gregg Baxter's sex life," Reuben said. "I don't mean to be prurient, but my intuition tells me it may be relevant to solving our puzzle."

"I'll tell you what I can, but you should know that I tried to stay out of Gregg's personal intrigues as much as I could. He wanted it that way, and I did, too. But you can't help seeing things and knowing things, especially when you're the one that writes the checks."

Abbott paused, took a large forkful of spaghetti and a generous swig of San Pellegrino.

"Start with the proposition that Gregg was homosexual. He claimed he always had been, and I never knew him to have sex with a woman. He didn't hide it, but he didn't flaunt it, either. And when he was working very hard, which was often, there was no time for sex.

"You know, some people have funny ideas about that. They think gays are in and out of bed all the time, without stopping. Just as people believe that alcoholics drink steadily. But that's not necessarily true. Take my ex-wife, or Doris Medford for that matter. Either one of them could go for weeks without a drink and then might go on a binge and stay plastered for two or three days.

"Sex can work that way, too. Gregg Baxter would have binges—seducing his models, cruising the trucks, calling hustlers who advertised in the gay magazines, running through his Filofax to find the numbers of former partners. He was so rich and powerful and famous that he could have the pick of the gay and bisexual boys that hung around. He'd take them out to his mansion in Quogue or have parties in the duplex up over his office in New York. Then, two, three, four days later, he'd be back designing, as celibate as a monk.

"I hope this isn't embarrassing you, Mrs. Frost," Abbott continued.

"Heavens, no. I was a dancer for many years, don't forget, so I have seen a bit of sexual 'bingeing' in my day," Cynthia said.

"Was Thursday night one of Baxter's 'binges'?" Reuben asked.

"I would say so. He knew he was in danger after the poison incident, but he went off anyway and there was no stopping him. I suspect he picked up the first piece of trade he met. And got himself killed in the process."

"You believe that?" Reuben asked.

"At the moment I don't have anything else to believe."

"I realize that," Reuben said, "but how do you fit the attempt to poison Baxter into the picture?"

"Yeah, that's occurred to me. Maybe someone else pulled that stunt."

"It's possible. But is it likely?"

Abbott looked crestfallen, though he brightened when presented with his San Pietro.

"Let me change the subject a little bit," Reuben said. "Tell me about the relationship between Baxter and Tony Garrison."

"That's more complicated. Gregg met Tony six years ago now, at the Fashion Institute of Technology. Gregg was teaching a course at FIT, and Tony was a student. A poor black kid, or half-black kid, who lived in Brooklyn. He had real talent and Gregg discovered that right away. Besides, he was smart, had a great sense of humor and was handsome as hell. Gregg hired him part-time when he was still in school and he started helping with the design work even then.

"Gregg was a New York City boy through and through. So he was glad to see another city kid with talent and ambition come along. But his relationship with Tony was complicated. Gregg was almost paternal, treating and loving Tony like a son. Yet there was the other side, the gay side, too. Tony used to go out on the trunk shows with Gregg—you know what they are, where a designer takes his new designs to stores around the country—and I knew they'd begun sleeping together on the road. But the sex was only a part of an intricate arrangement in which Tony was employee, partner, lover and son, depending on the time and the day of the week.

"About three months ago, Tony snarled things up but good by moving in with Tabita and announcing to Gregg that sex with him was over. I know Gregg was devastated but there wasn't much he could do to get back at Tony. He'd become dependent on his wonderful imagination—I won't say Tony had taken over, but he had become more than a paid helper—and the glamorous allure of Tabita was an asset for Gregg, too. The more Gregg felt helpless the moodier he got, ending up with his explosion Thursday night."

Abbott had been talking so much that he had fallen behind Reuben and Cynthia and now wolfed down his food to catch up. As they finished their coffee— they had passed up the *crespelli alla crema* urged on them by Alfonso Corrado, the owner—Reuben managed to work into the conversation a reference to the Orientale gondolier. It was an awkward one, but it alerted Cynthia.

"If you don't mind, I'm going to hurry back to those stands in the Piazzetta. There was some lace there that caught my eye."

"We should try to get the boat at two-fifteen," Reuben said.

"I'll only be a few minutes, dear, don't worry."

When Cynthia had left, Reuben returned to the matter of Baxter's sex life. "Did Baxter have AIDS? Or was he what they call HIV-positive?"

Abbott appeared uneasy with the question, but soon answered, "He didn't have either one. Gregg was a terrible hypochondriac. With some justification, given his diabetes. But I know that he had himself tested for AIDS every month. And the result was always negative. Why do you ask?"

"Mr. Abbott, a little more than three days ago you and the late Gregg Baxter asked me to help you out—help you discover a would-be murderer, which unhappily has turned into a search for a real one. I agreed, and I believe I've tried to cooperate with you. But I would not be frank if I didn't tell you that I have not been entirely pleased with how things have gone."

"What are you driving at?"

"What I'm driving at is that I haven't been given all the facts."

"I don't understand."

"Then why was I not told that Baxter had pretty strong words with Tony Garrison the night he was killed? Specifically, he told Garrison that he was HIV-positive. Not a very comforting revelation to Garrison, who'd exchanged bodily fluids, as they say, with Baxter."

"You get around, don't you?"

"I thought that's what I was supposed to be doing," Reuben snapped.

"It is. I was just admiring your technique. You're absolutely correct. I was less than candid with you about what happened at the restaurant Thursday night. Gregg told Tony that he was HIV-positive, and Tony and Tabita left, obviously mad as hell. Why didn't I tell you? As I said, the HIV business was a cruel joke of Baxter's."

"Garrison didn't know it was a joke."

"Granted. But I didn't tell you because it was irrelevant and would only get people going down the wrong track.

However bad the situation had gotten, there's no way Tony could or would have killed Gregg. I'm real confident of that. So I tried to save you—and the police—from wasting unnecessary energy.''

"That should have been my call, not yours,'' Reuben said.

"I see that now,'' Abbott said. "But I still say the fact that Baxter and Garrison had words is irrelevant. Hell, for the last few months Baxter was quarreling with everybody. Me included.''

"What about, in your case?'' Frost asked, thinking of what Gussie Morrison had said.

"About the direction of the business. Gregg had a very conservative approach. He wanted to design dresses and menswear, period. No perfume. No luggage. No cheap line run up in Korea by some schlock licensee. I was doing my best to persuade him that the money was out there hanging on the trees, ready to be picked. Can you imagine the millions that could be made from a Gregg Baxter perfume? A Gregg Baxter after-shave lotion?

"That's why Eric Werth was here. I wanted him to make a pitch to Gregg. But he wouldn't even *see* Werth, and even disinvited him from the big party. Said he didn't want 'the old runt' anywhere around.

"And look at this, Mr. Frost,'' Abbott went on, pointing to the small figure of a polo player on his sports shirt. "Ralph Lauren's logo. You look around at the Americans over here, you'll see it on about half the men's shirts. Do you know how many millions that means? Gregg Baxter could have had a logo and grabbed off part of those millions. But he wouldn't do it. That's a long answer to your question, but that's what we quarreled about.''

Cynthia, with impeccable timing, appeared as Abbott finished his response. Abbott, when he saw her, asked for the check. "This is on me,'' he said, as he flipped his American Express card onto the table. "A peace offering,'' he said quietly to Reuben. Then it turned out that the Ponte del Diavolo did not take credit cards, so all three of them had to pool their cash. Cynthia was the largest contributor.

"I'm sorry I couldn't afford lunch," Abbott said, smiling, as they walked back to the boat. "But thank you anyway. This has been an eye-opener for me."

Reuben smiled back and did not say anything. He would have liked to say, "Me, too," but he was not quite sure to what it was his eyes had been opened.

15

REUBEN HAD BEEN SURPRISED WHEN VALIER HAD TOLD
him, in a telephone conversation Sunday night, that Monday was his day off and that he could not be reached, except
in an emergency, until Tuesday.

"I spend the day with my older sister," Valier explained.
"She's a spinster, and I'm a bachelor, so we keep each
other company once a week. For better or for worse, she's
the only family I have, and vice-versa."

Frost reasoned that if the officer in charge could take the
day off he, as a put-upon vacationer, could do the same.
This left him free to go to the barbershop Monday morning,
to fend off increasingly strident pleas from Cynthia that he
get a haircut.

"At least I've got my own hair, not like Dan Abbott,"
he had grumbled before setting out for the shop in the Mercerie
recommended by Gigi.

Returning later, Reuben was satisfied that the result had
not been too disastrous; he had remembered to say a firm
"no, grazie" to each strange nostrum and novel styling
technique his barber had proposed. It was almost noon when
he reached the Cipriani dock, where there were four others
waiting, including Tabita. She was wearing tight-fitting blue
slacks, a red silk shirt and a wide straw hat with a red silk

band, not unlike a gondolier's. She was carrying several shopping bags, including ones from Fendi and Krizia.

Reuben greeted her affably as she said "hi" and smiled. "Buying out the competition, I see," he said.

"No, only some extras to perk up the clothes I've got. Even though I'm a prisoner, I want to look good."

"You bought some fancy paper," Reuben said, pointing at a bag with a marble pattern from Alberto Valese-Ebrû.

"Yes! It's the most beautiful stationery I've ever seen. It's fabulous!"

Lowering his voice, Reuben asked if she could talk with him for a minute, "to clear up a couple of things."

"Sure," was the reply.

"How about back there, where we can sit down?" Frost asked, pointing to the Giardinetti Reali behind them.

"Suits me," she said, as Reuben walked with her to a faded bench in an alcove at one side of the gardens.

"Tabita, I'd like to go over with you some details about what went on Thursday night," Reuben said.

"You mean about Gregg's death?"

"No, before that. You and Tony Garrison had dinner with him, then left suddenly. Do you recall the time?"

"It was about nine forty-five."

"You're certain of that?"

"Yes."

"How did you know? Did you look at your watch?"

Tabita shifted uncomfortably. "I just knew," she said, pouting slightly.

Reuben dropped the subject and continued, "Now, the police have learned, and I have also, that there were some pretty harsh words exchanged, including a belligerent announcement by Baxter that he was HIV-positive. Is that correct?"

"Yes," she said, without elaboration.

"Yet neither you nor Garrison told the police—or me—about any row taking place. Why was that?"

"It wasn't relevant. It had nothing to do with anything. It just would have been embarrassing."

Reuben was getting provoked by everyone's attempt to

decide "relevance." His impatience showed as he looked hard at Tabita. Again she squirmed edgily, perhaps because of the hard bench on which she was sitting, perhaps not.

"Had Baxter ever mentioned HIV before?"

"No."

"So what he said to you was a surprise."

"Not especially, given how he led his life."

"But it was the first time he'd ever referred to his condition, was it not?"

"Yes."

"And if he were HIV-positive, wasn't that a matter of concern to you and Garrison?"

"It's a matter of concern when *anyone* is HIV-positive, when *anyone* gets AIDS, Mr. Frost."

"Fair enough. But let's be blunt about it—Tony Garrison and Baxter had sex. And, unless my sources have been gossiping irresponsibly, Garrison has had sex with you. So weren't you and he at least a trifle worried, a trifle disturbed, at what Baxter said?"

"You seem to take a lot about our private lives for granted," Tabita said crossly. "Of course what Gregg said disturbed us. A lot. Even if we'd gotten sort of numb to his abuse." She paused, then continued in a very quiet voice. "You see, it blew Gregg's mind when Tony began seeing me. Then Tony warned Gregg that he'd gone straight and sex was over between them and, wow, I can't even describe Gregg's reaction."

"When did this happen?"

"Three months ago. We all got along professionally—it was to everybody's advantage to do that—but privately Gregg was real bitter."

"Let me ask you something else. When you left the restaurant Thursday night, where did you two go?"

"You know, Mr. Frost, you sound like a D.A.," Tabita said, not without resentment. "I thought you were supposed to be our friend, supposed to be helping us."

"I am trying to help. It's only that I can't do much unless I know the facts. So, I repeat, where did you go?"

"I made Tony take a long walk, to try to calm him down. We were both upset, but he was *really* upset. So we walked and walked, and he gradually cooled off."

"Where did you walk?"

"My geography's not so good. But I remember we went by the back door of the Guggenheim Collection and eventually came to that church right across over there."

"The Salute."

"We took the boat from there and then the other one back to the hotel. Like we said the other day."

"And you didn't see or hear Abbott that night, after you left the restaurant, except hearing his television?"

"You've got it."

"Shall we go back?" Reuben asked. Tabita followed him out to the Cipriani dock. While they waited, he asked her where he could find Garrison.

"He's down at Ceil's studio," she said.

"Will he be there later, do you think? She's invited Cynthia and me for cocktails this evening."

"It's not just you. There'll be others, though she did decide not to do a big party so soon after Gregg's death."

"Will you be speaking with Garrison this afternoon?"

"Maybe."

Reuben explained that he would like to talk to him before the party and Tabita said she'd give him the message.

Once the *motoscafo* headed out, Reuben tried to point out some of the sights. Tabita could not have been less interested.

Reuben, seated at his usual table with Cynthia, could not decide what to order for lunch. Finally they both settled on the Cipriani's elaborate buffet—"the Cipriani's blue-plate special," he had once said to a friend, "all you can eat for seventy-five dollars." There was some justification for the atrocious cost: the two dozen platters contained an exceptional selection of delectable items, ranging from a variety of mushrooms to three types of shrimp.

He told Cynthia that he was convinced Gregg Baxter's

colleagues were coordinating their stories about what had taken place on Thursday. She expressed surprise at *his* surprise that they were doing this.

"My dear, if you had five lawyers from Chase & Ward here, and one of them was murdered, don't you think the other four would try to get their act together? Before facing the police of a foreign country? Not to speak of an inquisitive old party poking about for information."

"Inquisitive old party. That's me, I suppose."

"Just kidding."

Before Cynthia could defend herself further, a porter rushed up and presented Reuben with an envelope.

"Fax for you."

Frost opened the envelope and took out four shiny pages.

"It's from Ted Demetrios," Reuben explained. "He worked fast." He stopped eating and quickly read the text. "Very interesting. All about the House of Werth, just as I requested: It has sales of roughly $1.5 billion a year—"

"—that's a lot of perfume," Cynthia said.

"It says here perfume, cologne, hair-care products, skincare products, lipstick, et cetera. It's not as big as Revlon or Estée Lauder, which have sales over two billion. But listen. Ted says that the analysts on Wall Street who cover the fragrance and cosmetics industries think Werth is stagnating. Competitors' sales are growing but Werth is standing still. A recent market letter said quote The House of Werth badly needs a new high-end, designer fragrance to anchor its line unquote."

"That sounds to me like one with Gregg Baxter's name on it," Cynthia said.

"Yes. Except he never would have allowed it."

"But don't we think Dan Abbott would have?"

"What do you conclude from that?" Reuben asked. "That Eric Werth killed Baxter, or more plausibly had Jim Cavanaugh or someone else kill him, so that he could make a deal with the survivors?"

"Stranger things have happened, dear."

"That would be terrific. All of us stewing around here

while the murderer is safe in New York, where Commissario Valier can't even question him.'' He sighed. ''I guess all I can do is pursue the leads that *are* here. And speak to Tony Garrison this afternoon. I figure I'll go down to Ceil's around five-thirty and talk to him. I'll meet you there.''

La marchesa Scamozzi lived and worked in a converted warehouse on the Giudecca Canal, at Fondamenta di Ponte Piccolo. After a brisk walk, Reuben came to the bright green door of the building and rang the bell. It was opened promptly by Tony Garrison, who admitted him to the ground floor where la marchesa had her workshops and dyed her fabrics.

''Rubes! Come in. We just knocked off for the day and Ceil went upstairs to get ready for the party. Let's go up and eyeball the sunset.''

Frost followed Garrison upstairs and the two men sat down opposite each other on facing sofas of cracked leather. The room was a jumble of antiques of uncertain age and drab fabrics that bore no resemblance to the bright ones Ceil produced for sale; *The Aspern Papers* came to mind.

The living quarters did have large windows overlooking the Giudecca Canal and the Zattere on the other side. They appeared new, though stains from old leaks remained around the frames; perhaps la marchesa's improvement funds had run out before she was able to replace the streaked wallpaper.

''Want a drink, Rubes?'' Garrison asked.

''Not yet, thanks,'' Frost replied.

''Spoken to the police today?''

''No. Commissario Valier has the day off.''

''Pretty casual.''

''I'll second that.''

''So you're the only guy working on the case.''

''At the moment, that may be right. Of course Valier probably has some of his minions out asking questions. He seems to have an ample supply of *ispettori, sovrintendenti, assis-*

tenti and what have you. I take it no one's been to see you?''

"Nope.''

"I'm glad for this chance to talk," Reuben said. "I apologize for going over old ground. I know you've made a statement to the P.S., but there are one or two details that I'd like to confirm. As I get the story from others, Gregg Baxter had some pretty rough words for you at dinner last Thursday. So rough that you and Tabita got up and left. Words about Baxter's health, about his being HIV-positive. Is that a fair statement?''

"Yeah.''

"Yet you didn't mention this to the police when you made your statement to them. Your *deposizione*, as they call it.''

"Sì, sì, la mia deposizione l'ho fatto alla Pubblica Sicurezza.''

"I'm sorry. I forgot you speak Italian.''

"The only wop-speaking spade in captivity.''

"Try Ethiopia," Reuben shot back. He did not like racist cracks, even when it was the putative victim talking.

"Anyway, Tabita warned me you were leaked off that I didn't tell anybody about our, um, misunderstanding.''

"My feelings have very little to do with it. What's important, to me and to the police, is knowing exactly what happened. But if you want to know my feelings, I'll tell you. I believe any reasonable man, to use an old lawyer's term, would think that what Baxter said to you the night he died was relevant." He could use the magic word, too.

"So that means I was an unreasonable man, right?''

"That's your conclusion.''

"Gregg mentioned AIDS, right? That's not cool. Not cool if it gives the police the idea that *I* might have AIDS. I don't need to be deported before I finish my business with Ceil, because some dumb Eye-tie cop thinks I might be infected. Nor do I need to be put in quarantine somewhere. Whether Gregg had AIDS or not had nothing to do with his being killed. Neither did his attempt to pick a fight with me at dinner.''

"My reasonable man might differ with that conclusion."

"Then your reasonable man is an asshole."

"Let me shift the focus a little bit. I also understand that Baxter and Dan Abbott were also quarreling before the murder. Why didn't anyone tell us that?"

"Look, man, nobody mentions that the sun comes up in the morning, either. Dan's fights with Gregg were as regular as the sunrise. Part of the atmosphere, like oxygen. Okay? Their arguments didn't matter. Just like his firing Doris didn't mean anything. Uproars like that flared up all the time. It never occurred to me to mention them, and I doubt that it did to anyone else."

"Abbott told me that his arguments with Baxter concerned a difference in philosophy about the future of the business," Reuben pressed. "Which side were you on?"

"I was for bigger and better, like Dan. If you've got a good thing and can grow it, I say do it."

"Now you'll have your chance, won't you?"

"I sure hope so. Thank the Risen Christ Dan made Fashions get that key-man insurance on Gregg. We can work things out smooth and not go crazy."

"Did you ever tell Baxter your views about bigger and better?"

"Endlessly. But he didn't listen—to me, to Dan, to anybody. He was set on keeping the business as it was. No Baxter jockey shorts, no Baxter underarm deodorants, no Baxter anything. Dan and I even had the idea for a line of pet clothing. Don't laugh—with all the animal-rights freaks around you could do it. Poor Gregg. You gotta understand his oddball ideas about money. He was actually afraid—and this is the truth, man—that he'd become *too rich*. He talked all the time about Ralph Lauren, who he said had made so much money he had an adviser to tell him how to spend it! Not how to *invest* it, man, but how to *spend* it!

"The screwy part was, if he'd been left alone, Gregg wouldn't have made *any* money. He had no commercial sense. None. Why, hell, if he were in charge, the rich bitches who bought his clothes would be sent a bill a year later—which they'd take another year to pay. If they paid at all. Dan finally changed that—those chicks couldn't get out the door with their new threads unless they paid first.''

''There must have been much tension.''

''Tension? Nah. Most of the time it was only talk and if it escalated, it cooled off right away. Look, Gregg Baxter was the goose and if he wanted to lay a little tiny golden egg, instead of a nice big fat one, there wasn't one damn thing Dan or Doris or I could do about it.''

Except kill him, Reuben thought.

16

FROST'S CONVERSATION WITH TONY GARRISON WAS CUT short when Luigi Regillo came into the room carrying several bottles. He had what Reuben believed was called a "boyish" figure; though he looked a good forty, he was still thin as a rail, without a hint of paunch. But if the figure was youthful, the manner was fussy.

"Now I can shake hands," he said as he approached Reuben after putting bottles down on a dark wooden table at the side of the room. "You'll have to excuse me while I get this place tidied up." He went out and returned with a bouquet of flowers—not a grand florists' spread but a modest assortment bought from a street vendor—and a small bucket of ice cubes. Based on experience with Venetian entertaining, Reuben knew, with a sinking heart, that he was looking at the evening's ice supply.

The doorbell rang and Regillo ran down to answer it. He came back with Dan Abbott and Tabita before disappearing again. When he returned, he had put on a double-breasted blazer but not a necktie. As he busied himself about the room, plumping a cushion here, straightening a picture there, the others were drawn to the front window. The sun was setting out of sight to the left, but they could look across the water and see the changing light on the facades

145

along the Zattere. The effect was mesmerizing to the visitors, and they stood and watched without speaking.

La marchesa Scamozzi broke the silence when she entered, wearing a royal-red silk caftan. She ignored Regillo, nodded to the others and greeted Reuben emphatically, receiving kisses on both cheeks in return.

"I tried to chase you at Gregg's dinner but I never could get through the mob," she explained, pushing back her cropped jet-black hair. "I'm *so* glad you're here. With all the trouble, I haven't even had a chance to call you. Is Cynthia coming?"

"Yes. She should be here any minute."

"It's *wonderful* to see you. And you look so healthy! You know, Reuben, you haven't changed in the—what? fifteen years?—I've known you."

Reuben remembered well the first time he had been introduced to Cecilia Scamozzi by mutual acquaintances from London and realized that, yes, it had been fifteen years ago. They were not fast friends, but usually managed at least one outing during the Frosts' annual visit.

The Frosts had never met Cecilia's former husband, Gianpietro Camboni. That font of information Gussie Morrison had once filled them in on the missing spouse. "Camboni is a banker in Milan," Gussie had said. "He's rich and married Ceil for her title. God knows *she* and her family didn't have any money. He had a girlfriend in Milan right from day one. The floozie put her foot down a few years ago and demanded that they get married, so Gianpietro divorced Ceil and married her. Ceil got that house and studio she's in, but she gets a pittance from Camboni. Hardly enough to keep her, let alone the gigolo. That's why the poor thing's been trying to get into the fabric business." The "gigolo" had been a relatively recent acquisition, Reuben recalled; at least he and Cynthia had become aware of Luigi Regillo only within the last couple of years.

The hostess insisted that her guests have a drink. Reuben inspected the bottles Regillo had arranged; the pickings were slim. There was no gin, only a half-empty litre of vodka and one of sweet vermouth. He noted that the bottle of Schweppes tonic was also half empty, meaning that it was flat, he was sure. The white wine looked newly opened, so he opted for that. It was lukewarm and almost sour.

The next arrival was Marie Tyson, a novelist and short-story writer Reuben had often seen in New York, where she was a PEN activist ("Poets, Editors and Novelists," she had once assured Reuben, not "Pricks, Eunuchs and Nitwits" as a grumbling author had once called the organization in his presence) and a fixture at its benefits and any other literary event of significance in the city. She was a chronicler of female angst whose novels were stuffed with walloping sexual exploits. One of them, written after a long visit, had been set in Venice and highlighted the sexual adventures of an American visitor (reliably thought to be Tyson herself). "Did you know that Marie Tyson writes on her back?" a bookish wag had once asked Reuben. Reading her output, it seemed entirely plausible to him.

"Reuben Frost!" she said, as she reached him while circling the room. "I didn't know you were in Venice!"

"I could say the same. You going to be here long?"

"No, sadly. I'm just noodling around Europe until the Frankfurt Book Fair. It's such a drag, but my publisher says I have to flog my new novel. Have you ever been?"

"No, it's not really my line," Reuben said.

Doris Medford came in while Marie Tyson and Reuben were talking. Even from a distance he could tell that she looked better than she had at Antica Besseta, when she had been drinking too much, and certainly at the Questura. Frost decided to talk with her before she got lost in another conversation, so he extricated himself from Marie Tyson and walked across to where she was standing.

"I'm sorry we missed you yesterday," Reuben said. "We had a fine excursion to Torcello."

Medford looked puzzled. "Dan told me about your trip. But I didn't know I'd been invited."

Now it was Reuben's turn to be confused. He was sure his written invitation to Dan Abbott had explicitly included

Medford, but obviously there had been some misunderstanding. He decided that it might be embarrassing to pursue the matter, so he changed the subject. "I understand you want to go to Milan," he said.

"Not *want* to go. I don't much like it. But I have to make sure a whole group of fabrics gets into production. I suppose I could call the manufacturers up and tell them the police won't let me leave Venice, so would they please come and see me here? But that's too shame-making."

Reuben did not know quite how to respond, so he let her remark pass. "Now that you've had a chance to rest, do you have any thoughts on who might have killed your boss?"

"Former boss, don't forget. This time Gregg didn't get around to hiring me back."

"That was the pattern, wasn't it?"

"God, yes. Once or twice a year, I'd be told to pack up and leave. Then a day, a week later—six hours once—he'd call me back. It was crazy, and not great for the old self-esteem."

Reuben saw no point in getting into a discussion of Medford's psyche and was trying desperately to figure out how to change the conversational direction when Cynthia arrived. She was with Ephraim Miller, a hardy old party they had known for years and the scion of a nineteenth-century New England shoemaking fortune. By the time the Miller millions had been passed down to Ephraim's generation, they had diminished considerably, but he had enough to live modestly in Rome and for the month of September each year in Venice at the Bucintoro, an unpretentious pink pensione near the Arsenale. A jolly sort, he made annual excursions to Glyndebourne, Bayreuth, Salzburg and other music and dance festivals around Europe. Today he was wearing a double-breasted white linen suit, so old that it was more yellow than white.

"Reuben, I just picked your wife up on the Fondamenta outside," he said, shaking hands.

"You make it sound as if she were soliciting," Reuben said.

"Oh, no, no, no. Our meeting was purely accidental. And platonic," he said, then added, "Why there's Valarie Keene," as he spotted a tall, awkward-looking American woman hesitating at the door. Keene, who was now on the far side of thirty-five, had come to Venice a decade earlier with two objectives—to find a husband and to become a famous artist. She had failed at both, though she continued to paint in a studio in the Dorsoduro.

She was not unattractive, even though she wore her hair in a single lumpy pigtail, but her height had scared off a succession of men, mostly shorter, macho Italians unprepared to cope with a taller companion. She specialized in realistic studies of local scenes. They were professional enough, but she had never been able to capture the magical light of La Serenissima, a failing she shared with many an artist more accomplished than she; her Venetian cityscapes were bathed in the bright, harsh light that might have prevailed in her native Tulsa, Oklahoma.

Valarie Keene was followed almost immediately by a trio Reuben did not know but who were shortly introduced by Ceil Scamozzi as Dalton Glover, an American film director, and Betty Staples, the blond star of his movies and his life. The third member of the party, who it turned out had arrived with the movie pair only by coincidence, was Enzo Marcatti, a reporter for the local daily, *Il Gazzettino*. The be-spectacled, graying Marcatti was ubiquitous on the local social circuit. As Erica Sherrill had once put it, he was always ready to go to a party at the drop of his wife. She was a long-suffering and invisible lady who lived with their four children in Treviso, on the mainland. He circled the room, kissing each lady's hand, and then requested a vodka to renew his strength.

"I say, Enzo, have you been covering the Gregg Baxter murder?" Ephraim Miller asked him.

"I've been involved, yes," the newspaperman replied.

"Well, tell us what's happening," Miller boomed at him.

As if they had been anticipating a discussion of the

murder—as indeed they had—the other guests grew quiet and waited for Marcatti's reply.

"I know very little. Commissario Valier is handling the *indagine*, the investigation. He's a clever man. He is being very silent and what is known is what we have had in the paper—the facts of the crime only, no speculation about criminality."

"But surely they must have *some* idea of who killed the poor fellow," Ephraim pressed.

Marcatti raised his hands palms upward and shrugged. "If they do, they have not told me. There has been only a small hint, a very small hint, that they think he may have fallen into bad company at Haig's Bar before he was killed."

No one at the party seemed to know of Reuben's interest in the Baxter case. This suited him fine, as it enabled him to listen unnoticed.

Miller, mentioning that he had read somewhere that Dan Abbott had been Gregg Baxter's business partner, now turned to him. "Mr. Abbott, what do you think?" Then, realizing that his craving for gossip had gotten the better of his manners, he added, "His murder was an outrage. I'm sure you have the condolences of everyone here. You certainly have mine."

"Thank you, sir," Abbott replied. "Several of us were close to Gregg and we appreciate your sympathy. All I can say is that I agree with Mr. Marcatti, that the probability is that Gregg Baxter met up with a bad character when he was at that bar Thursday night."

A few minutes later, satisfied that the murder talk was winding down, Reuben turned to Dalton Glover and asked him what he was doing in Venice.

"The film festival brought me here. What keeps me here is Betty," he replied, nodding at Betty Staples. "We decided—she decided—to stay on a few days."

"Dalton's movie *Oysters* was in the competition," Staples explained. Reuben had not seen it, but remembered reading about it when it opened in New York the previous spring. Ms. Staples played a fishing-boat captain, a modern Tugboat Annie, who fought the polluters of her offshore oyster beds.

"For all the good it did us," Glover said. "We didn't come close to winning the *leone d'oro*. The festival juries in recent years have never liked American movies. But this time they outdid themselves, as you probably saw. A *Dutch* movie winning the golden lion, for God's sake! I didn't even know there *were* Dutch movies!"

"*Good-bye to God*," Betty added. "About a nun who gets married. It was terrible. Dalton suffers because he makes movies about *serious* subjects like ecology and native American history."

Reuben made appropriate noises of commiseration and then excused himself to talk to la marchesa Scamozzi. "Cynthia and I are going to Da Ivo for dinner," he told her. "Would you and Luigi like to join us?"

"What a lovely idea!" she said. "Ask him. I'm sure it's all right."

Frost moved to where Regillo was talking to Marie Tyson and Dan Abbott.

"Ah, *Commissario* Frost," Abbott said by way of greeting.

"Commissario?" Regillo said, puzzled. "I don't understand."

"Mr. Frost, besides being an eminent lawyer, is a well-known detective in New York," Abbott explained. "Specializing in murder cases. Which certainly makes him at least an honorary Commissario and a valuable fellow to have around right now."

Reuben smiled tightly, not happy to have his cover blown.

"Participating in the Baxter case?" Tyson asked.

"From a great distance," Frost said coolly. After some further small talk, he managed to get Regillo aside and repeated the invitation for dinner.

"Let me ask Ceil," he said.

"I already have," Reuben was about to say, but Regillo

had quickly darted off to confer with her. The two of them had an intense conference, after which Regillo came back.

"Thank you for your invitation, Mr. Frost, *Commissario* Frost," Regillo said, "but Ceil is feeling very tired. She still has not recovered from the shock of Gregg's death, as you can understand. She feels that it would be better if we went out another evening."

Reuben gave Cynthia the high sign that it was time to leave. She was talking with la marchesa and he went to join them.

"It's all in here," Ceil Scamozzi was saying. She handed Cynthia a thick, leatherbound book.

"What's all in there?" Reuben asked.

"Everything the Venetians knew about coloring fabrics," Ceil said. "This monk, Angelo Natal Talier, gathered the existing learning—you can tell from the title, *Dell'Arte di Tingere in filo, in seta, in cotone, in lane ed in pelle*—The Art of Dyeing Thread, Silk, Cotton, Wool and Hides. This is the original edition, published in 1791, which I've had rebound. It's from this that I've found out what I know about dyes."

"Ceil has invited me to visit her workshop," Cynthia said.

"Yes, I mean it. Just call me when it is convenient and I will show you everything. You might even enjoy it."

"I'm sorry you won't have dinner with us," Reuben said.

"It's better, I think," she replied. "Luigi is right. We should stay here and be quiet."

The Frosts thanked la marchesa and then made their farewell rounds, kissing and shaking hands.

"I'm afraid Ceil's seen better times," Reuben said a few minutes later as they stood at the railing of the *circolare*, watching the Giudecca shoreline pass by. "No whiskey and that rot-gut wine."

"It was dreadful, wasn't it?" Cynthia said. "But none of the social Italians take drinking seriously. It's almost a badge of honor to be frugal."

"Perhaps so," he said. "Her living quarters certainly get shabbier year by year."

"It's a pity. Let's hope her business bails her out."

Reuben mentioned the puzzling and contradictory reactions to his dinner invitation. "If she's as hard up as she appears, I'd have thought she would have jumped at the chance for a free dinner."

"I have an explanation," Cynthia said. "Maybe not the right one, but an explanation."

"Which is?"

"It sounds to me as if Luigi Regillo did not want to be looked over too closely by the honorary Commissario."

"Hmn," Reuben grumped. "An interesting thought."

"CLAUDIO, WHAT HAVE YOU DONE TO GIVE US SUCH MAG-
nificent weather?" Reuben asked in the Cipriani dining
room Tuesday morning, as he and Cynthia had breakfast.
They had now been in Venice for a week and a day and the
weather had been clear, without even a threat of rain.

"You brought us good fortune, Signor Frost," the maître
d' replied diplomatically.

"Mid-September really is the time to come here, Cynthia," Reuben asserted. "The weather's good and the summer hordes are gone. That hokey regatta is over, and so is
the Film Festival. But as Erica Sherrill said the other night,
you're in time for white truffles and mushrooms. And she
forgot the wild strawberries. *Tartufi, funghi* and *fragolini di
bosco*—what more could one ask?"

"I have to admit that Signor Ivo's *tagliatelle con tartufi*
last night was delicious. White truffles on pasta are enough
to make the whole trip a success," Cynthia said. "And
since you're so taken with Venice in September, where are
you going today?"

"San Vitale and Santo Stefano. Assuming Jack Valier
doesn't have other ideas for me. What about you?"

"The Palazzo Grassi," she said, referring to Venice's
newest museum.

"Even if the current show isn't supposed to be much," Reuben said.

"If it's too bad, I'll just slip into their sweet lunchroom. Harry's Bar food without Harry's prices, if you remember."

"Yes. The cheapest Bellini in town. At least that I've found. Will you have lunch there? Or shall we meet up?"

"I don't know how long I'll be. Let's go our separate ways and I'll see you later."

Unable to reach Valier at the Questura, Reuben picked up his green bag and headed off to the Accademia, where he crossed the bridge and walked to the deconsecrated eleventh-century church of San Vitale. Here he looked over the carved commemorative portraits of Doge Carlo Contarini (1655–56) and his wife set in the Palladian-style facade. Frost recalled from his reading that Contarini had died after less than fourteen months in office, and his successor lasted barely a single month. The result was the election of the Commissario's ancestor, Bertucci Valier, who was a mere fifty-nine. Frost thought it resembled the "youth movement" at the Gotham, his New York club, with about the same notion of what constituted "youth."

Returning to the Campo Morosini, Reuben passed the tilting campanile of Santo Stefano and then went inside to examine the memorial set in the floor honoring Doge Francesco Morosini (1688–94), the last Doge who personally led an army in battle. He won against the Turks at Salamis, Hydra and Spetsai, before dying ingloriously of gallstones in 1694.

As Reuben stood by the slab cast by the Doge's cannon makers, he also read (in his Norwich, certainly not on the monument itself) of Morosini's ill-fated attack on Athens in 1687 when a Venetian cannon was fired at the Parthenon, causing an explosion that blew up its roof and fourteen of its columns. Not the most splendid achievement to be remembered for, Frost decided. If there were any parallel between *this* Doge and Chase & Ward's Executive Partner, Reuben could not think of it. None of the firm's disasters, of which there had been a few in its history, compared even figuratively with wrecking the Parthenon.

On his own for lunch, Reuben strolled to the Vino Vino, a modest *enoteca* near the Fenice with a variety of wines. He settled for a glass of rich, and expensive, Brunello di Montalcino, and a plate of *baccalà Montecato*, codfish with polenta.

Later, napping back at the hotel, he was awakened by a ringing telephone and the operator telling him he had a call from New York. It was Jim Cavanaugh. An angry Jim Cavanaugh. "Boy, am I glad you're still there," he told Frost. He went on to describe an item in Sharon Meagher's gossip column in the morning New York *Press* and read it aloud to Reuben:

"The jet set is buzzing about an angry feud that boiled over in Venice last week between Eric Werth, the perfume king, and slain designer Gregg Baxter. It seems Werth had gone to Venice to entice Baxter into putting his very hot name on a line of fragrances. The temperamental Baxter not only refused to see him but revoked his invitation to the fabulous dinner extravaganza the designer threw the night before he was killed. Nobody will talk, but we have learned that Werth returned to New York in a fury hours after Baxter was found stabbed to death near the Grand Canal."

"That's damn close to libel," Cavanaugh said.

"It's pretty raw," Reuben agreed.

"I called you because I figured you probably would know what's going on. If there's any thought of dragging my client into this, I want to hire a lawyer to look out for his interests over there."

Frost admitted that he had gotten enmeshed in the investigation, though he told Cavanaugh "there isn't much I can report now."

"Can I ask you to keep me posted, to let me know if the police are breathing down Eric's neck?"

"Or yours, I should think," Reuben said.

"Yes, I suppose mine," Cavanaugh agreed, after a pause.

"No, I don't see any problem with giving you a call if I hear anything."

"I sure would be grateful," Cavanaugh said. "What a tragedy, even if he was a shit. You know, we must have seen Gregg Baxter right before he was killed."

"Really?" Frost tightened his grip on the telephone, as if by squeezing it he could make Cavanaugh's words come faster.

"Yeah. After we left you, Werth and I had a drink on that porch outside at the Gritti. We had a late appointment with Tony Garrison and his girl—"

"—you had what?" Reuben asked.

"We had an appointment with Tony Garrison, to have a farewell nightcap. Garrison was on our side, trying to persuade Baxter to make a deal. We were prepared to extend our stay if Garrison had anything positive to tell us."

"You said you saw Baxter," Reuben said tensely.

"Yes. While we were sitting there, a gondola took off from next to the hotel. Baxter and some stranger none of us knew were in it."

"A man?" Reuben asked.

"Yeah. A young Italian guy. Anyway, as the boat got out into open water, he saw Garrison and Tabita with us and started shouting. I was sure he was going to capsize the gondola, but his sidekick—the one nobody knew—started petting him, like you would a dog, and he shut up."

"What was he shouting?"

"It was pretty incoherent, but part of it was 'You'll get AIDS, Tony, AIDS!' "

"How did Garrison react?"

"He just looked straight ahead, as if Baxter wasn't there. Tabita was stroking *his* arm and trying to keep *him* calm. Then, when the gondola disappeared, he said to us very quietly, 'I guess that's the end of it. You guys don't want to make a deal with a psycho.' We didn't disagree."

"How long did Garrison and Tabita stay with you?"

"Not long. There wasn't much to be said after that scene. I'd say we broke up around midnight."

"Any idea where Garrison went when he left you?"

"I assume back to the Cipriani."

"Baxter was murdered near the Gritti, you know."

"Jesus, I never made the connection. But what would have happened to Tabita?"

"Maybe she helped him."

"That's nuts. We've seen a lot of Tony Garrison over the last few months and I'd be amazed if he were a murderer. He'd like to be a tough businessman, or at least make a lot of money, but he's really a gentle, sweet kid."

"Right now the police are pretty interested in the two of them. And Doris Medford, too."

"Doris? That's even more ridiculous," Cavanaugh said. "From what I read, Baxter was killed sometime early that Friday, the day we left. Isn't that correct?"

"Yes. The police think between one and three A.M."

A pause followed, one so long Reuben began to wonder if he had been disconnected.

"Let me tell you something, Mr. Frost," Cavanaugh finally said. "Not for general consumption, and I'd be very grateful if it doesn't get back to the U.S. of A. To eight-two-five Westchester Boulevard, Scarsdale one-zero-five-eight-three, in particular."

"Of course not," Reuben said.

"I spent the night Baxter was murdered with Doris Medford in her room at the Bauer Grunwald. From, say, twelve-thirty or twelve-forty-five until around six in the morning. She was not out murdering her old boss during those hours, believe me."

"Would you make a statement to that effect?"

Another pause. "If it's necessary to get Doris out of trouble, I guess I'd have to. But I'd sure as hell like to keep it out of the papers and out of Scarsdale."

"I'll be as discreet as possible," Reuben said. "One question. While you were with Ms. Medford, did you have anything to drink?"

"We were drinking all night from her minibar."

"Do you remember what and how much?"

"Barely. If I had to guess I'd say Doris had three vodkas—she outdrank me—and I had two Scotches."

"Okay, thanks," Reuben said, itching to call Valier. "I'll be in touch if the police want anything else."

"Keep me posted and I'll be a very grateful fella."

"I have news," Frost said, when at last he got through to the Commissario.

"So have I. But you go first."

Reuben summarized what he had just been told by Jim Cavanaugh. "If Cavanaugh's telling the truth, and I have no reason to doubt it, Medford's in the clear. And, I'd say he's strengthened the case against Garrison. At least it puts him in the neighborhood at the right time."

"Well, I've got a piece of information that may or may not fit in with yours," Valier said. "One of my men found an antique shop this morning, near the Campo Santo Stefano, that sold a *pugnale di Venezia* the beginning of last week."

"Before Baxter was killed."

"Yes. The only problem is, the owner says the purchaser was an American serviceman."

"How did he know that?"

"Three reasons. *Primo.* He spoke English. *Secondo.* He was black—the fellow's assumption was that most American soldiers are black. *Terzo.* He was wearing an American soft cap that said PADRES on it."

"That isn't a serviceman, that's Tony Garrison!" Reuben shouted into the phone.

"Son of a gun!"

"He wears a PADRES cap most of the time."

"So it wasn't a GI, it was Baxter's assistant."

"That's what it sounds like. Which means, Commissario, you now have the motive, the means and the opportunity. It's time you arrested Garrison. He's not *il povero fornaretto* but Gregg Baxter's murderer."

18

"I'M BEGINNING TO SEE THE LIGHT," COMMISSARIO VA-
lier said to Reuben, who wondered if the detective was
about to burst into the Harry James song (*"I never cared
much for moonlit skies, I never wink back at fireflies . . ."*
Frost dimly recalled). Valier said he now agreed with Reuben and would set up Garrison's arrest as soon as possible.

"Cynthia and I have been invited out for dinner," Frost
said. "Is there any reason we can't go? Should I stay
around?"

"No need. To stay around, that is. *È finito.*"

Frost was relieved. Despite all, he "Rubes," had taken
something of a liking to Garrison—and to Tabita. He would
have found it embarrassing to be present when the young
designer was taken away.

He waited impatiently in the room for Cynthia, who soon
returned, wrestling with a package from Jesurum, the fan-
ciest Venetian linen shop.

"A new tablecloth," she explained.

"Well, put it down and let me bring you up to date." He
did just that, ending by saying that "all the pieces fit together rather neatly."

"Almost too neatly," Cynthia said.

"What do you mean by that?"

160

"You have at least two people, Dan Abbott and Jim Cavanaugh, telling you that killing Baxter was not in character for Tony Garrison. I wonder, too. Do you really think a black kid smart enough to avoid the streets and make a promising future for himself would turn to murder? It doesn't make sense to me."

"Murder seldom does, my dear. The evidence is overwhelming."

"Let's hope so," Cynthia said, sounding unconvinced.

The Frosts' dinner invitation was from Emilio Caroldo and Erica Sherrill.

"Calle Zucchero," Reuben said as they reached the address on the Zattere where the Caroldo apartment was located. "Sugar Street."

"I suppose they unloaded cargoes of sugar here."

"I guess. Isn't sugar one of the million or so things Marco Polo brought back from the East?"

"I believe so."

"Did it ever occur to you how big a fleet he must have had, to transport all his discoveries?"

With a clank and a crash, the decrepit elevator in the building took off and slowly went up to the sixth floor. Once there, a look around was enough to remind Reuben that Erica Sherrill had told him at the Baxter dinner that she and her husband had redecorated their apartment. It was now startlingly modern. In the living room one faced a black sofa, resting on bright red blocks, stretching across an entire wall. He asked her, when she came to greet him, who had designed it and who had painted the enormous canvas mounted behind it.

"The sofa's by Ettore Sottsass, as is most everything else," Dr. Sherrill said. "Surely you've heard of him. He's the *eminenza* of Memphis, the design group in Milan. The painting's by Domenico Bianchi, an artist from Rome."

"It's not at all what one expects of an art historian who specializes in the Renaissance," Reuben said.

"I see quite enough Renaissance art every working day.

That's why it's wonderful to come home and find this contemporary interior. For me it's like jumping into a deliciously warm bath." Her long chartreuse dress, while more traditional, contrasted well with the sleek decor.

Reuben ordered a Prosecco from the white-coated waiter and went over to the large window. La marchesa Scamozzi's view had been a spectacular one, but the Caroldos' was more so, with a panoramic vista that included three Palladian churches, the Redentore, the Zitelle and San Giorgio.

"Is *magnifique*, no?" came a voice behind Reuben in a stage French accent. He turned to face Marianne Wilke, international social gadabout and wife of Martin Wilke, a self-described "private art dealer," though others were never precisely certain in what he dealt.

Cynthia Frost, who had a retentive memory for biographical detail, had put together a mental dossier of the Wilkes years earlier, when she and Reuben had first met them at the home of a mutual friend in Paris. They were in large part pretenders. Martin, for example, claimed to be Dutch (they had apartments in Amsterdam and Paris) but was in fact German. "The only Wilke to be in the Netherlands before Martin was his father, who was there with the Nazi occupation forces," a Parisian journalist had once told the Frosts. Marianne, seemingly French to the core, was an American Army brat who had learned French moving around with her parents; home was technically Omaha, Nebraska, and her maiden name had been Mary Ann Budbane.

The Frosts often ran across the Wilkes, in one city or another. Despite their reinvention of themselves, they were amiable and always full of delicious stories concerning the rich and famous. And, as Cynthia once said, when the Wilkes were not being amusing, one could always laugh at them.

Conversation soon turned, inevitably, to the Baxter murder. Reuben kept a low profile, knowing that it would be improper for him even to hint at the impending arrest.

A mention of the police caused Emilio Caroldo to explode. "The police! The police! *Sciocchi!* Fools! Il signor Baxter has been dead almost a week, and nothing's happened. Absolutely nothing."

"You can't blame the police," Martin Wilke said. "There are so many constraints on them. Not as ridiculous as in your country, Frost, but still many inhibitions, many controls. The police *must* be permitted methods to get at the truth."

"What do you have in mind, Martin—torture?" Erica Sherrill asked. "That fine old Venetian tradition, the *camera del tormento,* the torture chamber?"

"No, nothing as extreme as that. But the right to interrogate, to ask questions without apologizing or bringing in lawyers, all that soft-minded nonsense."

Reuben thought Wilke hardly sounded the freedom-loving Dutchman he purported to be; other roots were exposed.

"Let's see who we're missing," Erica Sherrill interrupted. "Melissa Wheeler and Father Glynn. Melissa's always late, but Father Glynn's usually early. Do you think he's saying mass or something?"

Sherrill's worries were ended with the arrival, together, of Ms. Wheeler and the priest.

"Oh, thank God," Erica said. "Have a drink. We must sit down to dinner. Our cook lives over in Mestre, so she insists that we eat early."

While the new arrivals got their drinks, Erica led the others into the dining room, again an ultra-modern space with a black-lacquered table in the center, surrounded by black chairs with bright orange cushions and backs.

"Sottsass again?" Reuben asked.

"The table is, yes. The sideboard's another designer. Alberto Friso. What do you think?"

The piece in question was painted dark green with a *trompe l'oeil* orange ribbon, carved from wood, draped across the front.

"It's very striking," Reuben said.

"That's probably a diplomatic way of saying you don't like it."

"No, no. I'm partial to modern design, if the truth be known. What you have here is very good. Very good indeed."

Dr. Sherrill directed each guest to a seat, putting Reuben at her right. Ms. Wheeler, the newest arrival, was on his other side, with Father Glynn next to her.

"How's your Mayor Dinkins?" Erica Sherrill asked Reuben, as she attacked her prosciutto and melon.

"Surviving. Barely," he replied.

"Well, at least he's not promoting a world's fair."

"That's what's happening here, isn't it?"

"*Was* happening. Sense has prevailed. Actually, it wasn't our mayor that was trying to get the exposition here, but our foreign minister. A fat, vulgar man who dared to argue that the fair would *benefit* Venice."

Reuben tried to keep up his end of the conversation, but his thoughts kept shifting to what was perhaps taking place even now at the Cipriani. Then it dawned on him that *l'affare* Baxter was over, or about to be. He relaxed, and listened to his hostess with renewed interest.

"One of the worst aspects of the world's fair scheme," Sherrill said, "was that some supposedly cultivated and sophisticated New Yorkers *encouraged* our foreign minister— gave him a forum, allowed him to peddle his preposterous idea in the States. It was a disgrace."

"Erica, don't forget we both know people in New York who invite Claus von Bülow to dinner," Reuben said.

While talking with Dr. Sherrill, Reuben had been aware of a nearly unceasing chatter down the table. It was Father Glynn, who by Reuben's reckoning had scarcely stopped talking since sitting down. He was not surprised, for he had often overheard the priest at the Cipriani pool, where he had visiting privileges through his hostess, Lady Burbage. Reuben now overheard him explaining his presence in Venice to Ms. Wheeler.

"Lady Burbage takes a palazzo every September and invites me out for a week. Frightfully kind of her, but that's what you might expect from a true lady, don't you agree?

She's twenty-eighth in line of succession to the throne, you know.''

Reuben knew from occasional encounters that Father Glynn was an enthusiastic monarchist, as knowledgeable about the royal family as the lives of the saints. He was a Benedictine, at a monastery called Stanbrooke Abbey in Worcestershire, and taught in the boys' school there. Reuben calculated that he might not be disobeying his vow of poverty, since the generous Lady Burbage had surely paid his way to Venice. The vow of silence was something else; he either had not taken one or was in flagrant violation.

When the second course, spaghetti with a sauce of five cheeses, *spaghetti ai cinque formaggi,* was served, the priest turned to Marianne Wilke and Reuben quickly took advantage of the opening. He was curious about Ms. Wheeler, whom he had not met before. It turned out that the attractive young woman had first come to La Serenissima to spend her Radcliffe junior year, had fallen in love with it and vowed to return as soon as she could. A recent inheritance from a well-to-do aunt in Boston had made this possible and she had arrived in the early spring with the ambitious goal of writing a novel.

"Can you have writer's block before you've ever written *anything?*" she asked. "Or can you get blocked only after you've started?"

"I've never thought about it. I don't know the answer," Reuben said.

Ms. Wheeler explained that she had been unable to write a word and so had become interested in environmental issues. She was working as a volunteer with the local UNESCO office.

"Most of the locals don't care a *damn* about what pollution is doing to their city," she said indignantly. "Nor are they concerned that many of the restoration techniques do more harm than good, to things like the patina of old stones, for instance. If John Ruskin were writing today, he'd have to call his book *The Shards of Venice.*

"The foreigners—mostly the English and the Americans—are the ones who are concerned," she went on. "The great *industriali* are happy to live the good life here, but they're doing nothing, *niente*, to preserve its beauty."

"The government?" Reuben asked.

Melissa snorted. "Hopeless. A complete tangle, one agency tripping over another. The only consolation is that if there weren't absolute gridlock, what got done would be worse than nothing at all."

Father Glynn interrupted, turning back to Melissa Wheeler and expounding, for no apparent reason, his theory that the length of one's obituary in the London *Times* was a highly reliable gauge of eminence. Reuben could not think of a subject that might interest him less, so he quickly resumed talking with Erica Sherrill.

"We saw Ephraim Miller last night," Reuben told her. "If I'm not mistaken, we met him for the first time right here at your table."

"Dear Ephraim. He's ageless, don't you agree? He's as pink as he was when I first knew him. Probably as pink as when he was a baby."

"I agree. He looks very well."

"Where did you see him?"

"At la marchesa Scamozzi's."

"Ah yes, Ceil. How is she? We seem to be on the outs with her."

"Oh?" Reuben said. He had to wait for an explanation while Erica helped herself from the platter of sliced veal the waiter held at her place.

"Our trouble was over Luigi Regillo," Erica said. "I can't stand that mincing pansy and I'm afraid I've let my feelings show."

"Pansy?" Reuben said.

She laughed. "Good Lord, yes. He's one of the busiest pederasts in Venice, which is saying quite a bit. He thinks he's leading a secret life, but everyone knows about him."

"Interesting."

"Poor Ceil. Her first big break was linking up with Gregg Baxter. So what happens now? I've heard that his protégé, that black boy, Garrison, can carry on, but do you suppose that's true?''

"I don't know," Reuben said evasively.

"I truly hope so. Ceil has done wonders with those designs of hers. The most exciting thing in Venetian fabrics since Fortuny, seventy-five years ago. She deserves some success and I know she can use the money. Gianpietro, her husband, gives her nothing. What's sadder, since he has all the money, he's purchased the loyalty of the children. A boy and a girl, both adorable, in their teens. They're mercenary and selfish, like all adolescents, so they've gone where the money is and live with their father and his second wife in Milan.''

Melissa Wheeler claimed Reuben's attention once again as salad was served. She was eager to get away from Father Glynn, who was still talking, now about making goat cheese in Worcestershire. Reuben asked her if she planned to write about Venice's environmental difficulties.

"I hope to. What I'd most like to do is a real exposé of the polluters, who they are and what hypocrites they are. I've begun some digging and I hope it works out. I'm a little worried about the Italian libel law, though.''

"Can't assist you there," Reuben said. "Why don't you write your novel about the polluters?''

They discussed this possibility through dessert, a *budino di riso*, rice pudding, that they pronounced extremely tasty. Wheeler had been set on writing a novel about the Brownings in Italy—no wonder she had a block, thought Reuben, who found the Victorian Brownings tedious—but now allowed as how twentieth-century defilers of the environment might be promising subjects for fiction.

Then, following Erica, the guests returned to the living room for coffee and, if desired, grappa, though the sole taker for the latter was Martin Wilke. Reuben found himself next to Mrs. Wilke on the window seat.

"You know what I've missed this year?" Reuben asked. "What?"

"The Communist fair. It used to be held every September on the Giudecca, practically outside the Cipriani back door.

But not this year. I noticed on a poster the other day that they've even renamed the Communist Party. It's now the *Partito Democratico della Sinistra*. The Democratic Party of the Left, indeed. It's all too bad. The fair used to be hilariously funny.''

"Funny?" Marianne Wilke said, screwing up her face.

Another right-winger? Reuben wondered, recalling Mrs. Radley with a shudder. "Oh yes, didn't you think so? Totally nonthreatening. Usually featuring an exposé with photographs of unsanitary hospitals or garbage dumps. Hardly the stuff of a very bloody revolution.''

"It was naive to think they weren't a threat," she snapped. "For my money, they still are.''

"As far as I could see, the most dangerous thing at their fairs was the faithful's unbelievable consumption of food,'' Reuben said. "No surprise the party failed. The *salsiccie* were clearly more important than Lenin or Marx—sausage above ideology.''

"I'm glad it amused you," Mrs. Wilke said grumpily.

Given the contretemps, Reuben was relieved that the party had started to break up. He and Cynthia shook hands all around and thanked the Caroldos. They went outside to the Fondamenta and waited for the water-bus. Once on the boat, Reuben decided that it was a trip for which he would not pay, since they were only crossing the Giudecca Canal. The *marinaio* had a different idea, and nicked Reuben for two tickets, though not the 40,000 lire fine for fare evasion.

As they crossed, Reuben told Cynthia about Erica Sherrill's dislike for Luigi Regillo and her characterization of his sex life. And Cecilia Scamozzi's need for money. "If Tony Garrison hadn't been caught, I think I would have found what Erica had to say about Ceil Scamozzi's situation very interesting,'' Reuben said.

"But, darling, it's over," Cynthia said. "So there's no need to speculate any more. The only thing left to do is to enjoy what's left of our vacation to the fullest.''

"You're right, my dear," Reuben said, as they looked up at a full moon in a clear sky.

CASE NEARLY CLOSED

19

FROST WAS NOT SURPRISED TO FIND A MESSAGE FROM DAN Abbott awaiting him after dinner: "I am in the bar. *Must* see you tonight." THE BAR WAS NEARLY DESERTED. WALTER, the bartender, was struggling with the endless paper work that always seemed to need doing and Dan Abbott was sitting alone in one corner, a bottle of San Pellegrino in front of him. He nervously thanked Reuben for seeking him out and offered both Frosts a drink. Reuben declined, but Cynthia ordered an additional bottle of mineral water.

"Have you heard what happened?" Abbott asked.

Reuben shook his head, though he knew full well what Abbott was about to say.

Abbott maneuvered his glass to his mouth with a shaking hand and took a drink. Then he blurted out that the police had arrested Tony Garrison for Baxter's murder. "They came around eight o'clock. That guy Valier and three others."

"Where did they take him, do you know?" Reuben asked.

"That police station where we were the other day."

"The Questura."

"Yeah. I wouldn't have even known they were after him

except I heard voices outside—they arrested him in his room—and Tabita was raising holy hell.''

"Where is she?" Cynthia asked.

"She took a Seconal and went to bed. We were both pretty shook up. I still am." He looked morosely at Reuben. "Why the hell pick on Tony? He *can't* be guilty."

"Mr. Abbott, I know it must be a shock to you," Reuben said. "And I also can appreciate that it's going to devastate your business. But the evidence is pretty strong against Garrison."

"Evidence?" Abbott asked belligerently.

Frost quietly told Abbott about the purchase of the glass dagger, about Baxter's curses outside the Gritti before he was killed and about the vagueness of Garrison's alibi.

"What motive did he have?" Abbott asked, when Reuben had finished. "There was no reason on God's green earth for Tony to kill Gregg!"

"I'm afraid that's the easiest part," Reuben said. "There are almost too many possible motives." He spelled them out, to Abbott's discomfiture.

"Look, Gregg could be a sadistic son of a bitch, no question," Abbott said. "And he was savage to Tony Thursday night. But Tony'd been through that a hundred times. He disregarded Gregg's outbursts, just like we all did. And look at what Tony had at stake. I can't believe he'd risk his career by anything as insane as killing Gregg."

"I'd like to agree with you," Reuben said. "But I'm afraid I can't."

"I thought you were on our side," Abbott said crossly.

"I'm on nobody's side," Reuben shot back. "My only interest is seeing this drama completed and Baxter's killer brought to justice. I believe that's what's now happening, unfortunate as that may be from your standpoint."

"What's next?" Abbott asked.

"I don't know. I plan to call Valier in the morning."

"We attempted to get to him earlier. I had the concierge try. The big one."

"Gigi."

"Whatever. He couldn't track Valier down," Abbott said. "I think we've got to get Tony a lawyer, and damn fast. Can you help us with that, at least?"

Frost ignored Abbott's "at least." "I'll try my old firm in New York. It keeps a directory of recommended foreign lawyers. I'm not sure a name will show up for Venice, but I'm certain there'll be somebody listed in Milan or Rome who can steer us to the right person."

"Will you call New York to see?" Abbott asked.

"They're six hours behind us. I may not be able to reach anybody now, but I'll try when I get upstairs."

"It's none of my business, Mr. Abbott," Cynthia added, looking over at their distraught companion, "but let me be a nursemaid and suggest that you get a good night's sleep."

"That's not going to be easy."

"But you must try."

"I suspect that's good advice for all of us," Reuben said. With that, all three of them left, ignoring Massimo's impassioned version of "Strangers in the Night."

Reuben called Chase & Ward in New York from his room and was put through to Charlie Parkes, his old friend and now the Executive Partner of the firm. Frost described the circumstances, and asked if Parkes would check the foreign-lawyer file for a recommendation of Venetian counsel.

In less than half an hour, Parkes called back to report an absence of entries for Venice. However, there was a listing for a lawyer in Padua "who got that son of Rod Crutcher's out of trouble in Venice three years ago. You know the one I mean?" Parkes said.

"Yes, I do," Frost replied. "The lout."

"He got absolutely shit-faced and pushed a complete stranger into one of the canals," Parkes explained. "A native, not a tourist. So this fellow, Carlo Mancuzzi, had a real tough one, but he got Junior Crutcher off. I just talked to Rod and he said Mancuzzi did a first-class job. He was recommended by the American consul in Milan, speaks

English, all that. The only problem is, he lives down the road apiece."

"At least he's a known quantity," Reuben said. "Give me his phone number and address."

Parkes added that he had predicted that Frost would get involved in the Baxter affair. "I knew you were on your usual Venice holiday, so when I read about Baxter in the papers—with the tabloid war we're having, there was much coverage—I said to Betsy, 'I'll bet Reuben stirs up this pot before he gets through.' "

"I hope your wife defended me," Reuben said. "If I remember correctly, you ingrate, I've stirred up a couple of pots on your behalf in times gone by."

"I can't quarrel with that, Reuben. But now you be careful," Parkes said as he rang off.

Frost decided that it was too late to call Dan Abbott; there was a chance that he had followed Cynthia's advice and gone to sleep. They could discuss Avvocato Mancuzzi the next day.

Wednesday morning, Reuben was getting dressed when the telephone rang.

Cynthia answered. "Yes, he's right here," she said to the caller. Putting her hand over the receiver, she whispered, "Tabita."

"I must see you, Mr. Frost," Tabita said, sounding upset.

"Have you had breakfast? Why don't you meet me in the dining room in ten minutes?" Reuben asked.

"No! I don't want to see you at the hotel. Can we go somewhere where we won't be seen?"

"Well, there are the gardens over near San Marco, where we talked the other day."

"That's too close," she replied.

"How about the public gardens?" Reuben suggested after a moment's thought. "They're isolated and practically empty. It's mostly people who live in the neighborhood who use them."

Tabita agreed, and Reuben gave her directions to the Giardini Pubblici, and to the memorial statues near the Viale Trieste in particular. "I'll see you by the bust of Richard Wagner at ten-thirty. You can't miss it."

"Busy day," Cynthia commented, as Reuben hung up.

He told her of his appointment to meet Tabita. "Now I've got to decide what to do about this damn lawyer in Padua. It will be awkward to give him orders over the phone, but we may have to."

"This is my day to visit Ceil Scamozzi's workshop."

"Will you be back by lunchtime?"

"Oh, I think so. I can't imagine I'll spend much over an hour, and there was no mention of lunch."

"Then I'll try to see you back here around one. All right?"

"Unless Tabita casts a spell on you and spirits you away."

"One can always hope."

Before heading downstairs, Frost tried to reach Valier. He was told that the Commissario *"è in riunione,"* which Reuben puzzled out to be the Italian equivalent of that great American excuse, "He's in conference." Reuben left a message and said he would call again later.

After breakfast, Reuben ran into Dan Abbott in the lobby.

"I was trying to call you," Abbott said. "But your wife said you were down here. What have the police got to say?"

"I can't get hold of Valier," Frost replied.

"How about a lawyer? Did you get Tony a lawyer?"

"I've got a name. Unfortunately he's in Padua."

"How far away is that?"

"A half-hour on the train."

"Damn."

"This fellow comes well recommended, and he supposedly speaks English."

"How do we get in touch with him?"

"I have his office number."

"Let's get him over here quick. We've got to spring Tony."

"I haven't any idea about Italian criminal procedure, but I suspect that's easier said than done."

"Let's call the guy."

"He may not be in his office. The other thing is, he may want someone—you or me or both of us—to come to his office in Padua."

"For the fee I'm willing to pay him, he can damn well get his ass over here," Abbott said.

Reuben sighed. "Shall we use your suite?"

As luck would have it, Carlo Mancuzzi was at his desk when Frost and Abbott called. Yes, he was familiar with the police—and their methods—in Venice. He even knew Commissario Valier. Yes, he would be honored to work with an American lawyer from the fine firm of Chase & Ward, which had a worldwide reputation of the highest merit. Yes, he would come to Venice. No, he could not meet before early afternoon as he had an important appointment with a notary in Padua that morning.

Abbott, on the telephone with the two lawyers, did his best to persuade Mancuzzi to come sooner; he sounded like a sick patient pleading to see a busy doctor. Mancuzzi, in turn, resembled the jaded medical receptionist who had heard it all before. He would meet Avvocato Frost and Signor Abbott at the hotel at two-thirty.

"Guess we have to sit tight until then," Abbott said.

"Not me. I'm going to town. I'll see you later," Frost said. He did not reveal the nature of his excursion and saw no reason to.

20

ARRIVING AT THE GIARDINI *VAPORETTO* STOP, REUBEN strode the short distance to the rendezvous point. He had half expected Tabita to be on the same boat with him, but she had not been, so he sat down to wait. Very soon he saw her approaching fast along the waterfront. A fence blocked her way to where Reuben was sitting, but she found an entrance and walked down the Largo Marinai d'Italia toward him.

He was startled when she embraced and kissed him. He felt her bony model's body, encased this morning in dark slacks and a denim shirt, as she held on to him while thanking him for meeting her.

"Let's go over there," he said, pointing to a red wooden bench that would give them an unobstructed view of the water. When they were seated side by side, he asked her why she wanted to see him.

"Mr. Frost, there's something I want to tell you, but I'm almost too frightened to do it."

Reuben gave an encouraging grunt that was meant to keep her talking. It worked.

"The person who killed Gregg Baxter is still loose here in Venice. I don't want to be the next victim."

"The police have made an arrest, as you know," he said evenly.

175

"I don't care. Gregg Baxter's killer is still at large. *It is not Tony!* He owed everything to Gregg. Like he always said, he'd probably be a crack dealer on Forty-second Street if Gregg hadn't picked him out and made something of him."

"I appreciate all that, Tabita. But you can't deny that Baxter had been behaving badly to your Tony."

"Sure, I know," Tabita said. "But Tony was very mature about that and took Gregg's abuse. There was too much at stake not to. If Tony left, that would have been the end of Baxter Fashions."

"That's a pretty big statement."

"It's a true one, though. Gregg was losing his touch and getting more dependent on Tony. Tony knew it, too. He didn't need to kill Gregg to take over. All he had to do was be patient and wait."

"He *was* near the scene of the crime," Reuben said, as gently as possible.

"What do you mean?"

"I mean just what I said. Garrison—and you—were having drinks at the Gritti Palace an hour or so before the murder. Drinks with Eric Werth and his lawyer."

"How do you know that?"

"Tabita, there's a full-fledged investigation of Gregg Baxter's murder going on. Many things have been found out, and I'm certain even more will be. By the time this is over, there aren't going to be many secrets left."

"That meeting—Tony thought a deal with Werth was a good idea," Tabita said. "It would have meant money for everybody. All Tony was trying to do was figure out a way to make it happen."

"Even though Baxter was firmly against it?"

"Tony hoped he could bring him around."

"Another thing has come out, Tabita," Frost said. "The glass dagger that Garrison bought."

"I see what you mean about secrets," Tabita said. "It's about the glass dagger that I want to talk to you."

"I'm listening."

"Okay, then. The glass dagger. Yes, Tony bought it. Not to kill Gregg with, for God's sake, but as a souvenir."

"Odd souvenir."

"On one of his trips here, Tony heard the story of the glassblowers who fled from Venice being assassinated with a glass dagger. He thought it would be a kick to own one. Said he might use it on anyone who tried to pirate his designs. So he shopped around and finally located a dealer who had one—not three or four hundred years old, but still an antique and an imitation of the knives they used to kill with. But then, after he'd bought it, someone stole it from our room at the hotel."

"What! When?"

"We don't know. When Tony bought it, he made a joke about how he should hide it from me, in case I might want to use it, but he just threw it, in its paper wrapping, into his suitcase. Then, when we heard how Gregg had been killed, he looked and it was gone."

"Possibly because he had left it in Gregg Baxter's gut," Frost said sternly.

"No, I tell you! We were at the Cipriani when Gregg was killed."

"Hmn," Reuben said, pausing to absorb all he'd been told. Then he said, "You know, your Tony is the most likely suspect. That's why he was arrested. But if by some chance he's innocent, the *next* most likely one is the hustler Baxter picked up. You realize that your stolen-dagger theory not only rules Garrison out but the hustler as well. At least it seems very unlikely that a young operator off the streets would be rifling your luggage at the Cipriani."

"I can't help that," Tabita said. "I'm just telling you what I know."

"If it wasn't Tony, and it wasn't Pandini, the hustler, who was it?"

"I haven't any idea," she said.

"Who knew about the dagger except you?"

"Tony told everybody about it at dinner one night, before Gregg was killed."

"Who is 'everybody'?"

"Doris Medford, Dan Abbott, Ceil Scamozzi and Luigi Regillo. It was a restaurant right near here, I think. Franz's."

"Ah, yes, Da Franz. It's right back there," Reuben said, indicating the Fondamenta San Isepo.

"They all wanted to see it, so he showed it to them at the hotel the next morning."

"Let me go back. When did Tony buy the dagger?"

"Let's see. We got here Saturday. It wasn't the next day, Sunday, and it wasn't the day of the party. It must have been Monday."

"And when was the dinner at Da Franz?"

"That same night. Monday."

"And then Tony showed it around on Tuesday?" Reuben said. "After which he put it back in the suitcase?"

"Yes, to both questions."

"And did the others see him put it back?"

"They did. All of them—Doris, Luigi, Ceil and Dan. Gregg, too."

"The theft. You don't know when it occurred?"

"No."

"You say everyone saw the dagger last Tuesday. What were Ceil Scamozzi and Luigi Regillo doing at the Cipriani?"

"Our suites were kind of a headquarters, you know, for getting ready for the dinner. People were in and out all the time. Mostly we camped in Doris Medford's suite, planning the party, but we had the whole floor and we used all of it. Ceil hated the rooms because of the Fortuny fabrics on all the furniture. It was kind of funny."

Reuben paused and stared out at the water, ostensibly to watch a passing Yugoslav ferry, but really to give him time to figure out how to pose his next question. "You're absolutely sure Tony Garrison is not the murderer?" he finally asked, looking Tabita squarely in the eye.

"Positively, Mr. Frost. Don't you need a *reason* for killing someone? I can't think of a single motive for Tony to murder Gregg."

"I'm afraid I can," Reuben said. "I can even think of a motive for you—Baxter's ham-handed interference in your love life."

"You mean you think I might have killed Gregg Baxter?" Tabita said incredulously.

"It's perfectly plausible. Wasn't Baxter making your life miserable because you'd stolen Tony away? And you knew where the dagger was. In your case, you didn't even have to steal it."

Tabita laughed. "Do you really mean what you just said?"

Reuben didn't and realized it would be unfair to pretend otherwise. "No, I don't, Tabita. I don't think you killed Baxter. But I'm damned if I know who did."

They sat and contemplated the water for what seemed a long time. Then Reuben said he was going to try to find Valier. "The Questura isn't far from here, you remember. I'm going to tell him what you've told me, though I fear it won't be enough to spring your boyfriend."

"Can I come along?" Tabita asked. "I've got to see Tony if I can."

Frost told her of his efforts to get a lawyer for Garrison, and said, "Of course you can come. But do you want to be seen with me?"

Tabita shrugged. "I feel safe with you, Mr. Frost."

What a desperate creature, Reuben concluded. Looking for protection and comfort to a very old man and, at the moment, a very confused one.

21

AT THE SQUADRA MOBILE, FROST AND TABITA ENCOUN-
tered a communications problem. Reuben asked for Commissario Valier and received every kind of Italian negative
in reply. The officer who greeted them at least purported not
to speak a word of English; although, as Reuben now noted
for the first time and with some amusement, the building's
exit signs were both in Italian and English. Reflecting the
nationalities of the P.S.'s best customers, he thought.

Reuben persevered and eventually the uniformed *agente*
went to the phone and disgustedly told the party on the other
end about the *due inglesi* he was unable to get rid of.

After a promised—and long—*momentino,* a second officer, heavyset and also in uniform, appeared. Again Frost
was informed, as he had been earlier, that Commissario
Valier "*è in riunione.*"

"*Possiamo disturbarlo?*" Reuben asked, pushing to the
outer edge of the envelope that was his Italian. "Can we
disturb him?"

"*Non è possibile,*" came the direct, curt reply. Tabita
appeared to be on the verge of making a try of her own, but
decided not to. Frost ripped a sheet from his notebook and
wrote out another message for Valier, saying that it was
imperative that he call as soon as he could. Without any

great confidence that it would be delivered, he and Tabita went out to the Fondamenta.

"He's probably questioning Tony right now," Tabita said.

"I wouldn't be surprised," Reuben agreed. "Our constitutional niceties unfortunately don't have extraterritorial effect." If Valier were "in conference" all this time grilling Tony, it was the real third degree.

"Shall we walk back to the boat separately?" Frost asked. "It's up to you."

"Maybe we shouldn't be seen together," Tabita said.

"Okay, you go out there to the water and walk down the Riva degli Schiavoni," Reuben directed. "I'll go around the back way."

Eight minutes later, they arrived at the Cipriani dock at the same time. They greeted each other extravagantly for the benefit of the strangers who were also waiting. With similar excess they loudly engaged in empty conversation about the weather and the likelihood of rain.

Back at the hotel, Gianni told Reuben that Cynthia had been looking for him. "She's having her hair done now, but she said to be sure and have you wait."

Frost relaxed on the bed in 201 with the morning *Herald Tribune* until Cynthia appeared, hair neatly reorganized. "Shall we go down to lunch?" he asked. "I'm starving."

"First I've got to tell you what I learned at Ceil's this morning," she said. "It can't wait."

"Why don't you tell me over lunch?"

"No. I'm going to tell you here, now, and I want you to listen carefully."

"Yes, dear," Reuben said dutifully, wondering what he was in for.

"Let me begin at the beginning," Cynthia said. "When I got to the workshop, Ceil was there alone. There was no sign of Luigi. She began showing me around and it *was* fascinating, Reuben, what she's done with Friar Talier's techniques, all out of that book she showed us the other night. Absolutely gorgeous fabrics, mostly silks, but some cottons. Incredible, rich colors.''

"Anyway, while we were walking around, I noticed a shelf of old-fashioned bottles, including one that said AR-SENICO. That of course piqued my curiosity and I remarked on it. 'Is that poison?' I asked. 'Oh yes,' she replied. She got quite nervous and started babbling on, really babbling, about what it's used for. If you care, you apparently need something called a *mordente*—I think that's right—when you dye or print certain fabrics, because the cloth itself doesn't take the dye or the ink. So you treat the cloth with a *mordente*, which *does* absorb it. Do you follow me?''

"I'm not sure," Reuben said.

"It doesn't matter. The important thing is that she has used the arsenic compound as a *mordente* in some of the monk's old formulas. When she'd finished her explanation, Ceil still acted skittish—to the point where I asked her if anything was wrong. When I did that, she dissolved. 'I haven't told anybody this,' she said, 'but half the contents of that bottle disappeared not long ago. It is *molto tossico* and I'm very nervous about what might happen.' ''

"Does she think someone stole it?''

"Yes, but all she knows for sure is that some time between the first of the month and last Friday, when she went to use the arsenic with some of her dyes, the contents had depleted badly.''

"Was she aware of Baxter's poisoned insulin?''

"Unless she's a wonderful actress, I would say not. When I told her, she went into hysterics—dramatic, very Italian hysterics, but I'd say genuine ones.''

"I suppose everybody and his brother had been in and out of her studio.''

"All the ones we're interested in. I asked her specifically. Except Eric Werth and his pal. And Pandini.''

"I'd eliminated them already. It didn't seem likely that they would have stolen the dagger—''

"—stolen the dagger?''

"Oh my God, I haven't had a chance to tell you.'' He

made up for his lapse by quickly relating Tabita's story.

"Do you believe her?" Cynthia asked, once he had finished.

"I'm inclined to. Though of course it could be a red herring. It'll be interesting to see what Garrison tells the police about the theft. If there was one."

"What do you think?"

"I think I'll faint if I don't eat. I noticed that lasagna is the special this noon. That's what I need—and I need it now."

While eating, Reuben and Cynthia exchanged theories about Tabita's story in very low voices. Together they decided that it might be true, and X, identity unknown, had stolen Garrison's dagger and killed Baxter with it. *Or* Tabita might have invented the tale as a means of trying to clear Tony. *Or* she and Garrison might have conspired to commit the murder and were using the theft as a part of their alibi. *Or* Garrison might have killed Baxter and fabricated the theft to fool Tabita. *Or* Tabita might have done the killing and told the story to protect herself.

The possibilities seemingly exhausted, Reuben had an espresso. A double. As he finished it, Cynthia announced that she was going off to Burano.

"To buy lace?" Reuben asked.

"No, it's just that I feel like a long boat trip on this beautiful day, and I haven't been to Burano in years."

"Good—about the lace. I understand most of it comes from Hong Kong these days."

"If I feel energetic, I might even go on to San Francesco del Deserto. I could use a little calming today. If it worked for St. Francis, maybe it'll work for me."

"I have an idea," Reuben said. "Why don't you take Tabita along with you? She's nervous as hell—scared, too, I'm pretty sure—and you might cheer her up."

"It's all right with me. Actually, I'd enjoy the company."

"And who knows what you might learn."

"Ah, I should have known you had a hidden agenda."

"I have to wait for Avvocato Mancuzzi," Reuben said, as a porter came out to announce the lawyer's arrival at the front desk. Reuben called Abbott and again they arranged to meet in the latter's suite.

Avv. Mancuzzi turned out to be a dapper man of perhaps sixty, compact and balding and wearing an expensive olive-tan suit. He carried a sagging, soft-leather briefcase and turned out to be all business. From television, he already was aware of Baxter's murder and Garrison's arrest, but Abbott and Reuben supplied him with what details they knew.

"We're not even sure where Garrison is," Abbott complained, as the three men sat down in his suite.

"I would guess he is still at the Questura," he said, in clear English. "They have detention cells there and that is usually the first stop after being arrested."

"How do we get him out, counselor?" Abbott asked.

Mancuzzi gave a small, rather sad smile. "For twenty-four hours, there is very little we can do. The P.S. can hold him without any cause whatever."

"But what about questioning him? Can they do that?"

"I fear the answer to that is yes and no. If they put questions to him, he does not have to answer. Or he can refuse to answer unless his lawyer is present. Often, however, except for some motorboat questioning, the police do not interrogate a suspect but hold him for twenty-four hours. To give him a proper chance to ponder his situation."

"I don't understand your reference to motorboat questioning," Reuben interjected.

Mancuzzi smiled. "A term unique to Venice. A suspect must be taken to the Questura by patrol boat, no? This gives the arresting officers a brief opportunity to question him."

"You mean grill him without anybody watching? With perhaps a little physical encouragement to answer?"

"Precisely. Of course, any answers the fellow gives to such interrogations may not be admitted in court. But they may be helpful to the P.S. in their investigations. In this

case, since the person arrested speaks English, I doubt that
the P.S. would learn very much. There would be an inter-
preter present only at the Questura."

"Garrison also speaks Italian," Reuben said. "Of course
he may have been clever enough to conceal that."

"I see," Mancuzzi said.

"From what you say, I gather that Garrison may be sitting in some isolation cell—'pondering his situation'?" Abbott said.

"Yes. Or the Commissario and his colleagues may interrogate him from time to time. But, as I say, he does not
have to answer."

"How would he know that?" Abbott inquired.

"Oh, they are obligated to tell him, Signore."

"And there is nothing you, a lawyer, can do about it?"

"There are two things I can do. One is to call, or have
you call, the American consul general. His legal officer
can make known to the police his interest in the case.
Your government cannot seem to afford such an official in
Venice, so one must call Milan. It is, however, a useful
step. To let the P.S. know someone is watching them.
Also, if I am retained to look after il signor Garrison's
interests, I will bring that to the attention of the P.S. immediately. So they will be aware that I, too, will be observing their conduct."

"Avvocato Mancuzzi, what happens when twenty-four
hours are up?" Reuben asked.

"A new twenty-four-hour period begins. At this time the
authorities must give notice that they are holding a person
and within that second period must present a *rapporto* to the
Procuratore della Repubblica, identifying the suspect and
the accusations against him."

"Who the hell is he?" Abbott asked.

"The Procuratore is a magistrate, a judge, who super-
vises the investigation of the P.S. In actuality, his deputy,
a Sostituto Procuratore, will be in charge."

"Then what happens, after the *rapporto*?" Frost asked.

"The Sostituto Procuratore must decide whether to hold

the suspect. If he does, he will issue an order, an *Ordine di Custodia Cautelare*, remanding him to the *carcere*, the jail. In this case our Carcere di Santa Maria Maggiore."

"Pretty name for a prison," Frost said. "And what happens if an *Ordine* is not issued?"

"If an *Ordine* is not issued within the second twenty-four hours, the suspect must be released."

"And what is the likelihood of one of those orders in this case?" Abbott asked.

"Sadly, I must say very high," Mancuzzi said. "The P.S. will have the *deposizione* of the antique dealer that sold Mr. Garrison the *pugnale*, the instrument of death. That alone would be enough to hold him, in my opinion."

"For how long?" Abbott demanded.

Mancuzzi only shrugged. The shrug set Abbott off. He bounded from the chair and started pacing the room, then pounded the television set with his fist.

"What can we do?" he shouted. "How are we going to get a spring line on display?"

"Line?" Mancuzzi asked, puzzled.

"Clothes—a line of clothes. Baxter Fashions' dresses for next spring!" Abbott shot back.

"I cannot help with that problem," Mancuzzi said. "I can only notify my representation to the P.S., and try to find out what they are thinking. And if Mr. Garrison is imprisoned, to consider with you an appeal of the *Ordine* to the Tribunale della Libertà. That may or may not be a fruitful path. We must see."

"How long does such an appeal take?" Reuben asked.

"Not long," Mancuzzi said. "It is an appeal of an imprisonment, after all, so it is very quick."

"What chance would you have?"

"There would have to be doubts raised," Mancuzzi said. "If there was evidence pointing to someone else, for example. Not necessarily enough to have someone else arrested, but facts to make some smoke."

"Right now, though, you'll be talking to the police?" Abbott asked. "And to the American consul?"

"There is only one small detail, Mr. Abbott. Have I been retained?"

A short discussion of fees took place. Mancuzzi was hired, promised a six million lire retainer, his expenses, 250,000 lire an hour once the retainer was exhausted and a "success fee," amount to be negotiated, if Garrison were promptly released and allowed to return to the United States. The lire amounts sounded enormous, but Reuben realized they were reasonable by American standards—a down payment of $5,000 and an hourly rate slightly over $200.

The terms agreed, Mancuzzi shook hands and said he would make an appearance at the Questura at once. He also said he would call the American consul when he knew Garrison's exact status with the P.S.

After seeing Avv. Mancuzzi out, Frost remained behind for a moment to talk to Abbott. Both agreed the unclear situation was out of their hands and that they must, reluctantly, wait to hear from the newly hired lawyer. Unless, of course, Reuben could get through to Valier.

Eager for a change of scene, and having decided not to try Valier again right away, Reuben prepared to continue his visits to Doges' monuments. After consulting his map he set off on the *circolare* to the Ponte delle Guglie, the very bridge where the raucous students had shouted taunts at Gregg Baxter's party guests. From here he walked to the church of Gli Scalzi, or Santa Maria di Nazareth, which had been started by the discalced, or barefoot, Carmelites (the "Scalzi") in the second half of the seventeenth century. Much of the cost of the Baroque facade, Reuben read, was paid by one Gerolamo Cavazza, a wealthy social climber who had bought into the nobility. Reuben was reminded of Cavazza's striving counterparts in twentieth-century New York who had donated wings and galleries to the Metropolitan Museum; some things never change, he concluded.

Inside Gli Scalzi, he found the yellow and red marble slab commemorating Ludovico Manin, with its unadorned legend: MANINI CINERES, the ashes of Manin. Manin, who took office in 1789, was the last Doge. He presided over the dissolution by the Maggior Consiglio of the thousand-year-old Venetian Republic in the face of an invasion by Napoleon's troops, on May 12, 1797. His memorial was not much to look at, amid banks of hideous electrified candles and in front of a dreadful grass-green and yellow rug covering the steps to an altar.

Looking at this austere monument, Reuben remembered Manin's words as he handed his *corno,* his symbolic headdress, to his servant after the fall of the Republic: "Take it, I shall not be needing it again." The servant did so, and promptly sold it. No, Reuben thought once more, some things truly do not change.

Outside the church, Reuben was reminded of home by a line of African street peddlers vending their wares. Did they come here to practice before moving on to New York? Or were these deportees from the United States? Reuben wondered. What he did notice was a change in fashion. Fake Vuittons and Guccis had been replaced by counterfeit Timberland shoes. (He was later to learn from the Caroldos that Timberlands were currently the rage among Italian teenagers, hence the market for the ripoffs.)

Being almost next to the Ferrovia Santa Lucia, the railroad station, Reuben decided to go there and try to reach Valier once more. He walked across the plaza to the post-World War II monstrosity in search of a public telephone. He went inside, and eventually found a bank of them on a wall facing *binario quattro,* the departure platform for Milan. It was three-thirty, according to the large clock facing Reuben, who was about to turn his attention to the tricky business of activating a Venetian pay telephone, when he stopped abruptly. Across the way, at the foot of the platform, was Luigi Regillo, talking intently to a younger man Frost did not recognize. Curious, he pulled shut the door of the telephone booth and from this partially obscured position watched Regillo and the stranger a few feet away.

Their discussion was animated. Perhaps the reason was as simple as the fact that two Italians were talking. Yet the degree of volubility and gesticulation was such that Reuben suspected otherwise. The two had something stormy to discuss.

While he watched, Regillo removed an envelope from his loose, unstructured coat and handed it to the stranger, who put it in the pocket of his leather bomber jacket. Then he and Regillo embraced and kissed—straight on the mouth, no brushing of cheeks. The younger man went off down the platform.

Regillo hesitated for a moment and then turned quickly, placing him in position to look directly at Reuben. Frost turned at once to face the telephone and assumed, though he could not be sure, that Regillo had not seen him through the glass door of the phone booth.

Nonetheless, Frost was nonplussed. He did not wish to be seen spying by a possible murder suspect. Or suspects, as he soon discovered when he finally tracked down Commissario Valier.

22

Frost was relieved to find that he could use coins to make his call; it would not be necessary to undertake the difficult, and sometimes impossible, task of finding where to purchase a *gettone* for use in the pay telephone. He rang Valier. This time, to his relief, he got through.

"We have things to talk about," he said to the officer.

"I hope so," Valier replied. "Your friend Garrison certainly doesn't. Come *subito*."

So instructed, Reuben took the number two *diretto*, the fastest service to San Zaccaria. Here he disembarked and went across to the office of the Squadra Mobile. Valier was in shirt sleeves, tie askew, when Reuben was shown in.

"This Garrison is a tough nut. He refuses to admit anything. *Niente,*" Valier said. He looked exhausted.

"I assume he denies that he's guilty," Reuben said.

"Deny! He has more denials than St. Peter!"

"His girlfriend, Tabita, told me an interesting tale this morning," Reuben said, then repeated it to the detective.

"He's already insisted to us that his *pugnale* was stolen," Valier said. "Do you believe him?"

"If he told you that, it either means it really happened or that she's in this with him." Reuben then went over the other possibilities he and Cynthia had explored.

The wide range seemed to dishearten the worn-out Commissario. "If Garrison is not our pigeon, we have to start back at square number one," he said.

"Oh, not quite," Reuben said. "Or at least I'd start with Tabita herself, Luigi Regillo—and the hustler, Pandini. Speaking of which, I just saw Regillo at the Ferrovia. He was seeing off some young fellow to Milan. My God, do you suppose . . . ?" Sitting now in Valier's office, his mind fully concentrated on Baxter's murder, he had suddenly had a jolting thought.

"Suppose what?" Valier asked.

"That I saw Pandini? Could that be? Had I found your hustler without even knowing it?"

"You could recognize him again, no?"

"Oh yes, I think so."

"Good. I have a picture of the *vagabondo*. His dear mother gave it to one of my men." Valier rooted amid the disordered piles on his desk and eventually produced a framed photograph. The boy in the picture was younger than the man who had been with Regillo, but the resemblances were there, the hooded eyes, the cleanly angled face, the fleshy lips.

"This is Pandini?" Frost asked.

"Yes."

"That's who I saw."

Frost's announcement galvanized Valier into action. He first called for a railroad timetable, which a functionary, out of breath, rushed into the office.

"You sure you mean the train to Milano? Not Roma, not the local to Padova or Treviso?"

"I didn't see him get aboard, but he walked down the platform where the train to Milan was standing."

"Let's see," Valier said, studying the schedule. "Milano. A train at three thirty-five. Due in Milano at six-forty. That must be the one." He got on the telephone, barking orders. Then he began questioning Reuben about how Regillo's companion was dressed.

"He had on one of those World War II bomber jackets

the young people are wearing. It was leather and had several markings and insignia on it. I only noticed one I recognized, the old American Army Air Force emblem—a white star enclosed in a blue circle, with another red circle in the middle.''

Valier was puzzled, so Frost picked up a pad from the desk and drew an illustration. While Valier was studying it, the telephone rang and Reuben was able to overhear snatches of a conversation he guessed to be with a police officer in Milan. Another one, with a colleague in Brescia, followed.

"Let's hope your spotting Pandini hasn't used up our luck," Valier said, when he had finished. "*If* Pandini was on that train, and *if* he wasn't going only as far as Padova or Vicenza or Verona, where it's too late to catch him, and *if* there's no snafu and the police are wide awake when he debarks in Brescia or Milano, then we may have found our man. *If, if, if.*"

"Why don't you have them pull him off the train at Brescia?" Reuben asked.

"I'd rather deal with the P.S. in Milano. Besides, to delay a train long enough for a search is . . . is . . . Forget it.''

"Where was he hiding, did you ever find out?"

"No. Pandini's family is a bad lot. Big and bad. Some cousin had concealed him, I'm sure of it.''

"He certainly wasn't trying to hide at the Ferrovia.''

"Why should he?" Valier said, spreading his hands upward in a gesture of helplessness. "He knows very well that we don't have the manpower to spare to keep a constant watch for him at the station. And the young ones on the regular patrol, they'd be lucky to spot their own mothers.''

Valier got up and peered out his window. "Any other surprises for me, Avvocato Frost?" he asked.

Frost was chagrined. In the excitement of Pandini's discovery he had completely forgotten Cynthia's news about the missing arsenic. His memory was failing, he had no doubt of it; an unwelcome, quick vision of Edgar Filbert flashed through his mind.

Valier, made aware of the arsenic problem, looked perplexed, and then perhaps angry.

"This badly confuses things, doesn't it?" he said.

"How do you mean?"

"It makes Pandini a less promising alternative to Garrison. Is it not doubtful that he stole the poison from la marchesa?"

"Yes, no question about that. It's also unlikely that he poisoned Baxter's insulin. But how about this, Jack? *Regillo* takes the arsenic and poisons the medicine. Then, when that doesn't work, he steals Garrison's dagger, which he gives to Pandini. Probably telling him in the process that there was a good chance Baxter would be at Haig's Bar Thursday night looking for a pickup."

Valier lifted his chin and thoughtfully scratched under it with the fingertips of his right hand. Then he said slowly, "That may fly, my friend. Yes, it may fly. But until we talk with Eccellenza Pandini, Mr. Garrison will remain a guest of my government. Don't forget, in all those scenarios you worked out, he figured in all but one of them—the one in which someone else really *did* steal his *pugnale*."

"Where is Garrison now?" Frost asked.

"He was taken about two hours ago to Santa Maria Maggiore, down near the Piazzale Roma."

"You're aware that Garrison now has a lawyer?"

"Oh yes. Avvocato Mancuzzi has declared his interest. He need not worry. We have not abused Mr. Garrison. We will treat with proper respect a man who may have killed the richest person ever murdered in Venice. With all the notoriety, we'd be fools to do anything else."

"I'm reassured—I think."

"Personally, I wish la signorina Medford was the guilty one," Valier added, leaning back in his desk chair.

"Ms. Medford?" Reuben queried. "You must have taken a terrible dislike to her."

"Oh no, not at all. It's only that I've always wanted to arrest an English-speaking woman for a big crime."

"Dare I ask why?" Reuben asked.

"So I could sing to her—'*Lay that pistol down, babe/Lay that pistol down/Pistol packin' mama/Lay that pistol down.*' They sang that on the radio all the time in Arkansas," Valier said, laughing heartily.

"Good grief," was all Reuben could say.

Frost believed that he himself had not heard "Pistol Packin' Mama" in at least forty-five years, but the tune would not leave his consciousness as he walked to San Marco. Shaking his head, as if the physical gesture would rid him of the song, he thought about the day's events and was discouraged. There were too many pieces that did not quite fit together, too many signs pointing in too many directions.

What he needed, he decided, was a comfortable dinner with Cynthia. When he stopped for his room key, he asked Gigi to make a reservation at Harry's Bar. Then, once he'd climbed the stairs and opened the door to Room 201, he found an envelope on the floor. It was of luxurious stock, the sort that Tabita had bought the other morning, as was the single sheet inside it. The envelope was addressed to REUBEN FROST in block capital letters and the message inside consisted of one line:

DON'T OVERLOOK DANIEL ABBOTT

Frost hurried to the lobby and demanded to know from Gigi who had left the anonymous missive.

The concierge examined the envelope and said he'd not seen it before. "Besides, Signor Frost, if someone had given this to us, we would have kept it here in your mailbox if you were out. We would not have put it under your door."

Frost walked away, frustrated. Then he turned back and asked whether Gigi had seen la marchesa Scamozzi or Luigi Regillo that day. The concierge said he had not, but that it had been extremely busy—a large party of guests had arrived on the Orient-Express from London—and he might have missed them.

Frost murmured perfunctory thanks and returned to his

room. A few minutes later he fairly jumped at Cynthia when she returned. "Has Tabita been with you?" he demanded.

"Why, yes, dear. You asked me to take her, remember?"

"Of course. But I didn't know if she had gone along. She was with you all afternoon?"

"Yes. Why?"

Frost told Cynthia about the note he had found.

"If the note was left this afternoon, I'm afraid you'll have to look for a guilty party other than Tabita."

"That's what I was afraid of."

Since there was time before dinner, he decided to call Abbott, who turned out to be in his suite and invited Frost to come by.

"I got some mail," Reuben said, once seated across from Abbott, who was wary as he took the sheet proffered to him and read the brief message.

"Jesus Christ," he said. "Where did this come from?"

"The stork brought it, apparently. Or maybe one of those overweight seagulls out on the lagoon. In all seriousness, I don't have any idea and neither does the concierge." Reuben described how he had found it under his door. "I assume we can ignore the message," Frost said, looking at Abbott closely to study his reaction.

"What can I say?" Abbott replied with a tight smile. "It's too absurd to deserve comment."

"But it may be important—even crucial—to discover who left this thing."

"Who could it be?" Abbott said. "The obvious candidate, Tony Garrison, is still being held by the police. Doris Medford's in Milan. What about Ceil Scamozzi or Luigi Regillo?"

"I doubt that it was Regillo—or Pandini, the hustler Baxter picked up," Reuben said. He described for Abbott his encounter at the Ferrovia. "Maybe it was la marchesa, but Gigi said he hadn't seen her—or Regillo—in the hotel all day."

"Ceil or Luigi could have hired somebody to bring the message over," Abbott volunteered.

"I suppose. But it would have been pretty risky to send a stranger on such a delicate mission."

"That leaves only one person," Abbott said. "I hate to say it, but that's Tabita."

"Not possible," Reuben replied. "She was with my wife all afternoon, in Burano."

"She was?" Abbott said.

"That's definite. I just confirmed it with Cynthia."

"Perhaps Eric Werth and Attorney Cavanaugh came back here from New York," Abbott said, but without much conviction.

"Hmn," Reuben said. "Implausible, I'd say."

"Are you going to tell Valier about this?"

"Certainly," Reuben said. "If I can get hold of him, which hasn't been easy. Meanwhile, I suggest you ponder who your friend might be."

23

"A TRIP TO VENICE WOULDN'T BE COMPLETE WITHOUT dinner at Harry's Bar," Reuben said to Cynthia in their room, as he changed into a business suit for the evening.

"You and Hemingway," Cynthia said. "But I'm only teasing. Of course we should go. It's fun. Just bring money."

"I know, I know. Do you suppose it's the most expensive restaurant in the world?"

"Don't forget Tokyo."

"You're right. But it's still *troppo caro.*"

After his inconclusive talk with Dan Abbott, Reuben had received a call from Commissario Valier saying that Pandini had been collared in Milan; the P.S. officers had been alert and easily picked out the youth in the imitation American bomber jacket.

"We've already sent two guys to bring him back here," Valier had explained. "With luck, I'll have something to report tomorrow morning."

Then Frost told him about the missive accusing Dan Abbott, which provoked an Italian profanity on the other end that he did not understand.

"So you *have* become a *bocca di leone,*" Valier said. "Someone has slipped a denunciation into your open

197

mouth, or at least under your door." They discussed, inconclusively, what this development meant, before Valier asked if he could send an *ispettore* to pick it up. Frost willingly agreed.

"How's Garrison?" Reuben then asked.

"Stewing in his own juice—*sugo suo*," came the reply. "Don't worry, we're not torturing him. We don't want to upset Avvocato Mancuzzi. I should tell you, if Mancuzzi hasn't already, that the Sostituto Procuratore has decided to sign an *Ordine* remanding Garrison to prison."

"I can't say I'm surprised, but let's not lose sight of the love letter someone sent me."

Frost, once he had handed the note he had received to the *ispettore* from the P.S. who called for it, was satisfied there was nothing more he could do that evening. So he went off with Cynthia to Harry's in an ebullient mood, in spite of the day's confusing events.

Arrigo Cipriani greeted the Frosts as long-lost friends, which they weren't, quite. They usually made one visit to Harry's each year—and sporadically patronized Cipriani's two boomingly successful restaurants in New York. But their custom could not compare with that of the visitors who dined at Harry's each day. Or the doyens of the fashion industry who were regulars in Manhattan. Nonetheless, Arrigo seated them at a relatively uncramped table in the downstairs bar, where they could watch the hordes of the less fortunate on their way upstairs (to the grander of the two dining rooms, but not the favorite habitat of old hands, attracted by the more raffish bar).

Reuben without hesitation commanded a martini, a glory of the restaurant, mixed, stirred and refrigerated before being served. Cynthia had a Bellini.

"Oh my God," Reuben suddenly burst out, as they drank. "The Radleys. They're still here!" He had spotted, coming through the swinging doors at the front, Mildred and George Radley, their new "friends" from the Baxter dinner, who were shown to a table across the room. This did not prevent booming Texas "hi's" from being shouted, as if it were the most amazing coincidence in the world that the Frosts and the Radleys should be found together in the best-known restaurant in town. All suspicion of Reuben's leftism seemed to have passed and the Radleys acted as if they expected to be invited over. Fortunately, from the Frosts' viewpoint, it was too crowded for such moving around.

George Radley would have fitted right in at any suburban American country club, with his burgundy slacks and green jacket. Mildred, on the other hand, was wearing a proper couture Baxter, a navy cotton, elegantly simple and dotted with a pattern of small white flowers. Again, Reuben thought, here was living proof that you *could* buy elegance but (as in George's case) couldn't do much about acquiring taste.

The Radleys were heard clear across the room as they ordered their drinks—a double Jack Daniel's for him, a rum and Coca-Cola for her.

"It's a good thing Jack Valier isn't here," Reuben whispered to Cynthia.

"Why?"

"He'd be singing 'Rum and Coca-Cola.' I told you he's the Andrews Sisters' biggest fan. '*Both mothah and daughter/Workin' for the Yankee dollah.*' "

"Reuben, please. Maybe you'd like to join the Radleys."

"No, dear, I want to stay right close to you and have another one of these," he said, gesturing for a second martini. "How often do you have the chance to spend ten thousand lire for a drink?"

"We'd better eat," Cynthia said matter-of-factly.

Though they planned to dine lightly, they ordered enthusiastically. With little prompting, Reuben opted for the Carpaccio and Cynthia the lobster ravioli, to be followed in his case by the *risotto con carciofi* and in hers by *pollo al curry*, curried chicken, which she described as a "little change of pace," all to be washed down with a pitcher of the house Cabernet.

"That note you received doesn't exactly clarify things, does it?" Cynthia observed while they drank.

"I'm not sure I've sorted it out yet. What's your opinion?"

"It's probably all redundant now, but let me tell you what I thought about this afternoon, on the boat coming back from Burano. Tabita was very quiet, very subdued, so I just stared out at the water and tried to come up with a theory."

"I never did ask you, did you get to San Francesco del Deserto?"

"Oh yes, we did. It's really wonderfully serene, Reuben, just like Assisi. You can imagine St. Francis talking to the birds."

"Assuming he ever got there."

"He was supposed to have been shipwrecked on the island, isn't that the story?"

"That's the legend. But enough of St. Francis. Holy fellow that he was, I don't think he's going to help us find Gregg Baxter's murderer. So tell me what you worked out."

Valentino, Harry's most veteran waiter, served Reuben's Carpaccio, blood-red sliced raw beef with cross-hatched ribbons of mustard on top. Cynthia's four raviolis, in a light sauce, looked delicious but austere.

"You can't beat the Carpaccio here," Reuben pronounced, after his first bite. "In New York, everybody wants to junk it up with Parmesan, or hearts of palm, or God knows what else. Here they do it the way old Giuseppi Cipriani intended, God bless him."

"This ravioli isn't bad," Cynthia said. "It's scrumptious, if the truth be told."

"Don't let it stop you from telling me your afternoon thoughts."

"They're not remarkable, I'm afraid. I started with the idea that we have four actions that are most likely connected. Getting the arsenic from Ceil Scamozzi's workshop. Poisoning Baxter's insulin. Taking the glass dagger from Tony Garrison's suitcase. And the murder itself, of course.

"I went over the cast of characters that we know, to see who might have done all four things.

"As we've discussed, I eliminated Eric Werth and Jim Cavanaugh—and Nicolò Pandini. Granted they were all in the neighborhood when Baxter was killed, it's pretty hard to link any of them to stealing either the arsenic or the dagger, or tampering with Baxter's medicine. Agreed?"

"Basically, yes. I may want to come back to Pandini when you finish."

"Well, then, as for the others, all of them were in and out of Ceil's and the Baxter suites of rooms at the hotel. In other words, each one could have done everything except kill Baxter. So we have to look at that. Valier told you that Ceil Scamozzi and Luigi Regillo were seen going home on the *circolare* at ten forty-five. And we saw Dan Abbott in the bar at the hotel around eleven-fifteen."

"So we can eliminate those three, unless one of them sneaked back to Haig's Bar," Reuben said. "Valier says that Scamozzi and Regillo didn't, that no personnel on the water-buses stopping at the Giudecca saw them after they'd crossed to go home. As for Abbott, he would have had to slip past either the Cipriani boatman or the guard at the back door—and then slip by them again to come back when he had finished his dirty work."

"Which leaves us with three possibilities—Tony Garrison, Tabita and Doris Medford," Cynthia said.

"And Medford's out because she was busy making love to Jim Cavanaugh."

The serving of Reuben's rice with artichokes and Cynthia's chicken delayed conversation briefly.

"I think there's another possibility," Reuben said finally. "We've found out that Pandini and Luigi Regillo know each other. As Jack Valier and I agreed earlier, Pandini could have committed the murder after Luigi had done all the rest."

"So we have three suspects, counting Regillo and Pandini as one," Cynthia said. "But then we get the complication of the note about Abbott."

"Yes. I think there are two ways of looking at that. One is that some good citizen, using me as a *bocca di leone,* just as Valier predicted, really meant to denounce Abbott as the murderer. Which we agree is off-the-wall, right?"

"I certainly think so," Cynthia said. "It just doesn't add up that he was in the right place at the right time to kill Baxter. And look at all he's done to get Tony Garrison free. Not precisely what you'd do if the police would be likely to make you a suspect once they'd given up on Tony. And we can't forget his eagerness to find the guilty party—by involving you, for one thing—which doesn't gibe with his being the murderer himself."

"So far, I think we're on the same track," Reuben said, as the waiter interrupted to take orders for dessert. Normally, Reuben might have been tempted by Harry's extraordinarily rich chocolate cake, but in the present circumstances it would have been a needless distraction. He and Cynthia had only espresso.

"So we go to the second theory," Reuben continued. "That the actual killer sent the note fingering Abbott to divert attention from himself—or herself."

"Now it's getting interesting," Cynthia said. "Take the three suspects we had before the business of the note came up. Garrison is in jail—he couldn't have left it. The next most likely culprit, Tabita, was with me all afternoon, so it couldn't have been her. Pandini was en route to Milan. And just for good measure, Doris Medford was already there."

"So that leaves only Luigi Regillo, although nobody apparently saw him at the hotel today," Reuben said. "It may be worth it to have Valier check on his movements from the time I saw him at the Ferrovia."

"There's another ridiculous alternative."

"What's that?" Reuben asked.

"That Abbott wrote the note."

"Wrote the note accusing himself of murder? Ridiculous isn't a strong enough word."

"It was just a wild idea," Cynthia said.

"It seems to be a terribly serious conversation over here.

Are you working out your investments?'' asked Arrigo Cipriani, elegant in his customary double-breasted suit, who had come up to their table.

"No, no, just some speculating about recent events," Reuben said.

"Gregg Baxter's murder?" Cipriani asked.

"Yes."

"It would be nice if it were solved. Every tourist business in Venice would be grateful."

"I can't say it looks like it's affected you," Reuben said, surveying the packed room. Cipriani smiled contentedly and shrugged.

"Nor, I noticed, has anything occurred to cause you to lower your prices," Reuben added.

"Oh, Mr. Frost, please, please. I hear that so much, how expensive Harry's Bar is. How expensive Venice is. No one remembers one small fact—that everything here has to be brought in by boat. As someone once said, if you eat an apple in Venice, it means it has been shipped in. And once you've finished it, the core has to be shipped back out. It is very, very costly!"

"Well, Arrigo, we will do our little bit for you," Reuben said. "Our modest little repast—just what we wanted, no complaints—was splendid."

"Thank you. See you in New York soon, I hope," Cipriani said, before moving on to greet others.

"As Harry once observed, he's the only man in the world named for a restaurant," Reuben remarked after he had left.

"Not true," Cynthia said. "There's that waiter at Vico in New York who named his son for the place."

Reuben smiled, then sucked in his breath at the check that was presented, wishing that he received the *voce amica*, the discount at Harry's given to regular local customers.

When the check had been paid, the Frosts stood up, attracting the attention of the Radleys who waved at them vigorously. A cordon of diners still prevented the Frosts from nearing their table.

As the Radleys bade their long-distance farewells, Reuben noticed with horror that they looked like figures from some reverse minstrel show, with white skin and black teeth. They had clearly eaten the pasta made with *seppie*, and the sauce of black squid ink had grotesquely darkened their teeth. Why they were both oblivious to this was a mystery; perhaps too much Jack Daniel's and too much rum. From a distance, there was nothing either Reuben or Cynthia could do to tip them to their risible condition; they would just have to go on embarrassing their country and themselves.

The Frosts laughed over the Radleys on the trip to the hotel. As they reached it, Reuben noted that he'd had a very busy day. "I want a good night's sleep so I can dream about all those expensive apple cores being carted out of Venice."

RUSKIN GIVES A HINT

24

COMMISSARIO VALIER WAS AGAIN ON THE PHONE TO REUben early Thursday morning. He was calling from his apartment and said that he had been up most of the night questioning Nicolò Pandini. The streetwise Pandini had been eager to talk, but only to tell a story that distanced him from Gregg Baxter's murder.

As Valier recounted that story, Pandini had admitted going out in the gondola on the fatal Thursday night and had described how Baxter had spotted a dark-skinned couple, sitting with two other men, on the deck of the Gritti Palace. His English had not been up to understanding exactly what the nearly hysterical Baxter had shouted to the group, though it was sufficient to catch an impassioned reference to AIDS. That had been enough to inhibit any sex between them and the gondola ride had been a chaste one, except for a few feints by Baxter under the blanket covering their laps and a few calming caresses by Pandini.

Sex or no sex, Pandini had felt entitled to full payment at the end of the ride. The frustrated Baxter had first disagreed, then relented, when Pandini threatened to make a scene outside Haig's. According to Pandini, the last time he saw Baxter was when the designer headed back into the bar at roughly twelve-fifty—"after which our angel Pandini went straight home to his mama."

The next day, hearing about the murder, Pandini ran off to a cousin's (as Valier had suspected). He made the mistake of telling the cousin why he needed shielding so that, when the murder started dominating *Il Gazzettino* and the television, his protector decided he should pay for the privilege. This easily exhausted the money Baxter had given him, so he had needed to find help elsewhere to finance a trip to Milan, where he could lie low until the furor over Baxter's death had abated.

Pandini had contacted Regillo, whom he first described as a friend and then admitted had been a furtive client for his services as a prostitute. He did not, of course, suggest that he was attempting to extort money from Regillo; his former customer was making a "loan" to him at the Ferrovia when Reuben had seen them together.

Then there was a long pause in the conversation. Neither Valier nor Frost could think of an enlightening comment about Pandini, or about the letter accusing Dan Abbott. Reuben finally suggested that Valier have someone check on the movements of la marchesa Scamozzi the previous afternoon and of Luigi Regillo once he had made his "loan."

"Unless you have a better idea, I plan to visit Mr. Garrison this morning," Valier said. "It is very Christian to visit those in jail, no?"

"You're filled with the milk of human kindness, Jack."

"*Grazie, Avvocato Frost.*"

Reuben repeated to Cynthia what the Commissario had told him, then announced that, since there didn't seem anything useful he could do immediately, he was at last going to San Zanipolo.

"Unless something breaks, I may spend the whole day there," he said. "But I'll leave word downstairs in case anyone wants me."

"I'm off to the Fortuny Museum. Ceil Scamozzi got me

so interested in Venetian fabrics that I want to see what Fortuny did.''

''Don't find any more arsenic,'' Reuben commanded her.

Frost walked from San Marco to Santi Giovanni e Paolo, the church named for two (alleged) fourth-century martyr brothers and called by all Venetians San Zanipolo. It was a brisk walk, taking him along a series of inland canals where he eyed the traffic; he thought again of the apple-core theory as he saw a barge fully loaded with cartons of Kleenex and was very much amused as he spotted a young gondolier rowing some early-bird tourists along—while listening to a Walkman. Not to mention the burly operator of a motorized barge who had a teddy bear propped up next to the tiller.

Frost reached the Campo in front of the church, from which he approached the red-brown brick facade, noting in his Lorenzetti that it had been built by the Dominicans and consecrated in 1430. As the ''Pantheon'' of Venice, it was said to contain the tombs or monuments of 25, 45 or 46 of the 118 Doges, depending on which source one consulted. Whatever the figure, Frost had narrowed his search down to the three or four that he thought would be the most interesting; he would do more if there was time, perhaps when the church reopened in the afternoon.

Out of loyalty to the Commissario, Frost headed to the huge Baroque mass against a high brick wall of the nave that constituted the monument to Doge Bertucci Valier (1656–58) and his son Doge Silvestro (1694–1700). It also honored Silvestro's Dogaressa, Elisabetta Quirini, the one whom Jack Valier said had driven her husband to a terminal paroxysm of apoplexy. Turning to *The Stones of Venice*, Reuben could only conclude that John Ruskin had viewed the monument on an off day: the statues of the two Doges were described as ''mean and Polonius-like,'' and that of the Dogaressa as a ''consummation of grossness, vanity, and ugliness,'' the figure of ''a large and wrinkled woman, with elaborate curls in stiff projection round her face.''

Reuben wondered if Commissario Valier had ever read Ruskin's description.

Frost moved on down the aisle to the choir and the monument to Doge Michele Morosini (1382), with its elegant gold background, which Ruskin had apparently seen in a better humor and had called the "richest monument" of the Gothic period in Venice. It was a splendid memorial for a Doge who had died of the Black Plague less than five months after his election.

From here Frost was drawn to the opposite wall and his principal objective for the morning, the tomb of Doge Andrea Vendramin (1476–78), a collaborative effort of Pietro and Tullio Lombardo, father and son. Although one modern critic called the huge work the "manifesto of Venetian classicism," it had sent Ruskin into even higher orbit than usual. He pointed out that Vendramin died "after a short reign of two years, the most disastrous in the annals of Venice."

> "He died, leaving Venice disgraced by sea and land, with the smoke of hostile [Turkish] devastation rising in the blue distances of Friuli; and there was raised to him the most costly tomb ever bestowed on her monarchs."

Then Ruskin relates how he borrowed a ladder from the sacristan, climbed up on the monument and discovered, horrified, that the recumbent figure of Vendramin had been carved only on the side that showed to the viewer below. The other was completely blank. To Ruskin this was a "lying monument to a dishonored Doge," "dishonesty in giving only half a face" when one "demanded true portraiture of the dead," the product of such "utter coldness of feeling" as could only grow out of an "extreme of intellectual and moral degradation."

Frost stepped back and took a final look at the enormous monument, just as the church was being closed for midday.

As he walked outside, Reuben kept thinking about the half-completed likeness of Vendramin that had so troubled Ruskin. To the ordinary observer, it was whole and com-

plete, but if one looked behind, if one looked carefully . . .
Was there a lesson here to be applied to the pursuit of Gregg
Baxter's murderer? Could looking at the facts in a new and
skeptical way be illuminating? The idea was intriguing. He
decided to eat simply at a small bar nearby.

Frost sat at an inconspicuous outdoor table and ordered a
simple *foccacia con frittata,* an omelet with herbed bread,
and a small carafe of white wine. As unobtrusively as
possible—the restaurant was not crowded—Frost tore out
some sheets from his notebook. As he ate, he wrote down
a separate, possibly useful "fact" on each scrap of paper.
Then he sorted and resorted the pieces, climbing a figurative
ladder to look over, under and around each shred of information, to doubt and question what it appeared to convey.

By the time he finished, he had arrived at a theory of who
had killed Gregg Baxter, and just how the murder had been
accomplished.

Eager to get back to the hotel, and the telephone, he
waited impatiently while the padrona fiddled with his Visa
card. All thought of returning to San Zanipolo for the afternoon had vanished. A dead fashion designer had top
priority for the time being.

25

RETURNING TO THE CIPRIANI, FROST WAS ANXIOUS TO CALL New York but realized it was six hours earlier there and that it would be too early to reach his party. So he telephoned Alfredo Cavallaro to satisfy himself on another point.

Cavallaro met Frost in the lobby. "Your question is, what are the ways in and out of the hotel?" Cavallaro asked.

"That's right. If someone comes here, he has to leave again. How can he do it?" Reuben was tempted to refer to the apple being brought in and the apple core being hauled back out, but decided not to complicate matters.

"You know them all, Signor Frost. There are only three exits, two by water, one by land—the front landing stage, the landing stage by the swimming pool and the back door, that takes you out to the Fondamenta San Giovanni."

"No other doors, no secret side entrances?"

"Nothing like that. Only the ways I told you."

"Are you absolutely sure, Alfredo? There's no other way out?"

"Mr. Frost," Cavallaro said, showing slight impatience. "Two of your presidents, Mr. Carter and Mr. Reagan, stayed here, when they attended the economic summits over on San Giorgio. Both times your Secret Service swarmed over this hotel like a thousand ants and both times they complimented us on how safe it was, with only the three means of ingress and egress.''

"I'm not doubting your word, Alfredo. I just wanted to make absolutely certain, that's all,'' Reuben said. "Now, tell me, what happens to these entrances at night?''

"It's just as you know. The front landing stage is closed after ten-thirty—''

"—not physically closed, is it? A boat could still bring someone in or take someone out?''

"Technically, yes. But the entrance is under surveillance by the roving guard. Also by the closed-circuit TV at the concierge's desk. Besides, all the doors, except the one here to the lobby, are locked, so anyone going out or coming in would have to pass by reception and the concierge.''

To prove his point, Cavallaro led the way into the front garden and showed Reuben that, when the other doors were locked, the garden became a completely closed space, except for the single entrance to the main building.

The assistant manager then took Frost to the swimming-pool landing stage. "The hotel boat runs to and from San Marco all night, leaving and arriving from here, as you are well aware,'' he said.

"That leaves the gate out at the back,'' Reuben said. "Can we have a quick look at that?''

They did so and Cavallaro explained that this approach was watched at all times. The guard on duty operated the electronic gate and scrutinized each person going in or out.

"Thank you very much, Alfredo,'' Reuben said, as they went back inside. "I think you've told me all I need to know.''

"Pardon me for asking, but does this have anything to do with Mr. Baxter's murder?'' Cavallaro asked.

"I'm afraid I'm not quite ready to answer that,'' Reuben said. "Will you be around later? I may need your help again, and I may be able to give you an answer then.''

"I'll be here all afternoon and all evening. At your service, as always.'' Cavallaro bowed stiffly as he left Reuben at the elevator.

* * *

Frost made his call to New York from his room. The recipient was barely awake, early morning not being her best hour. All of Reuben's charm was needed to get her to answer the question he posed. But the effort was worth it. The answer was the one Reuben wanted or, more precisely, the one he expected.

Cynthia returned just as he was hanging up the phone.

"How was it?" he asked.

"Fascinating! I had no idea what a versatile fellow Mariano Fortuny was. It wasn't just those divine silk dresses at all. He was also a stage designer and lighting expert, a photographer, a painter—not his strong point, I might say—and an architect. Quite amazing."

"Well, I've had quite an amazing time myself. I think I now know who murdered Gregg Baxter." He tried out his theory on his eager wife and described the confirmations of it he was seeking. Then he explained his one dilemma—getting his hands on an extremely unusual photograph of his targeted suspect. "It's too much to hope that such a thing exists," he said. "We can make do without it, of course, but it certainly would be easier to have a picture."

"There is such a photo," Cynthia said. "You'd have seen it if you read *Spy* magazine."

"You know how I feel about that sheet."

"All right, my dear, but they ran a story a few months back that featured pictures of the sort you're talking about—including one of the person you're so interested in."

"How the hell can I get a back issue of *Spy* here in Venice?" Reuben asked, groaning.

"I doubt that you can. But, as you may remember, Arthur Qubrian's daughter went to work there when she got out of Wellesley."

"Do you suppose . . ."

"Why don't you call Arthur? If his daughter cooperates, you could have a picture tomorrow."

"Or perhaps even a fax," Reuben said. "If we're lucky, the fax would be clear enough to use."

He soon was talking to his old friend, Qubrian, a New York architect, who confirmed that his daughter, Jennifer, was still employed at *Spy*.

Frost described what he wanted and, when he hinted at the purpose—"Having the photo right away might be very helpful in a police investigation here"—Qubrian said he would try to enlist his daughter's help.

"She never gets up before eleven, so I should be able to catch her," Qubrian said. Reuben carefully dictated the Cipriani's fax number and thanked his old friend.

"Let's hope it works," he said to Cynthia. "I'd better get Valier before he goes home for the day." He called the Commissario, who was eager to tell him that the movements of Luigi Regillo and Ceil Scamozzi on Wednesday had been "fairly well" documented.

"I don't think it matters any more," Reuben said. He added that it might be worth the Commissario's while to join him at the Cipriani. "And don't forget your handcuffs."

Frost's come-on brought Valier to the hotel with remarkable haste. Before he arrived, Reuben had taken counsel again with Cavallaro, explaining the need for a private room in which to meet. After scanning the chart at the reception desk, Cavallaro said that a front suite was vacant and proceeded to show it to Frost.

"This will do nicely," Reuben said, looking around the large living room. "Commissario Valier is coming. I'll wait for him here, if that's all right."

"The suite is at your disposition, Mr. Frost," Cavallaro said.

"Oh, and there may be a fax for me from New York. If it comes, will you make sure it gets delivered right away?"

"But of course, Mr. Frost."

Then, anticipating Valier, Frost asked Cavallaro to check the hotel's records to see which *motoscafista* and which back-door guard had been on duty the previous Thursday night.

"You will want to see them?"

"I'm pretty sure Commissario Valier will, yes," Reuben said.

Soon after Valier arrived, Cavallaro called to say that the *motoscafista* and the guard working at the very moment were the ones who had been on duty exactly one week before.

"We're in luck, if only that photograph comes from New York," Reuben said to Valier, who had reacted with mild enthusiasm and a raised eyebrow to the theory that Reuben had propounded—neither doubting it nor suggesting that the murder was unquestionably solved.

They agreed that a "discreet" search of one of the Baxter group's suites probably would be necessary and, to that end, Reuben called the concierge to see if Dan Abbott or Tabita had asked to have restaurant reservations booked for the evening. The answer was negative, but a second inquiry to the dining room was more productive; Abbott had made a reservation there for three people at eight o'clock.

"Who's the third, do you suppose?" Valier asked.

"Doris Medford, I assume," Reuben said. "She was due back this afternoon, I was told." Reuben looked at his watch. "I guess there's nothing to do but wait. Shall we order a drink?"

"A nifty idea—but we shouldn't," Valier said.

Reuben called Cynthia in their room to ask her if she wanted to join the party. When she found out where her husband was, she said she would be over shortly.

"No hurry," he said. "If there's any real excitement I'll let you know."

To pass the time, Valier turned on the TV, to CNN. "I wish I could see your CNN every night," he said. "But it's only in the hotels, you know. I like to see the news from your country, even when your politics is crazy."

"Our politics crazy?" Reuben asked. "Compared to yours?"

"Italian politics is not crazy, Avvocato Frost, just ineffectual. Unlike you, we have no pretensions, no illusions.

We *know* that government will do nothing, or at least nothing of any value. Unlike your government people, who insist that they've got a method for solving things.''

"Hmn," Reuben said.

Their discussion was interrupted by the delivery of an envelope. It was a fax of an eight-by-eleven-inch photograph—Jennifer Qubrian had obtained an original print, not the reduced image from the magazine. Both men looked at it with satisfaction. Considering the method of transmission, it was an excellent likeness.

"All right," Valier said. "Let's get the fellow from the boat up here." He called Cavallaro to arrange this.

Soon Silvano Tagliapetra, the leathery-faced *motoscafista,* knocked at the door, marine cap in hand. He shook hands awkwardly with Valier, whom he did not know, and flashed a grin at Frost, whom he recognized.

Reuben did not take part in the conversation and wondered if perhaps he was not inhibiting matters by staying in the room. He did so anyway, curious to glean what he could from the conversation.

It seemed to him that Valier was almost trying to hypnotize Tagliapetra, to bring him back a week in time. Going over old ground, he confirmed that on the fateful Thursday night he had recognized Abbott, and Tabita and Garrison, when they returned to the hotel. When asked if any of them had showed up a second time on the boat—either going out again or coming back—the answer was negative.

Then the fax of the *Spy* picture was produced. Had he, Silvano, seen this person that night?

This question produced a different reaction—*può darsi di sì,* perhaps so.

Valier quietly explored the "perhaps." The *motoscafista* recalled again how hectic the evening had been, with the American businessmen and their wives to be ferried across the water, complicated by the drunken safari to Il Campiello. Many had straggled back to the Cipriani boat after the foray to the late-night bar, exuberantly drunk, from about one-thirty until after three.

Tagliapetra thought that a person resembling the man in the photograph had been on a late shuttle trip back to the hotel. How could he remember this? Valier asked, ever so gently. "Because he sat away from the others. Most were drunk and sat outside. He went inside and wasn't singing and shouting," came the reply, as translated by Valier for Reuben.

"As if he didn't know them, you mean?" Valier asked.

"Yes."

"Ask what he was wearing," Reuben said, once he had been brought current with the translation.

"All the men were in *smoking*," the *motoscafista* said. "*Molti pinguini*," he added, grinning his twisted smile.

"All were wearing dinner jackets? All were penguins? Even the man in the picture, sitting by himself? Ask him all that," Reuben said to Valier.

Yes, he was sure of that. All were formally dressed, though some had taken off their ties, even their jackets. The man in the photograph? Yes, he now remembered, he had been wearing black tie but carrying his jacket.

"Could you identify this man again?" Valier asked.

He thought that he could. And, yes, now he was sure, the man was the one who had been on his boat a week earlier. After two in the morning, and perhaps even closer to three. Tagliapetra was thanked and sent back to work.

It was now almost eight. Cynthia arrived and was told of the positive identification that Tagliapetra had made. Then, after another call to Cavallaro, arrangements were set up with the bartender and the maître d' downstairs to notify Frost and Valier when the Baxter group came into the bar or the dining room.

As they waited, Valier said he had "a technical detail" to take care of and called at home the Sostituto Procuratore in charge of the case. He received from him permission to search the Baxter suites.

"We will not have his *mandato di perquisizione*, his signed search warrant, in hand, but I am satisfied he has given his approval," Valier said.

*   *   *

The phone call came a few minutes after eight, relaying a message from Walter, the bartender. The Baxter party had arrived, which meant their rooms were now vacant. Cavallaro was summoned and told that it was most important for the Commissario to be granted entrance to them. He said he would conduct Valier there personally.

"Should I wait here?" Reuben asked.

"Nosiree," Valier said. "You're going to be the look-out. One of them might decide to come back, you know. I'll be the Lone Ranger. You're Tonto, my scout."

Cynthia did her best to keep from laughing when she heard her husband referred to as Tonto. "I'll stay here and wait for you," she said. There was no room for a woman in a Lone Ranger adventure.

Downstairs, Reuben was not precisely sure how to carry out his assigned duty—especially what he was supposed to do if Abbott or Medford or Tabita should appear, other than distract them somehow. Cavallaro, once he had given Valier access to the upstairs rooms, came back down and said that he would go and keep Mrs. Frost company, an assignment he seemed eager to carry out. Meanwhile Reuben waited, apprehensively but obediently, at the foot of the stairs leading to the Baxter suites.

Valier returned ten minutes later, his features set. "You were right, *amico mio*," he said quietly. "Dan Abbott is Baxter's killer, I have no longer any question."

26

EVENTS MOVED RAPIDLY AFTER VALIER'S ANNOUNCEMENT. He and Reuben returned to the borrowed suite. Valier immediately telephoned the Questura and called for a detail to come to the hotel *subito*. He also rang up the Sostituto Procuratore again. Then he explained that he had asked that the *Ordine* regarding Garrison be rescinded and that the former suspect be released from Santa Maria Maggiore at once.

"Will you have Claudio call us when Abbott leaves the dining room?" Valier said to Cavallaro, speaking English for Reuben's benefit.

The reception manager seemed puzzled and hesitated, causing Valier to lose patience. "Look, I'm doing you a favor by not arresting Abbott in your dining room." Cavallaro, now realizing what was going on, hurriedly left to deliver Valier's instruction.

The Frosts and Valier waited nervously, making small talk. The Commissario startled Reuben and Cynthia by asking if they thought Bing Crosby was as good a singer as Sinatra. Reuben, who quite honestly said he'd never considered the question, nonetheless had no trouble in concluding that the answer was "no." Once Valier had been set off, Frost was afraid they would have to comment on every crooner who had been heard on the man's prison-camp radio. The queries had reached Perry Como ("Bland," said Reuben) and Vaughn Monroe ("Couldn't carry a tune," said Cynthia) when the squad from the Questura called on their cellular telephone, announcing that they were in a patrol boat at the back landing stage.

Valier instructed them to stay where they were and then, when word came that Abbott and his party had moved to the bar near the pool, he told Reuben to "come on" and they went off to rendezvous at the police boat. Cynthia's admonition to her husband to "be careful" echoed in his ears as he followed the Commissario out.

"I don't want to be in the way," Reuben said, as they walked through the lobby and out a back door, so they would not cross directly in front of the bar where Abbott was sitting.

"Don't worry, I don't think he's going to shoot. Just stay a few meters behind us and if anything happens—duck," Valier said.

The Commissario's three colleagues resembled professional mourners in their dark suits when they came up the stairway from the back landing stage. Left aboard the blue boat, with POLIZIA and the identification "PS 475" painted in white on the sides, were three younger *agenti* in uniform, two men and a woman. The plainclothesmen conferred with Valier and then went with him to the bar. Frost stayed outside near the pool and observed the scene through the broad windows.

The Squadra Mobile officers went directly to the table where Abbott, an American coffee in front of him, was sitting with Tabita and Doris Medford. To the accompaniment of "Raindrops Keep Fallin' on My Head," played by Massimo, Valier spoke to Abbott, who got up and went out peacefully with the police. The maneuver was carried out so deftly that only Abbott's companions were aware of what had happened.

Medford rose and started to follow the arresting party outside, but the police had moved so fast that they had Abbott inside the cabin of their launch before she could intervene. The boat left at once, a blue emergency light flashing atop the cabin roof.

For the subject of a surprise arrest, Abbott had remained calm and offered no resistance. He had said nothing except, "Thanks very much for your help," as his captors and he swept by Reuben. His look had not been altogether friendly.

No sooner had the boat with Abbott aboard disappeared toward San Marco when a second blue-and-white craft, also a P.S. vessel, pulled up. Engines running, it stopped only long enough for Tony Garrison to jump clear. He saw Reuben and ran toward him.

"Rubes! Is it you I have to thank?" he said, embracing Frost.

"In part," Reuben said. "Me and Dan Abbott—who was just arrested for Gregg Baxter's murder."

Garrison, wearing his shirt open and carrying a blue blazer, appeared unaffected by his confinement, his handsome features intact and unmarked. "So it's Dan, is it?" he said very quietly.

"I'm afraid so, young man," Reuben said.

"How do they know?"

"Look, the hotel has put a suite at our disposal up on the first floor. I haven't eaten, Cynthia hasn't and I'm sure you haven't—"

"—I have. But if you're talking about *real* food, I'm ready."

"Let's go upstairs, where it's quiet and private, and I'll reconstruct the story as best I can. Tabita and Ms. Medford would perhaps like to join us, too. They're right inside."

Frost repeated his plan to the two women, who, still shaken, seemed grateful for the chance of company. Back upstairs, he found Cynthia sitting uneasily across from Cavallaro, who was doing his diplomatic, hotel-school best to make diverting small talk.

Reuben quickly asked him if he could arrange for dinner and drinks in the suite. Cavallaro said he would tend to it at once, though he pressed Reuben for details of the arrest before leaving. His relief was palpable when Frost told him and Cynthia what had happened and he was reassured that the operation had been carried out without undue alarm to other guests.

A waiter and a bar cart appeared with extraordinary speed. Reuben requested a martini and oversaw its preparation. Then a captain came and took orders. Reuben, Cynthia and Tony Garrison all settled on fried calamari and broiled scampi, to be accompanied by a white Durello the captain recommended. Tabita and Medford passed.

"How did they figure out it was Dan?" Garrison asked.

"They didn't. I did," Reuben said. "I'll tell you how if you promise to stop me when the tale gets boring."

Reuben began by describing the epiphany he had experienced earlier in the day, after viewing the incomplete likeness of Doge Vendramin and reading of John Ruskin's shock at discovering it.

"Suddenly I was determined to look at the facts of our case in a new light, to turn all our assumptions upside down or inside out, however you want to put it. So I began with the most recent surprise, the note accusing Dan Abbott." He described the note and how it had been found under his door the previous afternoon.

"Cynthia and I had agreed last night that to accuse Dan was preposterous. Today, I made myself assume that the note, wherever it had come from, pointed to the truth—that Dan Abbott had killed Gregg Baxter and earlier had tried to poison him.

"Before going any further, I reviewed Abbott's possible motives again, and realized that, when you thought about them carefully, they were pretty powerful ones. Gregg Baxter and he differed on the future of Baxter Fashions and how it could be expanded and exploited. If Baxter's conservative views prevailed, Abbott, as a one-third owner, stood to lose millions—many, many millions—in unrealized profits. Then there was the whole matter of Baxter's erratic and contentious behavior—plus his sexual escapades—which could only cause harm in the future, and which were surely personally unpleasant to Abbott.

"I concluded that at some point Abbott might well have

decided that Baxter had to be eliminated. But wouldn't this destroy the very business Abbott wanted to expand? Not from what everyone said. The prevailing opinion, and certainly Abbott's, was that you, Tony, could carry it on. Even before Baxter's death, I had received hints, especially from you, Tabita, that Tony was already doing much of the design work. And Abbott and you, Tony, told Cynthia and me that there were buyout arrangements for Baxter's share of the business—a key-man insurance scheme—that would prevent financial disruption.

"By last Thursday night, I think Abbott was in a desperate state of mind, evidenced by the fact that we saw him in the bar late that night having a good strong drink, and ordering a second one. This although he claimed to be a nondrinker."

"That's true," Medford said. "Unlike some of us, he never drank at all."

"Look at his situation, while he was sitting there drinking: The poison attempt had not worked, and Baxter was determined to find the poisoner. The chance for a lucrative perfume deal with Eric Werth had exploded. His partner, Baxter, was in a vile mood after his less than successful dinner party and had complained to him about how he was running things. And then the two had their bitter confrontation over Baxter's going off to cruise at Haig's Bar.

"My guess is that Abbott, drinking in his bleak mood, remembered your glass dagger, Tony, and decided to steal it. That is what he did, climbing over the balcony from his room to yours—just like the pool boy who opens the umbrellas in the morning.

"Abbott probably figured that he could 'borrow' the dagger and return it later. The problem was that it broke when he stabbed Baxter, so he couldn't return it. This must have made him realize that the police would almost certainly finger Tony as its purchaser. Anybody buying such an oddity was likely to stand out in the memory of the seller."

"Particularly if the buyer was black," Garrison said.

"Exactly," Reuben said, turning toward Garrison. "Having you arrested didn't fit with his plans. Again, twisting the facts around, it suddenly dawned on me—if Abbott had a plan to get Gregg Baxter out of the business, *its success depended on you!* Your design talents were essential if Baxter Fashions was to keep operating—and you wouldn't be able to do very much if you were locked up in Santa Maria Maggiore. So Abbott not only had to keep others from suspecting *him* but *you* as well.

"He had started the process, as far as he was concerned, after the poisoning had failed. He knew that Baxter would be obsessed about finding the poisoner. What better way to appear innocent than to lead the investigation himself? Which he did by rather ostentatiously seeking my help. Probably on the assumption that I was a harmless old man, especially when operating in foreign territory."

"Boy, was he wrong, Rubes," Garrison said, provoking laughter all around.

"Then I tried to analyze his conduct over the last week in light of my hypothesis that he had a dual goal—to keep the spotlight off both himself and you, Tony. The result amazed me. Almost everything fit the pattern. It began the morning after the murder, when Abbott spread the rumor that the killing had been a homosexual one, planting the idea with Alfredo Cavallaro here at the hotel and Commissario Valier, before Abbott even knew that Baxter had met up with the dubious Nicolò Pandini. He also floated the theory with Cynthia and me, on a trip to Torcello last Sunday, and to anyone who would listen at Ceil Scamozzi's cocktail party.

"Then there was his almost fanatical defense of you, Tony. Look at what he did. He deliberately concealed from the P.S. and me that Baxter had been abusive to you the night he was killed—not that you didn't do the same, I might say. And he said repeatedly that you could carry on the business and that you had too much at stake to kill Baxter. Plus, of course, insisting on getting you the best possible lawyer. This had the double purpose of trying to get you off the hook and of making him look like a disinterested Samaritan.

"But trying to defend you, Tony, was only part of his tactics. He also had to get the P.S.—and me—looking at other suspects."

Reuben told the group about his call from Jim Cavanaugh and the item in Sharon Meagher's gossip column in New York, which at least hinted that Eric Werth had been involved in the murder. "Meagher is an old friend and when I called her she told me Abbott was her source. She was reluctant to tell me, like the good reporter she is, and only did so when I laid out the problem for her. The plant with Meagher had been another attempt to divert attention.

"Then he tried to do a job on you, Doris, to make me believe that you were an irresponsible drunk and quite capable of killing Baxter. When we invited Abbott to go to Torcello with us, I specifically asked him to invite you along. But then, when I brought the subject up with you at Ceil Scamozzi's party, I could tell that he had never done so. Now I figured out why—so that he could make his insinuations to us about you throughout the day."

"My God, he was an even bigger son of a bitch than I imagined," Doris said.

"Then we come to the most desperate act since the murder," Frost went on. "Look at the picture yesterday as he would have seen it. The Sostituto Procuratore was satisfied that you, Tony, should be charged with homicide and held in prison and, frankly, your situation looked pretty bad. I'm sure Commissario Valier explained that to you."

"Yes. Like about fifteen times," Garrison said.

"The lawyer Abbott hired, Avvocato Mancuzzi, said the most effective strategy for overturning the *Ordine* against you on appeal was to arouse suspicion concerning someone else, to create uncertainty in the minds of the magistrates over whether they were holding the right person. To make some smoke, as Mancuzzi put it.

"What surer means than to cast doubt on himself? So, in his urgent need to free Tony, he took the chance and sent me that anonymous note naming himself."

"That was pretty dangerous," Doris Medford interjected.

"Dangerous, but gutsy and clever. He knew I didn't suspect him, and I'm sure he was confident that view would carry the day. But meanwhile there would be the 'smoke' Mancuzzi wanted to support Tony's appeal."

"Question," Doris Medford said. "Why wasn't Abbott afraid that people would suspect him of sending the note?"

"Two reasons. One, it would normally be so completely improbable that anyone would accuse himself of murder. Second, I'll wager a healthy sum that he thought Tabita here would be tagged as the author. Unlike the rest of you, she was not accounted for Wednesday afternoon. Or so Abbott believed. What he didn't know is that she was with Cynthia the whole time and couldn't possibly have left the poison-pen letter under my door."

"*Shooot*," the model said incredulously.

"Before I forget it, I'm reasonably sure, Tabita, that you'll find an envelope and a sheet of paper missing from that box of stationery you bought the other day."

"Rubes, I've got a problem with what you're saying," Garrison commented. "You said yourself you saw Dan here at the hotel last Thursday night. How did he get back out of here without being identified? That's next to impossible."

"Maybe for you, Tony," Tabita said, laughing.

"I confirmed a few hours ago that late at night there are only two ways out and in, the landing stage by the swimming pool and the back gate. The *motoscafista* of the boat could not remember seeing Abbott any time Thursday night, except when he returned on the boat after dinner. This is where poor old John Ruskin really helped, with his example of looking on all sides of Vedramin's statue.

"Can anybody doubt that Abbott wears a wig? Wasn't it just possible that he had moved around unidentified while *not* wearing it? Luckily Cynthia remembered a piece in *Spy* magazine about well-known bald men who wear hairpieces. The real targets were the likes of Michael Milken and Sinatra, but one of the dozen or so indiscreetly pictured without his wig was 'fashion fixer' Dan Abbott. Were these photos real or doctored? I don't know. But the faxed print we received was enough for Mr. Tagliapetra, the *motoscafista*, to identify Abbott as a passenger he had brought back early on the morning when Baxter was murdered.

"You may remember that a week ago tonight this place

was going mad with a huge black-tie party. My hunch is that Abbott had the inspiration to take advantage of this. He had his tuxedo here, having worn it to the dinner the night before. So he put it on, removed his wig, blended anonymously with the black-tie crowd and went and stalked Gregg Baxter with Tony's glass dagger.

"He waited for Baxter outside Haig's, I'll bet, and then, when he came out, told him it was time to go home and led him back toward the Cipriani boat. Then he diverted him into the deserted Calle dei Tredici Martiri, killed him, and came back here on a crowded boat without being recognized—until we got the *Spy* photograph, that is.

"Just to wrap it up, the final piece in the puzzle was finding Abbott's dinner jacket rolled up in his suitcase, which Commissario Valier did tonight. There were small bloodstains on the sleeve that I have no doubt will be identified as Baxter's."

"Why didn't he have his tuxedo cleaned?" Tabita asked.

"And have the laundry or the chambermaid find the telltale stains? He had to hide it," Reuben said. "And maybe he'd seen that movie *Don't Look Now*. He might have been afraid his tuxedo would float to the surface and haunt him if he threw it into a canal somewhere."

The group, mesmerized by Frost's account, did not notice Valier's entrance, but Frost saw him and said, "Do you agree about the bloodstains, Jack?"

"I have no doubt they are Baxter's," Valier replied. "But it does not matter. Your friend Abbott has confessed. He actually seemed relieved to have the chance. He wanted to talk even before we got to San Lorenzo."

"Motorboat questioning?" Reuben asked.

"No. It was entirely voluntary," Valier said.

"*L'indagine è chiusa*," Tony Garrison said.

"Meaning what, Tony?" Reuben said.

"The case is closed," Garrison explained. "It's one of the local legalisms I've picked up in the last few days."

"Or as Irving Berlin wrote," Valier added, "the song is ended."

A SECRET MISSION

27

FRIDAY MORNING, FROST, AT DORIS MEDFORD'S REQUEST, called Avv. Mancuzzi and asked him to represent Dan Abbott. Having arranged a meeting between Medford and the lawyer, he made plans for spending the entire day at the Cipriani pool. He was going to rest and bake in the sun, free at last of both worry and surprises.

His one engagement was an appointment to visit the Manfredini Collection in the Seminario Patriarcale. Frost had set Gigi to work to obtain permission for a visit. This had proved more difficult than anticipated, but the word had finally come that Frost could see the collection precisely at five that day.

The seminary was next door to the Salute. Reuben allowed plenty of time, as he was unsure where exactly he was meant to present himself at five o'clock. Eventually he found a glassed-in reception booth, where the building's custodian summoned an eager seminarian to escort Frost to the collection on the upper floor.

Reuben had not come to see the entire collection of paintings and sculptures but, as he told his guide, "*Vorrei vedere soltanto il busto di Doge Da Ponte.*" The youth looked puzzled that Frost wished to see only one object, but dutifully led him to the room where the bust was located and pointed it out. Realizing that it must have some special significance to Frost, the guide quietly withdrew.

The terra-cotta bust by Alessandro Vittoria of Doge Nicolò Da Ponte (1578–85) showed a distinguished old man, wearing the *corno* and a vestment of a rich fabric that Reuben thought resembled one of la marchesa Scamozzi's.

If anyone had asked Reuben why he wanted to take the trouble to make this pilgrimage, he probably would not have told them. The truth was that he had come to gloat. Da Ponte, elected the Doge in his eighties, had developed the unfortunate habit of falling asleep in meetings. To keep him from slipping to the ground, a velvet-covered *appoggio*, a supporting shelf, was built across the front of his throne, creating in effect a high chair for the senile leader.

Frost wanted to exult because he was still in possession of all his faculties—hadn't the events of the last few days proved it?—and intended to continue to be.

He thought of the dreadful Filberts and their condescension to him, unlike the young novices he saw moving about the seminary, smiling and properly deferential. The Filberts be damned, he thought. Sustained and encouraged by his beloved Cynthia, he planned, *grazie infinite,* to go on for many more years. There was no need to build a high chair for him quite yet.

APPENDIX

Reuben's Book Bag

The Hotel Cipriani, ever accommodating, allowed Reuben Frost to keep a box of books at the hotel from year to year. As he made his sightseeing excursions around Venice, he selected the appropriate volumes to put in his green book bag from this collection. In the box were:

Da Mosto, Andrea. *I Dogi di Venezia* (Florence: Giunti Martello, 1947).

Hale, Sheila. *The American Express Pocket Guide to Venice* (New York: Prentice Hall, 1991).

Honour, Hugh. *The Companion Guide to Venice* (Englewood Cliffs: Prentice Hall, 1983).

Lauritzen, Peter. *Venice: A Thousand Years of Culture and Civilization* (New York: Atheneum, 1978).

Links, J.G. *Venice for Pleasure* (New York: Farrar, Straus, 1979).

Lorenzetti, Giulio. *Venice and Its Lagoon* (Trieste: Lini, 1985).

Morris, James. *The World of Venice* (rev. ed.) (New York: Harcourt, 1985).

Norwich, John Julius. *A History of Venice* (New York: Knopf, 1982).

Pignatti, Terisio. *Venice* (New York: Holt, 1971).

Ruskin, John. *The Stones of Venice*, edited and introduced by Jan Morris (Boston: Little, Brown, 1981).

HAUGHTON MURPHY
and
MURDER

TAKE A PEEK...
IF YOU DARE